If They Squeal

The Tag Series, Volume 2

Nolan MacKenzie

Published by Nolan MacKenzie Books, 2024.

IF THEY SQUEAL

First edition. February 13, 2024.

Copyright © 2024 Nolan MacKenzie.

ISBN: 978-0473704841

Written by Nolan MacKenzie.

Also by Nolan MacKenzie

The Tag Series
Eenie, Meanie, Minie, No!
If They Squeal

To my daughter, without whom this novel would not have seen the light of day.

Author's Note

This is a work of fiction, inspired by a Flash Fiction piece of writing from several decades ago when I was working on a skifield in New Zealand. While Melbourne, Adelaide, Mildura, Wagga Wagga, Sydney, Fernshaw and the Black Spur are all actual places, only Fernshaw and the Black Spur reflect any actual resemblance to the places named.

This novel could not have become what it is today without the generous and most appreciated help of many people who helped me with the topography, vegetation, aircraft and aviation, editing and general advice and encouragement. So my many thanks to the following - in alphabetical first name to avoid accusations of favouritism – Alistair Sarre; Allan McDonnell; Barry Tod; Bill Johns; Carolyn Asquith: Kiersten Leslie; Liam Sullivan; Lindsay Gerraty; Pat Quaid; Roe Cumming; Tony with no surname, who helped me via FaceBook.

Prologue

Bruce Gentle, quiet lad in school,
Teased by girls, the ridicule cruel,
His name, a target for their fun,
"Brucie Gentle" their laughter stung.

"Brucie Gentle, shy and meek,
Gently Gentle, give us a peek.
Brucie Gentle, you're a freak.
Gentle Gently, why don't you speak?"

Taunting words that cut him deep,
Kept him from his nightly sleep.
He kept a record, kept it well,
Kept in a book as a sentinel.

But time will come, oh yes, it will,
When those who teased will feel a chill,
For memory reigns, it has its say,
Bruce Gentle's revenge won't fade away.

-Anon

Chapter 1 – 1966

Bradley Gentian had been on this stake out for months now and not once had he sighted anything which could be used to tarnish the community. He could feel the latent resentment starting to collect and churn in his stomach. It should be he, not them, ensconced there. He hated them all with a passion—unintentionally foisted upon him by his parents—that he could not be put into words. Though bitterness came close, with jealously a near second. That was why, rather than enjoying full time employment he spent his time watching the commune and waiting. Initially he had hoped to be able to prove that the hippies were simply squatting, and he could use the law to be rid of them. But that endeavour had been fruitless. So now it was a matter of patiently waiting to see something concrete, such as a pot plantation, that he could report to the council and use to force their eviction.

Reluctantly he lowered the binoculars. Nothing was happening on the commune so there was no sense in his staying where he was getting cold and hungry. He bent down and stowed the binoculars in his backpack and swung it over a shoulder, then blended back into the bush. There was always tomorrow, or the day after. He was confident that one day his patient vigilance would pay off and he would regain what was rightfully his. Little did he know that his life would soon change. He could never have anticipated how fate would soon intervene in his plans.

3

Tess hurried along the path that wound through the outbuildings, looking back every few steps. It wasn't that she was doing anything wrong, it was simply that she didn't want anyone knowing, or seeing what she was doing, and she certainly didn't want anyone following her. Not this time. She stopped at the edge of the bush and took a final look back at the cluster of buildings. Then, feeling safe, she quickly walked into the bush, following the track that would lead her to the road into Hemlock; she did not want to be late for her assignation, after all, time was of the essence.

He watched mesmerized—as he did every time he was caught short and had the need to pee—as steam rose from the stream of his urine. He delighted in hearing the faint hiss as it arced out onto the dry leaves and bark at the base of the mountain ash. It never did that when he was inside the comfort of a bathroom. A blur of movement caught in his peripheral vision, and embarrassed, he grabbed 'the old fella' and gave it a 'how do you do' before ~~he~~ slowly ~~turned around~~ turning to see what had disturbed his ruminations. There, no more than four metres from him stood a young woman, staring at his appendage. He was reminded of the proverbial doe caught in a vehicle's headlights and felt the stirrings of exhilaration. He could see that she was from the commune, and he felt his pulse rise. Not that meeting her in the bush held any 'reason' for eviction, but, he might be able to at least extract some self-gratification from the situation. Keeping his eyes trained on the woman and with a faint smile on his face he fantasized as he encouraged his member into an upright salute.

"Is that the best you can offer?" The young woman laughed. What she saw was nothing new to her, and with a toss of her head she turned, and walked away.

Deflated and incensed Bradley quickly put his 'old fella' to bed and zipped up his jeans before reaching round and removing a pocketknife from his backpack. What right did she have to laugh at him? The best he could offer? Indeed! He would show her what he could offer. He would follow her and when the time and place were right, he'd show her. He'd not only offer, but he would deliver till she begged for release.

Tess, her mind a jumble over what had just transpired combined with her errand was unaware of the shadow she had acquired, so stealthily was Bradley following her.

Bradley too, was being shadowed. Tess's younger sister, ever curious, had followed Tess, and was about to become a silent witness.

Ray Daniels shuffled his feet and looked at his watch for the umpteenth time. She said that she'd meet him here; that she had something she needed to tell him. He hoped that it would be that she had finally gained the courage to leave the commune and go away with him. After all she was 18, just, and didn't need permission to leave. And he would not force her, much in all as he wanted to. It seemed so unfair that she, and the others of similar age, were compelled to remain at *Shangri -la* under duress. Surely even the inhabitants of the commune knew that eighteen-year-olds were now legally considered to be adults and so they did not need to follow the dictates of the commune.

He gazed up the road that she would come along and looked at his watch again. It would not bode well for either of them if he hung around for much longer. Every minute he stood there increased the likelihood of someone seeing him. And even worse, what if they stopped to engage him in conversation? Neither Tess nor he could afford that chance. Their meeting, as always, had to be secret. Certainly no word of it was to filter back to the commune. Not yet.

Chapter 2 - 1982

Tim McNaulty was a man of average height, and ever so slightly overweight which was something, along with his swarthy complexion, that had plagued him all his life.

He stood outside the front door of Paul Edgar's family home in suburban Melbourne. It was much like the other houses in the quiet tree-lined street—redbrick and domesticated, sitting behind a low brick fence. He sighed and took in a deep breath in the vain hope that by doing so he could better accommodate his hand into the pocket of his black jeans as he rummaged for the keys. It really was time, he thought, that he bought himself a new pair of jeans—the ones he was wearing had obviously shrunk in the wash. He managed to rescue the keys from falling through the hole in the bottom of the pocket, and pulled them out, the pocket lining and a variety of fluff accompanying them. He unlocked the door and pushed it open.

Leaving the keys jangling in the lock he kicked the solid wood door with its two cantilevered vertical glass panels closed behind him and stood listening in the dim vestibule. He could hear the muffled rumble of some appliance back in the kitchen and smiled. He was happy not to be the first one home—a quirk of his dating back to being the only latchkey kid in the street. Bernie, an erstwhile friend of his used to regale him with tales of hatchet men who laid in wait for fat little boys coming home to empty houses. He'd never forgiven Bernie, nor had he ever been comfortable with unoccupied houses, not even after his parents' careful scrutiny with him of all the obvious hiding places, and the instillation of security systems.

7

Tim pushed his fingers through his short crinkly black hair and whistled his way down the hallway and through to the kitchen which looked out onto a bricked, and fern-filled courtyard with a sleep-out hidden behind the ferns.

"What's cooking?"

Paul Edgar looked up from the workbench, and grinned. "Dinner. Did you leave your keys in the door again?"

Tim frantically patted his pockets down then looked sheepishly at Paul.

"Really Tim, I do wonder about you sometimes. You are so conscientious about the security of the house, yet you nearly always forget to extract the keys." Paul shook his head.

"Must be something to do with always having had them attached to a chain hooked over my blazer or shirt button. I couldn't get away from the door and into the house until I'd removed the key. Without that reminder ... I'll go get them."

When Tim returned to the kitchen he walked over to the fridge and took out a can of beer. He pulled the tab and sat on a barstool at the breakfast bar. "Busy day?"

"Huh! What do you think?" asked Paul, pushing another carrot into the blender. "It's a real quiet time for me at the moment. No pop stars visiting, no football games, no models, no idols, nothing." Several heads of broccoli followed the carrot. "No, been busy reading recipe books. This is a new, multi-blend soup. Says to eat it cold, but I think I'll heat it."

"Sounds good to me." Tim drowned his beer and sat pensively watching Paul feeding eggplant and celery into the blender. He wondered how the soup would end up tasting and wasn't sure that he wanted to know. If he hadn't just come home, he might have considered going out for some fish and chips. "What else are we having with that?" he asked tentatively.

"Toast with the soup, then jacket potatoes."

He nodded his head. Jacket potatoes. He could handle that. "Anything I can do?"

Later that evening Tim and Paul relaxed in the living room. It was a large room that hadn't changed much in the years he had been a visitor—homely after a fashion that had grown on him and reflecting the personalities of Paul's parents. The wall at one end, except for opaque double doors that allowed access to a formal dining room that was never used, was floor to ceiling home to books uniformly shelved according to genre. The feature of an adjacent floral wallpapered wall was the fireplace in the middle of tiled surrounds. As was the norm in this home, the fire was set patiently waiting for the colder weather to make an appearance. It would not be long before its services would be required. The main furnishings were an old, but comfortable lounge suite upholstered in now faded and worn wool at one end and a rectangular pine dining table and six straight-back pine chairs with now thinly padded seats at the other.

Tim was sitting at the dining table with his back to Paul, reading the newspaper. Paul was stretched out in one of the low armchairs, his long frame clad in faded blue jeans extended into the room as an exclamation mark. His arms were folded behind his head so the rolled-up sleeves of his plaid shirt cushioned his head with its receding hairline. A couple of magazines lay open, balanced across his stomach.

"You know," he mused, "it's really pathetic what gets printed these days. Not just in the monthly glossies, but also in these weekly for-the-masses magazines."

Tim, his Walkman plugged in and *Iron Butterfly* throbbing into his head, didn't look up from the racing pages of the paper. He hadn't heard.

"I mean, of what earthly interest is it what the elite wear to the races? Or which rock star's marriage is floundering? Who the hell is *Smegma* anyway? What was wrong with *The Beatles*? Look," he picked up the magazine and read "'Rod and Alana cruise the Aegean' Who gives a fart?" Paul flipped over a few pages. "Or what about this one? 'Liz lifts her face'. So what?" He looked over at Tim, the tip of his tongue had escaped the confines of his mouth again. It was a habit of Tim's when he was concentrating. Why, or how, anyone could concentrate over horse races was beyond Paul. He extended his leg even further and gave Tim's chair a prod. Tim looked up and pulled the earphones out, "huh?"

"I said," Paul enunciated clearly, "so what?"

"So what, what?"

"So what if the pope's wife runs off with the Bishop of Rome?"

"Can't."

"I know she can't," Paul said exasperatedly. "The pope..."

"The pope is the Bishop of Rome." Tim looked at Paul innocently. Paul sighed.

Tim had always exasperated him. Right from when they had both started secondary school. Two lost boys in a tornado of grey shorts and knee-high socks. As luck had it, they both started at the same school, in the same class on the same day a week after the rest of the school had started. Not through any fault of their own. Paul had been overseas with his parents and had not got back in time for the beginning of the school year. Tim had been recovering from a belated attack of chickenpox. One boy, tall and tanned, the other dark and portly. Both standing out from the rest and targeted for instant harassment. Paul could handle it, Tim became the butt of every prank, and the one who was always left to hold the baby. For some inexplicable reason Paul always felt responsible for Tim, and was continually irritated by Tim's ineffectual means of counteracting contempt and target practice.

"Why is it that all this tripe gets published, yet I cannot get my in-depth interviews with the bourgeois literati and excellent photographs accepted, not even by the weekly non-glossies?"

"Because you are too good for them and too picky for your own good." Tim returned to the form guide in the paper.

Paul smarted. He knew it was true, the bit about his photojournalism being of a high calibre, but he didn't like anyone else to even hint that his ego was a problem. "Well you sure as hell can't pick them," he snapped.

"Pick what?" Tim asked in all innocence, his mind focused on Race Five.

"Well, girls for one thing," he fluttered his hand in the general direction of the newspaper Tim was reading, "and horses for another."

"Speak for yourself," Tim muttered. "When was the last time you went out with the same girl more than once?"

Paul should have seen that one coming, but his own preoccupation with the unfairness of the publishing world had left him with his guard down. Inspired by Tim and the form guide he decided to steer onto less shaky ground. "Do you remember Horse?"

"What?" Tim was unprepared for the change in tack. "Horse?" Tim looked down at the paper spread across the table. What race is he in?"

"Not a horse you donkey."

"Then what page is he on?" Tim asked, thinking that Paul was referring to a character in the comic strip *Footrot Flats*.

Paul groaned out loud. "Don't you remember? That senior prick from school."

"Which one?" Tim was totally confused.

"You know, the one who gave you so much trouble." Paul ground his teeth. "The juniors, we all called him Horse, think the seniors did too. But not to his face."

"What's his name?"

"Can't think beyond what we called him. Tall guy, arrogant as hell, thought he was god's gift to the girls, and they did too. Built like an Adonis."

"You mean Gee-Gee?" Tim frowned in confusion, and Paul sank back into the chair with a sigh. "What about him?"

"I said," Paul hauled himself to a sitting, rather than sprawled, position. "Do you remember Horse. I just wondered what had become of him?"

"Don't know. Don't think he was at the reunion last year," Tim's face was crinkled in concentration. He stood up and walked out of the room mumbling something, which Paul didn't catch, and didn't know if he wanted to.

Paul stood up, the magazine falling to the floor, and reached over for the newspaper that Tim had left on the table. He shuffled it back into some semblance of order and sat down at the table to read the news. As usual it was all trifling tabloid stuff. Nothing of substance or noteworthy. Puerile political squabbles which wasted taxpayers' money and distracted the public's attention away from the real issues. It seemed that every time something of national, or international importance was brewing the government would throw in a red herring. So while bills of magnitude were surreptitiously passed, the public was totally unaware, being preoccupied with trivia like MP's salary increases, or petty cash spending.

He flipped the page over. The editorial was lambasting the pro-life forum—flogging a dead horse more likely, thought Paul as he scanned the remainder of the pages. Even the funnies were re-runs. Was there nothing which he could follow up and create into a prize-winning piece?

He turned the pages again and perused the international page. Nothing much there either. Starving millions still littered the globe as famine, drought, flood and war ravaged the place. He sighed. No pending coups, no nuclear dumping of wastes, no new rainforest demise. He may have to resign himself to peddling more trifling piffle for the women's magazines to tide him over till 'the big one' came along.

He'd done it before, and he'd do it again. He wasn't too proud for that, but it didn't really do much for the reputation he was trying to foster and maintain. He acknowledged that other big-name writers, and photographers, had cut their teeth on the local papers and mass magazines, but they were those who had gone through the cadet system of servitude. He was one of the first of the new breed. Those that had tertiary qualifications. He had an image to maintain. Or thought he did.

He turned the page again, then flipped it back. His eye had caught something at the bottom of the page. A short paragraph. He read it carefully, and slowly a smile spread across his face. He tapped his finger on the paragraph and grinned. Here it was. The piece that he was waiting for. This was a news item worthy of his pursuit.

With that Tim returned, a number of books and papers in his arms.

"What have you got there?" asked Paul.

"Oh, these are some Old Collegiate magazines, and stuff from that reunion last year." He flopped them down onto the table and pulled out a chair and sat down. "Thought there might be something in them about Gee-Gee. Here," Tim tossed half the pile over to Paul, "take a look through."

But neither of them could find any mention of the old boy they sought.

While Tim retired for the night Paul sat disconsolately at the table and wondered about the item he had read in the paper. There must be some way in which he could run that to his advantage. He carried the newspaper out to the kitchen and took a pair of scissors out of the third drawer down in the dresser. Carefully he cut out the short paragraph and slipped it into his wallet. He would visit his agent in the morning and see what could be done.

Chapter 3

"Damn it Fletcher. Enough with the arguments. The decision has been made, and if you don't like it then that's tough, you still have to work with it." And with a wave of his hand Gary G. Fletcher was dismissed.

Gary G. Fletcher stood and stared at the suited man seated at the immaculate desk in front of him. The man's attitude said it all. Head down to reveal his thinning thatch of greying crown, hand busy dragging the gold fountain pen over the bond paper. The interview was over. Gary Fletcher had been given his orders and he was no longer an entity in the insular office. His eyes swept once more around the room and shuddered at its austerity. A hallowed office where countless assignments had been meted out, for better or for worse.

Fletcher had been the recipient of many of them, but never one such as this.

Slowly he shook his head as though to clear his thoughts. He stared once more at the doyen in front of him. The great man himself. Edward Maxwell, the name unuttered by the public because it was unknown to the public. The emotions which the man conjured in Gary sped into a whirlpool of distaste. Unconsciously he swallowed and then slowly he turned and walked silently across the plush carpet to the door. He reached out for the gold-plated handle and hesitated, he turned his head for one last look at Maxwell, half hoping that the man would rescind at least some part of his order. But the older man remained, head bent and writing. Gary opened the heavy door and pulled it towards him.

15

"Fletcher!" Maxwell's voice sliced across the room and speared Gary to the spot. Slowly he faced back into the room. Edward Maxwell sat primly at the desk, his arms resting comfortably on the edge while he seesawed his pen between his fingers. Fletcher could feel his flesh creep in a ghastly wave, but he didn't have time to speculate on what this new summons was for. "You're on your own remember. Totally on your own. No one, not even me. I don't want to know anything." Maxwell smiled sardonically. "No matter what happens, we'll deny any knowledge of you."

Fletcher shuddered inwardly as his stomach congealed into a lead weight. He inclined his head in acknowledgment, but Maxwell had already returned to his work.

That was all he needed. A job that was not only beneath his abilities and expertise, but one that left him dangling at the end of a weak bungy cord. And, if the cord snapped, they were not going to provide him with a safety net. He didn't need this kind of treatment. Put him in the field carrying out assigned missions formulated by others, and he would deliver. He was a man of action. That was his forte. He was good. He, and they, knew it. He was not a lackey into planning and logistics. So why fob him off on some wet-nurse task? A puppet is what he had become. He should have told old Maxwell to stuff it, there and then. Hang the consequences.

Instead, with concentrated resignation Gary quietly left the room, closing the door behind him. Maxwell's secretary looked up at him with a smile which he didn't see as he ground his way to the lifts, stepped into the waiting cavern and rode the mirrored cage to the ground floor.

The reflection showed a man, a finger short of six foot, and normally brimming with confidence, determination, and pride. In his early forties, he wore his dark-blonde hair cropped short and his face, though somewhat weathered, and starting to crinkle around the green eyes, had a natural tan, which didn't sit comfortably with the business suit and dark tie. He had often been mistaken for a champion athlete, but his strength and expertise were not used in the sports arena.

When the lift reached the ground floor he strode purposefully across the foyer of the building and out into the balmy autumn afternoon. Looking neither left nor right, and totally unimpressed with the early tints of the deciduous trees that lined the street, he walked across the multilane arterial road. He didn't hear the raucous tirade of abuse that accompanied the strident scream of horns as cars in all lanes braked, swerved and slewed around him. Fortunately there was no scrunch of metal against metal and all participants in the crossing were able to proceed unscathed. Not than Fletcher noticed. His mind was in such angry turmoil that no extraneous stimuli penetrated his consciousness.

As his agitation wore off his pace lessened. The low clatter of a ride-on mower trimming lawns further afield jarred him to full awareness of his surroundings. He was somewhere in the Botanical Gardens. He stopped and looked around him. Not in surprise, but in appreciation of the work by the city gardeners. He enjoyed nature, whether it was wild or cultivated. Slowly he walked past the regimented beds of Chrysanthemums, Marigolds and Nerines.

The 'mums' reminded him that Mother's Day was not too distant, and he thought about his own mother. Maybe this year, with this assignment being on 'home turf', he would be able to spend some time with her over the autumn months. Together they could work in her garden. It was a pastime which they had enjoyed in the past. Now both found gardening difficult. His one-bedroom penthouse did not extend to the luxury of garden space, and he was so often absent that satisfaction could not be gained from window boxes or patio planters. His mother had the garden, but with increasing years and failing health there was little that she could do in it these days. Sure, he had arranged for a man to come and cut the lawns, and do a regular general tidy-up, but other than the perennials in raised pots little could be said about the garden back home.

Fletcher sat down on a park bench in the sun and stretched out his legs. What was he to do about this latest assignment? He knew, if he wanted to keep his position in the company, he could not turn it down. Whichever way he looked at it, this job was his. So, despite his initial anger, he would do the very best that he could. Nothing less would be acceptable. Yet he did still wonder what he could possibly have done to deserve such a menial task as this. He thought back over his last assignment. Had he muffed up somewhere? Or trodden on any toes?

The game was getting more and more political. He had enjoyed it more when his section of the company had been an autonomous unit. Answerable to no one, but your back was always covered. Now there was Accountability, and there always seemed to be paperwork. He thought of his desk, the one that he used, like now, when he was between fieldwork assignments, hidden under a blanket of forms and reports. Once all it had contained had been the current file and a telephone. Now he had a word processor, a fax machine, *and* an answering machine attached to his phone. He could see no reason for that to be cluttering up the desktop, after all now he was hardly out of the confines of the office. And why did he have a VCR? Then there were the drawers of printouts and forms for rubber-stamping. They called it progress. But he preferred the older methods where all his day-to-day workings had been taken care of by a pretty little strumpet whom he'd shared with a couple of others, in more ways than one. He smiled. Now he was expected to front up to the office every day that he wasn't outside the country and put in a decent appearance. Maybe, if he played his cards right, he'd be able to turn this assignment into a field assignment and he wouldn't have to confine himself to the four walls of the office. After all, that was what he'd been trained as—a field officer.

He tried to recollect all that Maxwell had said to him. There hadn't been much, and it hadn't been committed to paper either. Naturally. He was meant to be working without their backing. He'd never heard of anything so inane. Surely all the cloak and dagger stuff was now obsolete with talk of the cold war's demise. He massaged the back of his neck and stretched his shoulders. There was definitely something more to all this than Maxwell was letting on, and he wondered what it was.

All he knew was that he had to arrange the transfer of some unknown person from some unspecified place to a safe house; all of which he had to arrange. Maxwell had made it sound so simple. Too simple. Fletcher sighed. He hadn't been given any dates, just told that someone would be contacting him 'at home' the next day. Fletcher noted wryly that he obviously wasn't wanted back in the office. He really must have squashed and ground someone's toes to powder. He assumed, from the directive, that he would need to have his plan formulated by tomorrow. He looked at his watch. 4.30. He didn't have much time.

Chapter 4

The television screen erupted into a frenzy of violence. Yet another demonstration, Fletcher thought as he reached for his iced herbal tea. His colleagues always razzed him about his non-alcoholic lifestyle. But he invariably got the better of them every 'morning-after'. He had found, early in his career, that he did not need the stimulating euphoria of alcohol to help him in his work, nor did he need its blotting effects to ease the pain. His healthy lifestyle with its puritan diet was all that he needed in order to survive the rigors demanded from his line of work. Not that this present assignment needed strict adherence to diet, exercise or ... anything. This was real couch-potato stuff.

He took a long draught of his drink and pulled a writing pad towards him. Logistics and statistics. That's all this job needed. The logistics of getting whoever from wherever to some other, wherever. Any rabbit from the section could have done that. Even the statistics of how many men—no, they were now 'personnel' he reminded himself—were needed didn't need an Einstein. He doodled on the pad. The television screen now showed a reporter embraced by the usual rabble of children grinning at the camera. His pen poised in mid-air as Fletcher realized that he knew the reporter, and the embassy outside which the demonstration was taking place. He dropped his pen and reached for the remote and depressed the mute button.

"*Once more Demetrius Popolo has incensed the fabric of decency in yet another country.*"

21

The television showed a much-publicised photograph of Popolo, not the usual head and shoulders portrait that the media kept on file, but the one favoured by the man himself where he was leisurely leaning against a Doric column in some ancient ruin. He was dark haired and swarthy skinned, of average height and weight. He wore pristine white slacks and shirt, open nearly to the waist, a large gold medallion and the usual assortment of chains hanging around his neck. The photo must have been taken years ago. No one went around with their animal chests displayed like that since the Bee Gees. A white slash of teeth was spread across his face in a plastered smile.

"*The question which begs to be asked,*" continued the reporter, "*is 'why does he do it?' When he knows what the reaction will be before he puts pen to paper, why does he insist upon following the thought with the action?*"

The camera panned away from the reporter and zoomed in on the demonstrators who were now turning nasty, hurling stones into the embassy compound.

The reporter continued as a voice-over. "*Popolo's latest book, a novel of some length, is a flimsy attempt to portray his country's oppression of women. For this he is now no longer welcome to remain here, his sanctuary, for the past two years. One wonders where he will next reside and what further books he intends to write. This is Jefferson Reynolds of...*"

Fletcher punched the mute button again and Jefferson was left to silently mouth his by-line.

"Damn fool of a man," Fletcher muttered as he reached for his pen again. "What does he write such things for? He must have a death wish, or something. Sure, things are bad in his home country. But every country has its problems. What gives him the authority to air his? It does no good. Never will." Fletcher rummaged through the piles of papers on the table, looking for a calendar. He hadn't really been given a timeline for this assignment.

He found the calendar. Now it was time for statistics and probability. Fletcher leant back in the chair, raised his hands above his head and stretched. He addressed the ceiling. "Let's say this person is to disappear in a week's time. Then what would I do? Depends where I pick him up," he answered, sitting back up. "Okay, suppose I pick him up at a hotel." He wrote 'hotel' on the pad. "Okay. Pick him up in a dirty early model ... no, too conspicuous these days." Fletcher doodled a vehicle on the pad. He scratched it out and stood up. He covered his face with spread hands and ran them up and over his hair. He shook his head and walked into the kitchenette.

He liked this room. Small, compact with a view to kill for. All along one wall was window. Below was the workbench, so whenever he was home and preparing meals, he could stand there and gaze out across the bay to the You Yangs, the series of granite ridges that appeared as two joined peaks on the horizon across Port Phillip Bay. He'd often contemplated investing in a high-powered telescope, that would not only bring them closer, but which would also enable him to bring his neighbours into his life and home through the lens. He'd never bought the telescope, it was voyeurism, and too much like work, so had contended himself with speculation and enjoying the sunrises and weekend yachties. Not that there were either right now. Tonight the water was flecked with white horses and the darkening sky was dappled with darker clouds scudding towards the setting sun.

He had intended to boil the kettle for another pot of tea, but instead he filled a glass with water from the filter and picked an apple up from the carved wooden fruit bowl which he had brought back from Bali one year. Bali. Now there was a place. Maybe he could secrete this anonymous person there. That would be safe. But how to do it? Now there was an exercise in logistics!

Fletcher walked back into the living area, set the glass down where it was sure to add to the collection of rings on the table, and sat down again. He sighed and took a bite out of his apple. Nothing could beat a Fuji apple, he thought, as he nibbled the skin off around the equator. He pulled his pad towards him again, picked the pen up and staccatoed the nib against the paper, leaving an ant trail in its wake. He circled the word 'hotel' several times.

"Yes, pick up from the hotel in an inconspicuous late model car and drive to..." Safe house. Safe house. Which one? Where? For how long? Fletcher patted the pockets of his jeans in frustration. It was times like this that his colleagues would reach for a cigarette. Instead, he withdrew a crumpled packet of chewing gum. He looked at it glumly and pulled out a foil wrapped strip, unwrapped the gum and wadded it into his mouth. How was he supposed to formulate a plan when he had nothing to go on? Fletcher ripped the doodled pages from the pad and furiously scrunched them up in a ball and tossed them across the room. He finished his apple, turned the lights out and retired to bed.

Chapter 5

True to Edward Maxwell's word, not that Fletcher had ever had cause to doubt it, Fletcher was contacted the next day. When the call finally came, he had been up and dressed for the better part of three hours. He had watched as the horizon had lightened and heralded the gentle emergence of a battery-hen yolk sun. He had completed his regime of morning exercise and meditation, along with his fruit-full and high-fibre breakfast, and had washed, dried, and put away the dishes.

He was leaning against the workbench in the kitchenette, glad that he was at home, but wishing that the call would come through and put him out of his misery. It was shortly after nine o'clock, when the phone finally rang. 'Someone's in early and on the ball', he thought, as he rushed through to the other room and lifted the receiver from off its rest before the answering machine could kick in.

"Fletcher," he growled into the mouthpiece. That was all he ever said when he answered the phone. His mother found it most disconcerting and went to great lengths to tell him so whenever she rang him. The telephone was set austerely on a marble pedestal. It encouraged short conversations. He drummed his fingers on the cold stone surface and waited for the caller to identify themselves.

"Er, Mr Fletcher, this is, er,"

Silence.

"Mr Fletcher? Are you there?"

"Yes." Fletcher bristled at the voice. He could see the minor minion. Sitting sweating at some obscure desk. Hardly out of nappies and already raking in the girls with tales of his important corporate position.

"I've been told to ring you and give you some information."

"Go on." How he hated being beholden to this disembodied voice for information pertaining to his assignment. What was Maxwell playing at? Couldn't he have been given his directive face to face like usual?

"Er, do you have a pen and paper?"

"Just give me the message." What did the idiot think? He was a professional. And if this job was so clandestine to warrant a departure from routine, then why would he write something down that would lead to a paper-trail? He was listening to a juvenile flunky for sure. Fletcher listened intently for 30 seconds then dropped the receiver back onto its cradle.

Great. Just great. He now had the information. And he wanted it less than he had wanted the assignment in the first place. Again, he wondered what he had he done to antagonize the powers that were to such an extent that he would be landed with this.

He thought back to the previous night and his jottings on the pad. He laughed at his childish ideas. This was going to be much bigger than first impressions. Damn Maxwell.

Fletcher stormed across the room and into his immaculately tidy bedroom. He sat down on the neatly made bed tossed his Dr Scholl sandals off and thrust his feet into running shoes. He flung open the cupboard doors and dragged his training jacket off its hanger and struggled into it as he strode across the floor and out the front door. He shoved his hands into the pockets and clumped down the ten flights of stairs to the street level. He shouldered his way out the main doors of the apartment block and without a glance around the environs he jogged off down the street towards the beach.

Two hours later a very weary and sweaty Gary Fletcher sank into the overstuffed, floral upholstered armchair in his living area. It was a relic from his youth, childhood in fact. He could remember the cosy evenings spent coiled in its embrace. While the rest of the family puttered around doing their own things—his mother in the kitchen creating wafting fragrances of baking and dinner; his father wheezing over crusty books and papers at the roll-top desk over by the window; his brother listening to the crystal set he'd made; his sister playing dollhouses in an old orange box—he had pretended to be a lone sailor braving the Atlantic, or an explorer in deepest Africa. Always an adventurer. The memories were what had induced him to lug the armchair with him wherever he had lived since leaving home. His fingers lazily traced a shabby lily on the arm of the chair. He knew what he had to do, even if he still didn't know who the V.I.P. was. More importantly, he now had a timeline. He slapped the palms of his hands down on the floral arms, pushed himself out of the chair and went into the bathroom to shower.

Chapter 6

Christie Rowlands and Melody Arnold were whispering across a book-strewn study table in the university library. They were oblivious to the pointed stares from the students, unused to seeing admin staff in the five-storied concrete edifice.

"But I tell you Melody," Christie leaned closer to her friend, her dark hair reaching the pages of the opened books on the table and so shielding her flawless English complexion and the clear blue eyes which danced like leprechauns at a fairy's wake. Two attributes which she had inherited from feuding ancestors. "There. Is. No. Ghost." She slid down her chair till her shoulders rested on the lip of the backrest, her feet crossed at the ankles and almost reaching the midpoint of the floor under the table. How had the topic of ghosts even come up, she wondered? Why had her friend even brought up the subject of ghosts? Ghosts had no bearing on either of the topics they were working on for their individual department heads. "I don't believe there ever was."

"How can you say that?" scoffed Melody, deaf to the muted muttering about libraries being places of silence, as she rested her elbows on the table then folded her arms. Her curly cropped auburn hair was in stark contrast to Christie's. Her hair wasn't exactly red, but she had the expected freckles peppered across her face; and the temper to match a redhead. "Everyone knows that the girl was murdered there." She flashed a broad smile at Christie, as if to say, 'so there!'"

29

Christie gaped at Melody. First ghosts, and now murder? Neither had any relevance that she knew of, to what they were in the library for. Whatever was her friend talking about?

"What girl, where?"

"The girl who was murdered in Hemlock. That's where you're from, you must know her."

"Which girl?"

"The one that was murdered."

Christie could feel herself starting to sweat. Had there been another murder? She told herself to calm down, it could not be possible. "Melody, how would I know her? I left home years ago."

"I'm not talking about now. This is the one that happened years ago. It's all here in the article about the haunted house."

Christie blanched, that murder had been something she had worked hard to forget. She involuntarily shivered. She'd barely been a teenager when it had happened. While there had been plenty of local speculation at the time, it had not been reported in the national papers. So how could Melody, a year younger than her twenty-nine years, know about that? She shook her head.

Christie sighed and rubbed her fingers against her temples. "There are no ghosts."

"But everyone knows that murdered people leave a ghost. It's because their spirit has never been set free. It happens whenever anyone has an abrupt and untimely end to their life."

Christie straightened up and lent in towards Melody. "Oh sure, and last week you were telling me that you believed everything was destiny, even the time when one died."

"That was last week," Melody scoffed as though it was the most natural thing in the world to change one's philosophy on life as frequently as changing one's underwear.

"So what changed your mind?" Christie cooed.

Melody, never taking her sparkling gold-brown eyes off Christie pushed a magazine across the table to Christie. "Here, read this."

Christie broke her stare across the chasm between them and looked down at the magazine in front of her. She flipped the pages back to read the cover, and then flipped it back to the page that Melody wanted her to read. "Don't tell me that you read these types of magazines and then believe this stuff?" Christie slapped her palm down on the magazine. "It's rubbish. It's only written to make a profit off stupid housewives who've got nothing better to do than eye-monger the rich and famous. The women who read these magazines don't think about things, they simply absorb the trash as verbatim truth." She pushed the magazine away.

"But Christie," Melody looked hurt. "It's a true article. Investigative reporting, and it has good quality photographs to go with it."

Christie felt a niggle of compassion and drew the offending magazine back towards her. She looked at the article again and saw the by-line. She raised a Brooke Shields eyebrow. "What's Paul Edgar doing writing for a woman's weekly magazine?"

"Who?" Melody's freckles merged as she puckered her face in confusion.

"Paul Edgar. He's a freelance photojournalist. Writes good stuff and is a terrific photographer."

"How do you know?"

"I know because I don't waste time reading this stuff." Christie tapped the magazine with her nail-bitten finger. "His work appears in a number of quarterlies. You know, the magazines that cost heaps to buy. The ones that deal with international issues. Or he used to, I haven't seen any of his work recently, not for a few years. I wonder what happened?"

"Ah, but if you only read those types of magazines, how do you know that he doesn't now write for other types, like this one?" Melody sat back and grinned triumphantly across the table.

"Any reputable photojournalist wouldn't lower himself." Christie also sat back, crossed her arms over her chest and glared at her friend.

"Everyone has to live."

"What do you mean by that?"

"Oh, come on. You know what I mean. It's called 'bread and butter' money. The jobs that keep you in pin money while you wait for the big breaks." She smiled as she gathered her books into a tidy pile and collected her personal papers up and put them into a carry-all at her feet. "Come on." A smidgen of smugness had crept into Melody's voice, as though she knew something that Christie didn't. She scraped her chair back and stood up. "Time for a coffee I think."

Chapter 7

"Tell me about it."

"What?" Christie had no idea what Melody was talking about. They were still in the campus cafeteria and onto their second cup of coffee. Evidence of their first being two shredded Styrofoam cairns in the centre of the table.

"You know, the ghost of that dead girl."

Christie laughed, "I told you Melody, there is no such thing as ghosts."

"Then why does everyone still talk about it?" Melody swirled the coffee in her cup, staring at the whirlpool intently.

"What do you mean *everyone*? No one has mentioned the murder since it happened, and ghosts are not real. Where are you getting all this from anyway? Not that magazine you were reading upstairs?" Christie shook her head sadly.

Melody put her cup back down and lazily drew circles with her finger on the surface of the table, then looked up defiantly. "And what's wrong with that?"

Christie shook her head again, clasped her hands behind her head, and stretched. "Really, do you want me to go over it all again? Come on let's get back to those books before we get into strife for skiving off work. Don't know about you but Prof Swank's expecting my findings before his meeting starts." She stood up and swept her cairn into the empty whole cup she held in her hand.

"But it's interesting." Melody stood up too, slugged back the dregs of her coffee, and cleaned up her cairn as well. "You should read it," she said as she followed Christie across the cafeteria floor.

33

They dropped their rubbish in the bin by the door and rode the elevator up to their floor. "No, I mean it. You should read the article. Did you know that the property where it all happened is up for sale?"

Christie looked sharply at her friend. No, she did not know that. Was it that long since she had been home? Why hadn't anyone told her? Who would buy it? Who would want to buy it, with its history of murder, mayhem and haunting? She blushed as she realized that her thoughts contradicted her earlier denials to Melody. Maybe she ought to read the magazine.

Chapter 8

Refreshed and invigorated Fletcher sat down at the table and arranged pens, pads of paper, maps, a calendar and a diary before him. He sighed. He had less than three months in which to execute the perfect deception. It had to be meticulous and fool proof. Nothing could afford to go wrong. He was on his own and there was to be no fall guy, other than himself, and there was no way that he could allow that to happen.

He opened the calendar up to the current month. Today was Wednesday the 10th. He circled it. An auspicious start—if his memory served him that was the day a decade or so ago that Martin Luther King Jr's murderer was sentenced to 99 years in prison. He hoped that his own involvement in this assignment would not lead to the same result for him.

He had exactly eight weeks to prepare to work a miracle. Nine to be on the safe side. He looked at his watch. It was well past lunch and so he'd be better off working through to dinner. He reached for a pen and pad and started to list the people and areas of expertise he would need. He estimated that the assignment would require at least thirty people, of whom the fewer on the 'need to know' list, the better. He thought he could probably get away with maybe only one or two being privy to what was happening. But, if he managed to keep as many as possible separate, he might be able to swing it that no one other than himself need know the full extent of the project. There would always be some who would speculate. Hell, they would all try to guess. But nobody would guess the whole truth. He couldn't

35

afford for that to happen. He tapped the end of his pen against his teeth. Maybe he could work this a different way. On another page he divided the task into six areas for ease of organization.

It was dark well before Fletcher finally dropped his pen on the tabletop. "Done," he said with tired satisfaction. He rubbed the bridge of his nose with the middle fingers of his hands as they cupped over his face. He was dog-tired, but he'd got it sussed. He clasped his hands together and stretched them out in front of him, yawned, and brought them back over his head. He let them go and shook his head. Then stood up, straightened the papers on the table and smiled. He had done it. It was all sorted. Now all that was left was to put it into operation and starting on that could wait for tomorrow.

Gary Fletcher looked at the photograph that had been couriered to him earlier in the day. It showed a man that was nothing like the publicity photographs he had seen. He remembered the one that he had seen, quite a number of years ago, when Fletcher's mother had described the man in question as 'rather dashing'. Fletcher shook his head, he was hardly 'dashing' now. The man now staring glossily at Fletcher was of average height. That had not changed. He was now of more than average girth, to say the least. The belt with which his body was bisected had never, so the owner proudly proclaimed, changed notches. It was the same as it when he left school. However, by looking at this photograph his body had not kept up the pretence. Folds of flab bulged out from either edge of the belt, and had he been a girl his mother would have fitted him out with a D-cup bra years ago.

Fletcher sighed. It was going to be more difficult than he had first thought. He scribbled 'dietician' and 'aerobics' on the pad before him. That just added to the numbers and increased the security risk. Security, that was turning out to be the real bugbear of this operation. How could he best pull that one off? He shrugged his shoulders. Well, it was simply too bad. At least he wasn't the one who had to foot the bill. And he was happy to pad the bill out as much as possible, it would be payback for allotting him this task.

He stood up and stretched. He looked at his watch and noticed that it was getting late. He had a dinner date and needed to get ready. He meticulously stacked the papers on the table into a pile, returned the photograph to its envelope, and placed it on top. He then went through to the bathroom and ran the shower. Cold. Five minutes later he stood in front of the mirror and splashed aftershave along his fair beard line.

Fletcher dropped the towel from around his waist, stepped out of the folds on the floor, and walked through to the bedroom where he had set out the clothes that he would wear. Business like, yet casual. After all, this was a working dinner date. Beige slacks coupled with a pale green shirt. He picked up the paisley tie and walked back into the bathroom. He stooped down, picked up the towel and carefully folded it in half lengthwise and hung it over the heated towel rail. He then turned to look at his reflection. His hair was slicked back off his face and his green eyes, made greener by his shirt, pierced back into his soul. He held the tie against the front of his shirt. Would he wear it, or not?

It had always been a problem, trying to decide what was the correct effect to create when dressing for wheeling and dealing. He could never afford to be too intimidating nor compliant. Just how far could one go? That was not something that they had taught him at school, nor had he been able to pick it up from his father who had been absent from pre-birth. And this was one area where his mother had been of no help. His mother's women's magazines, glossy or otherwise, were never any help, and he'd always believed himself to be above purchasing the men's magazines. Double breasted suits he felt were always too pretentious, and jeans too casual, so his wardrobe consisted of a numerous array of smart slacks, sports coats, and shirts. Ties were one area where he allowed his personality to show. But even then, he always deliberated at length over which one to wear before venturing out. Nude ladies and flamboyant cartoon characters were not to be worn to five-star restaurants. He removed the paisley tie and decided that he liked the effect better without the noose.

Chapter 9

Fletcher lay in his bed staring at the pale reflection of streetlights on the ceiling. Only the muffled vehicle noise from the street below penetrated the room and he was reminded of how insular his life had become. Few friends, and other than his mother, no family. Even his penthouse was sterile. Back in his childhood home, if he lay in his bed he was always surrounded—the scrape of the almond tree against his window; the wind in the trees beyond the garden fence; the whine of the dogs as each vehicle whooshed past, their headlights casting moving shadows across the ceiling and walls; bird call at dawn and dusk. He really would have to go back home and visit with his mother. Soon. Before this current assignment got too involved.

Fletcher sighed. The evening had been surprisingly pleasant. The food had been most enjoyable, and the time spent with his contact had not been as arduous as anticipated. Except when McFadden had called him out. He smarted as he remembered the malicious jibe. McFadden had placed his hands flat on the edge of the table and leant back in his chair, staring at Fletcher. 'You really are a jaundiced prick. You know that don't you? All right, she divorced you. But that was a decade ago. Get over it, and do your job.' McFadden having relieved his spleen and said his piece had then been most accommodating and agreed to approach the potential security team members on his behalf.

So why could he not get comfortable and get to sleep? He ought to feel pleased with his progress. Not be consumed with prickly feelings of unease. Such unsettling and sleepless nights usually occurred when he was well into an assignment and were recognizable as harbingers of pending shambles to his plans. But it was not that way this time. Things were going smoothly. It was still early days and there was nothing of substance yet to support a hiccup. He was still in the planning stage. So why couldn't he get to sleep? He ran through the scheme again.

Favours had been called in. The caterers and transport were sorted. Tonight's dinner had called in another favour and set further wheels in motion—the medical team would soon be under control. Everything was now nearly all in place. Overall, it hadn't been as hard as he had first imagined. Except for the one call that he had yet to make. The one that he had been avoiding from the beginning. The security detail was yet to be secured. He gave a little laugh at the thought, "Security to be secured. That's a good one!" He chuckled.

So what was bothering him and keeping him awake?

Exasperated with himself, he kicked off his childhood quilt and swung his legs over the side of the bed. Thinking that a cup of tea might help his thoughts he walked through to the kitchenette. The more he thought about it the more he realised that whichever way he looked at it he was bound to lose. If the assignment failed, his position in the section would be precarious, to say the least. More likely he would be finished. He grimaced. He did not need a career change at the current moment. If he succeeded, his position was secure. But he would be unable to operate again. At least to the extent that he had prided himself. He would have called in all his favours. No contacts, no work. Simple. There was nothing he could do about it. It was the only way to accomplish this current project.

Damn Maxwell. Sitting there, in his untouchable palace. Totally impervious to any pull of the tide. Totally removed from all persuasion or predicament. A master at putting others in peril and making life hell for those who crossed him and to Maxwell went the accolade, within the section at least.

Fletcher leant against the workbench and stared out the window. The bay was a blotch of black that sporadically twinkled as the scudding clouds let the moon shine through. His thoughts ran through the list of things he needed to do. His security detail was the one that aggrieved him the most. With who he was going to be responsible for, he would need something special as the media would be more than anxious to uncover the pending deception. He sighed, and looked into his cup. It was sitting there on the workbench top, cold and still clasped in his hands. Fletcher heaved himself away from the window, tipped the cold tea into the sink before making his way back to the bedroom.

He still worried about what it was that he had done to be landed with this assignment. Maybe he'd never know, but he would show them all that he could rise above the snub and succeed beyond their wildest hoping.

Fletcher yawned, flopped onto the bed, and dragged the bedcovers over him. Having sorted all that out maybe now he could sleep.

Chapter 10

Christie had not slept well. Images of tie-dye, incense and bells had haunted her dreams, along with those of murderous long-haired ghosts. She was glad to wake up and see the sun streaming weakly through the curtains. She never closed the curtains, unless she was sleeping on the ground floor, and then only if the window looked out onto a thoroughfare. But last night, at about 2 am she had ventured out of her bed and snapped them closed. She laughed at the memory. As if closed curtains would keep the monsters away! It had been years since she had last had a devastating night like last night. That was after she had found Steve in bed with another man. That sure had brought her up short. There she had been, blithely dreaming of the perfect couple, and so, apparently had he, only unlike her the couple didn't contain a she and he. The nightmares had been her companion then, and she didn't like the thought that they had returned. What she needed was some knight to slay her dragon.

Fat chance of that, she thought to herself, as she got up. Who would want to look at me, far less help me? She avoided the mirror as she showered and dressed in what her colleagues deemed as unsuitable attire for a campus lecturer—baggy jeans and voluminous sweatshirt. The less seen the better, she thought. Why else would Steve have sought recreation elsewhere? No one else shared her perception of herself. She was padded petite, with very shapely curves, in all the right places, including her calves. The envy of many a waif around campus. But she only saw an unattractive blob.

43

She caught up with Melody after her second lecture. "Let me see that article."

"Which one?" Melody asked in all innocence. They followed the paved path as it wound across the open space between lecture blocks and offices towards the Student's Union with its accumulation of services.

"There's only one article that I could possibly be interested in," Christie almost shouted. "The one you were showing me yesterday. The one written by Paul Edgar." She didn't want to mention the topic. She didn't want to tempt fate, at least not until she had read the article.

"Oh, I threw that out when I got home last night. I'd finished reading it." She pushed open the large glass door into the Union building and walked into a wall of noise. "Don't you just hate this place when its busy?" she asked as she held the door open for Christie. "I wonder if we'll find a quiet seat?"

"You what?" Christie screamed above the chatter. "Never mind, I don't want to know." She led Melody across the foyer, sidestepping the barrage of garrulous students exiting the building, and entered the main cafeteria. The two of them made their way through the tables of talk, heading for a table in the far corner. A group of students was also heading in that direction. She eyed the distance and decided to change course. They found a couple of lounge seats tucked in near the entrance to the bookstore.

Christie dumped her bag and a ring binder on the stained nylon fabric and rummaged in her bag for her purse. "Mind these will you." It was a statement rather than a question, and Christie was already moving away before Melody had a chance to either answer or to sit down.

"Where are you going?" she called after Christie.

"To buy a magazine you goat," Christie said over her shoulder.

Melody sat down; her bulging holdall haphazardly balanced on her lap. She let out a sigh and waited, not understanding what the fuss was about. Christie had not been interested, even if the article was about her hometown, and she'd done with the magazine, so why keep it? She shrugged her shoulders. Maybe Christie was suffering PMT, that would explain a lot of things. She watched as Christie returned, holding the magazine rolled tight and against her chest. What could have happened for her to suddenly be so interested in the article that she would lower herself to buy what was for her such an obviously distasteful publication?

Christie smiled as she thrust the magazine at Melody. "Where is it?' she demanded sotto voce as she swept up her bag and ring binder and sat down. "Well?"

Melody had never heard Christie be so impatient before, she battled the coil in the magazine and flipped through till she arrived at the article. "Here it is." She passed it across. "What's this all about?"

Christie didn't hear her. She was busy hiding the magazine in her ring binder and reading. Melody simply sat, her hands clasped in her lap, and tried not to appear uncomfortable. She glanced across at Christie, her lips were moving faintly, following the words on the page. Finally she closed the ring binder, leant back and closed her eyes.

"Mind telling me what this is all about?"

"Nothing, really."

Melody waited, but Christie did not elaborate, immediately.

"Yesterday you asked me to tell you about it. Today I will."

Melody gaped.

"Well, I'll tell you what I can." She hoped that by telling Melody what she remembered, and knew, that she could excise the nightmares. "You must remember that I was very young when it all started. In fact, it probably began even before I was born." Her voice drifted off to nothing and she opened her eyes and sat back up. "I don't really know, and the article doesn't really say. Not exactly. It is accurate, as far as my knowledge goes. But then," she almost sniffed derisively, "I'd expect nothing less from Paul Edgar."

"Well?" Melody turned towards her friend grasping at her holdall to stop it falling to the floor.

"Okay. Paul says," she tapped her ring binder reverently, "that in the mid-1950s the owner, Jim Gentian, died. He wanted *Braedon* ..."

Melody opened her mouth to say something, but Christie, anticipating her, filled in the blank.

"If you had read the article fully before throwing the magazine away you would know that that's the name of the property that the Gentian's had. Anyway, old Jim Gentian wanted it to remain as a testimony and monument to his family, so he left the whole thing to the council for it to developed into a park. Suddenly some long lost and dubiously distant relations decided that they would challenge the will."

"He wasn't married then?" Melody asked, already caught up in the story.

"Yes, he was married. The extended family wrangled with the courts for a couple of years over the will. They may have been distant, but they still wanted to be part of the action. You see *Braedon* was prime grazing land, with stands of native forest, and it fronted onto the lake. They could see profit in bundles, especially if they subdivided it into lifestyle blocks—hobby farms they were called back then.

"The council weren't particularly impressed by the bequest, and not interested in the wrangle. They were in fact quite happy for the family to have it. Finally, in 1958, the courts decided that the property should be sold and the proceeds to be split, after costs, between the council, who could build a suitable memorial, or establish a scholarship or trust or something in memory of the Gentians; and the family who would have liquid assets to dispose of as they felt inclined."

"What about children? Didn't they have family that the property could have been left to? Melody was feeling horrified at the unjustness of it all. Greedy, uncaring relations and an ungrateful council.

"Not really. You see, there was, I guess still is, a lake there. They all drowned."

"Who all drowned?" Melody prodded Christie, and her holdall fell unheeded onto the cushioned area between her and Christie.

"It took six years to wipe out the Gentian family. His wife drowned, trying to save their daughter. She was thirteen, and a good swimmer too."

"How many were there?"

"What?" Christie didn't like her narrative to be disturbed.

"How many were there? Children." This was like pulling weeds out of kiln dried clay, thought Melody.

"Five. Four boys and a girl."

"What happened?" Melody was anxious to hear the whole story, all at once, yet with all the details fully embossed.

"How should I know? I wasn't there," Christie snapped. Between her nightmares and the incident that had put her hometown on the world map, and reading it as written by Paul Edgar, she was reliving the whole past, and did not like the interruptions. It was her story, and she would tell it like it was, her way.

"I know that, but you're the one telling the story, you must expect questions. Besides, you live there for goodness' sake. You must know."

"I don't live *there.*" She had often thought that she would have liked to. Despite all the dire warnings and threats that she had grown up with, she had been human enough to hanker after the things that were forbidden. But it had all happened when it was still a time that children, especially rural children, obeyed, unquestioningly, their all-knowing elders.

"Oh, for goodness' sake, don't go all pedantic on me, you know what I mean. The daughter drowned, but what happened to the sons?"

"They drowned."

"All four of them drowned?"

"Yes. No one knows why or how they drowned. But that is what happened. It was pretty much a mystery. You see, the whole family were good swimmers, so there was talk about foul play, either by the family, or others. But as far as I know there were no investigations. Or, if there were the town's people were never informed so the whole area around the property and that part of the lake became shrouded in a pall of mystique and menace." Christie's eyes took on a faraway look. Melody felt that she was losing her.

"But what about the girl who was murdered?" Melody asked.

"That didn't happen till later," Christie quietly reflected.

"So, what did happen?" Melody tried to keep the exasperation out of her voice.

"Well, the property was put on the market, so that the rellies could all get their bit. Only trouble was, there are no buyers. Everyone knew about the history of the place, or soon learned about it once they got interested, and no one wanted to buy a place that was shrouded in mystery. Word gets around that the lake was a death trap and the home of a monster akin to Loch Ness. Who'd want to buy that?"

"Wouldn't that have attracted overseas buyers? Americans love that sort of thing, surely. Look at all the old castles and bridges they buy in England and relocate to the America."

"And when was the last time *you* tried to move a lake overseas?" snapped Christie. Honestly, sometimes Melody could be so thick. Here she was, weaving this tale of intrigue and all Melody could do was interrupt with nonsensical notions totally unrelated. "Be sensible. This property had a mozz on it well and truly. It was a pariah. No one wanted it."

"Okay, where does the murdered girl fit in?" Melody had not fully read the article. She had only read the headline and the caption on the pictures. All she had taken in was that the property was where Christie came from, that it had a mysterious murder, and that it was for sale.

"Well, the place sort of went backwards as there was no one looking after it. The braver town boys would take dares to go out and fish in the lake, or sleep in the house, but mainly it became a sanctuary for wildlife. Then, I guess it was about 1959, the article says the end of the decade, *Braedon* was finally occupied, by a commune of, well, I guess now we would call them hippies.

"They weren't perturbed by the rumours of hauntings and such, they just laughed at the locals and said that peace and love would destroy all hate, and besides, the rumours would work to their benefit. It would keep the 'prying eyes of perverted scaremongers' away. They would welcome those interested in joining their community of peace, free love, and tranquillity but they would not welcome those only interested in pursuing their own depraved voyeurism. Over the years stories of nudity, drugs, and orgies filtered into the town community, and the property became even more off limits. Boys who were game enough to take up dares came back with tales of witchcraft, incantations to the devil and child sacrifices.

"Little wonder that I grew up in an era of horror and distrust of the peaceful members of *Shangri-La*—that is what they re-named the property. What with the unexplained drownings of Jim Gentian's family, rumours of monsters in the lake, and the enigma of the members of the commune, my generation was terrified of the place. It became a convenient 'bogeyman' for our parents to threaten us with. And we believed them.

"Then in, oh, it must have been 1965, or '66. There was the murder. That really put the wind up everyone."

"Was it a local girl? What happened?"

Chapter 11

It was sad about the Gentian family, and the attitude of the townspeople was laughable, but this was the real meaty stuff. This was more recent history and Melody wanted all the gory details.

Christie sat quietly and stared into the distance. She could remember the day well. Not necessarily the time, or actual date of when it happened. But the day that sent the whole town into a panic and turned parents into vigilantes.

One minute she had been playing happily under the plum tree with her younger sister, the next she and her sister had been whisked up by her parents and unceremoniously dumped inside the house and told not to move. Her parents had then left the room, shutting the door behind them, but not before securing the windows. She and her sister had sat, stunned for fully thirty seconds then burst out howling. Her mother had called out to them to be quiet, and then came back into the room. She'd sat down on the floor in front of them, drawn them into her bosom and hugged them fiercely. Christie could remember feeling her ribs pushed in and being scared that she would not be able to breathe. Her mother had been crying and tried to shush them between hiccups.

"Yes, she was local, as far as the townspeople would accept her. She came from the commune. A beautiful love child. That's what the locals called her, a love child. In fact, that's what they called all the children from the commune, and there were a lot of them. We didn't see them that often, really. They didn't regularly come to school in the town, usually only when there was talk of an inspector coming to visit. *Shangri-La* had its own school, supposedly. I wouldn't know.

51

And they were pretty much self-sufficient, so they didn't come into town to shop, or anything. But we would see them at the town's annual fair. All longhaired and barefoot. Bright clothes and beads. They would come and set up stalls and sell things, crafts, produce, furniture even. And some of them would braid our hair and paint the younger children's faces. There was even one family who had a circus of mice,"

Christie smiled at the memory. She had loved the circus of mice and would patiently stand in line waiting to be let into the small red and white tent which served as the big top. She would sit through the show as mice ran down the arm of the ringmaster and jump from his hand onto a platform then climb ladders and run through hoops. Then, when there were a number of mice cavorting around the table the ringmaster would bring out some more mice, this time with little jackets on, and then a ball would be introduced, and the mice would play soccer. She would watch the show then run outside and line up again.

"It was really good fun, the annual fair, and I missed it when they stopped coming to the fair. That was after the murder. The townspeople didn't really make them feel welcome much after that."

"But what happened?" Melody glared at her friend. Really, Christie could be so infuriating at times. Times like this she always needed prompting to complete the task.

"What?" Christie was still back in the circus tent. Her mother would never allow her to keep mice.

"Who murdered her? How was she murdered? Why?"

"Oh. Well, first off it was simply a missing person case. A girl from the commune, so it wasn't as if it had anything to do with the townspeople. Then she was found, not at *Shangri-La*, but in scrub beside the roadside just out of town. That brought it a bit closer to home. It was no longer something that happened 'out there' with knowing nods and winks. It was no longer obviously an 'inside job'. But then again, those people at the commune were considered capable of anything. It might be a plant, made to look as if the townspeople were responsible. The town was suitably outraged and incensed.

"Then bits and pieces started to filter through, along with an influx of strangers: the police, reporters and the usual rubbernecks. The girl had been murdered. And the parental vigilance increased. The police had little to go on. Then we heard that she had been raped, and mutilated. More locks were applied, and distrust spread like slime in a stagnant pond, insidiously creeping into everyone's lives.

"The locals were shocked, and more than willing to demonstrate their innocence and ignorance of the crime by embellishing all the fabricated stories about the unnatural activities at *Shangri-La*. Hemlock suddenly became a media mecca."

Christie went silent again as she remembered. The town had been in hysterics for days after the body had been found, and the media didn't help. Prowling paparazzi, only they weren't called that then, were excessive in their zeal to scoop an exclusive. They were all after a story that would sensationalize the depravity of the commune. Had anyone been out to *Shangri-La*? What were the initiation rites like? Did it include group sex? Was there really a marijuana factory? The tales that the reporters told were even more bizarre than those told by the parents. The youth were starting to wonder what utopia they had missed out on by not sneaking off to *Shangri-La*. It did not sound at all macabre. Better than stuffy old Hemlock with it's no cinema, no disco, no nothing.

A young reporter had accosted her and her mother one day. She had wanted so much to go outside, but her mother would not let her, finally relenting, only if she promised to stay on the front veranda, and not to talk to anyone. She had eagerly agreed, but wondered why she couldn't talk to anyone, or how she could, from the veranda. Still, she gratefully sat out on the veranda and soaked up the fresh air. Her mother had come out to sit with her when the journalist brashly waltzed up the path. His name was Paul Edgar, and he wanted to interview the two of them. Christie remembered her mother being uncharacteristically rude and dragging her inside, leaving the journalist standing trout-mouthed on the bottom step. She had never forgotten him.

"But who murdered her? How was she murdered? Why?"

"Oh." Christie was brought back to the present. "Well, that's the funny thing. It has become one of those everlasting mysteries. You know, no solution. Case never closed.

"For sure they figured out how she died. That was the easy part. She had had her ears cut off, and her lips had been severed. Huge slashes had been made across her cheeks, a bit like the striations that you see primitive cultures sporting as part of their initiation ceremonies. Of course, by the time she had been found the flies had found her first and her face was a seething mass of maggots. Ugh!"

Both girls shuddered.

"Gross," was Melody's sole comment.

"Yeah, well, that wasn't all," Christie continued. "They worked out that the wounds had been inflicted by a knife. Nothing special about it, just about everyone in town had one. It could have been your average pocketknife or kitchen vegetable knife. Big help. That made all of us suspects. But there was also a small puncture mark on her neck, as though she had had a knife held to her throat. Know what I mean?"

Melody nodded and raised her hand up to her own throat. It was all very ghastly, but she didn't want to say anything to stop the tale. She hung onto every word.

"And she was pregnant."

"Oh no, the poor girl."

"Why? Because she was pregnant or because she was murdered?

"Christie! That's not funny."

"I wasn't trying to be. It was you. Of course she was an unfortunate girl. No eighteen-year-old in their right mind, certainly not back then, would want to be pregnant, far less mutilated, raped and murdered. Honestly Melody, you can be so crass at times."

"Okay. I'm sorry. Continue, please," Melody rearranged herself on the seat and faced Christie.

"She died from haemorrhaging." Christie said it with such finality that Melody simply sat and stared at her. What a horrible way to die. Alone, on the side of the road. What sort of person could do that to a fellow human being? A teenage girl, and pregnant as well. Melody's mind scrolled a mental video of the girl, struggling against her assailant, and being attacked with a knife in reply. The poor girl. How alone she must have felt. Did she cry out for help? Why didn't anyone hear? Where were her parents? Did they care? Who was the unborn child's father? Why wasn't he with her? The questions whirlpooled in her head.

"She had been dead for about three days before she was found. No weapon was ever found, nor the murderer. Theories flew and settled on both the commune and the community like swallows roosting at dusk on the powerlines running above the side of the road.

"The commune kept very much to themselves and grieved and mourned on their own. That didn't endear them to the community who felt it an affront to withdraw when so many questions remained.

"The townspeople were outraged that the commune members would allow an unmarried girl to be impregnated, completely forgetting their own wayward daughters. They smeared the commune with allegations of their own prejudices.

"With an atmosphere of resentment, fear and hatred the police could get nowhere with their investigation and our parents were given yet more ammunition to use in their battle to keep control of their children. Especially after rumours of the maldape started to circulate again."

"Maldape? What's that?"

"You don't know what a maldape is?"

"Na-ha," Melody shook her head.

"You know about Big Foot, and the Yeti, right?"

"Of course I do. Everyone knows about them. Oh, you don't think one of them emigrated here, do you?"

It was Christie who was now, mentally, shaking her head in disbelief. "What about Bunyips? You've heard about them, haven't you?"

Melody's eyes became saucers. "It was a Bunyip?"

Christie laughed, then shook her head. Melody, who believed in ghosts, was so gullible, even at her age. Of course she herself had believed in bunyips, and the maldape, when she was a young girl. But not now. She was well and truly past child's play, ghosts and bogeymen, she had even outgrown those who inhabited the travelling fairgrounds and Luna Park.

"Melody, Bunyips are as real as Big Foot and Yetis. And no, it was not a Bunyip. But Hemlock had its own bogeyman to scare us kids. And back then our parents used it, the maldape, with a vengeance. They conjured up and embellished the local Aboriginal myth and endowed the maldape with murderous attributes. It sure set the interlopers into a panicked withdrawal, and the whole incident died down.

"Slowly the commune members drifted away. The property once more fell into the hands of nature, another terror was added to the legend and another generation of townspeople were born to fear the property."

Christie fell silent. That was the end of the tale. Except, she looked down at the ring binder in her lap. Slowly she opened it up and turned the pages of the magazine to the double page spread written by Paul Edgar, part of a larger article covering properties with occult connections. Except the place was news again. Paul's article covered the Gentians only briefly. It focused on the commune and *Shangri-La*. But then of course it would. That was the more recent occupancy, and he had been there after the girl had been murdered.

It was a good article, and the photographs, though old, were excellent. She looked at them again, never realizing that the place could be so beautiful. Well how could she? She'd never been there. But it was beautiful, probably more so now that it had reverted back to nature. The lake was pictured as idyllic, with the still water reflecting the trees on the further shore and ducks cruising the expanse.

Another, older black and white photograph showed the house, a two story, once white and proud wooden structure, overgrown with ivy and honeysuckle. An erect figure with fair hair and long braided beard, swathed in a vertical striped caftan and pith helmet stood on the middle step of the stairs that were aesthetically placed in the centre, leading to the veranda and front door. A young girl stood on the step below him so that his one hand could rest on her budding breast, his arm possessively over her shoulder. His other hand held onto the balustrade.

Christie puckered her forehead in contemplation, and she wondered what secrets the house and *Braedon* held, and if would they ever be relinquished. Other photographs showed aspects of the countryside around the property. Thick stands of timber heavy in undergrowth and wildlife, evidenced, according to Paul Edgar, by their numerous 'calling-cards', nests and burrows.

According to Paul Edgar the property exuded an atmosphere of quiet serenity and none of the macabre vibes that the townspeople had bestowed it with.

With the photographs being old, she wondered when they had been taken, and by association, when the article had been written. Reading it had not given her any indication. She looked for some reference to the date. But she could not find one. Surely Paul Edgar had not written it way back when she had seen him in Hemlock all those years ago. How long did it take for an article to be published after it had been written?

Still, you wouldn't catch me going there, she thought vehemently. No way. Not with the killer still on the loose, and ... no, there were no such things as ghosts.

According to Paul Edgar, the property was on the market again. He made it sound so tranquil and idyllic, but would anyone buy it? They hadn't before, when there had only been six unexplained drownings. Now there was the legacy of a hippie commune, and a murder to dull the appeal. Still, she supposed that there were sufficient macabre people around that the place might just sell.

"Could we go and take a look at it?" Melody sounded bright and not at all put out by the tale.

"What?" Christie stared at her friend. She did not think that she could have portrayed *Braedon*, or *Shangri-La*, or whatever name it went by now, in a less glowing light. But Melody still wanted to see it for herself?

"I thought we could go and take a look at the place."

"Are you kidding?" Christie removed the magazine from her ring binder and flung it at Melody. "There it is, take a good look. It's the closest I'll take you."

"No, I'm not kidding. Are you scared?"

"Of course not," Christie spat, then felt herself cringe inwardly. Could her reluctance be because she was afraid? Afraid of what? Her mind trawled through what she had just related to Melody and willed herself not to shudder.

"Don't tell me that you really do believe all that stuff that your parents told you about ghosts and whatever it was that they called the bogeyman?"

"The maldape? Of course not." She no longer believed in the maldape, or bogie-men, so why was the inner cringe becoming an unwelcome a niggle in her mind? She thought back to before she left Hemlock, had she dismissed their existence as she had her earlier belief in Father Christmas? She had maintained that fabrication longer than normal to keep his existence real for her younger sister. But the maldape, when had she lost credence in his reality?

"So why not go there?"

"What purpose would it serve?"

"Oh, I don't know. So that you can prove to me that it is harmless. To see if we can find any mature marijuana plants to harvest and sell to cover the cost of that cruise you keep saying you can't afford. To tempt fate? I don't know, it seems a good idea."

"Well I don't think it is," Christie said emphatically, though she could feel the fabric of her resolve starting to unravel and tried to quell the sensation. She did not want to be forced into proving to Melody that ghosts were merely a figment of the imagination.

"Well, when was the last time you visited your parents?" Melody was changing tactics and took Christie by surprise.

"What's that got to do with it?" Christie felt the fingers of guilt starting to tighten. When was the last time she had gone home? Shamefully she could not remember. It had been a while. She tried to avoid asking herself why that was. What was it that was keeping her from visiting her parents? It was not that she did not love them, after all she spoke to them on the phone, regularly, and saw them every time they came to the city. Though that was usually only for medical appointments, birthdays and such. But for her to actually go and visit them? She mentally squirmed, reluctantly remembering the last time she had gone home. A visit that had been overshadowed with talk of the re-emergence of the maldape. To Christie that was 'old hat', the maldape was like a broken record, always returning. That was something she did not want to revisit, and she had made a hasty retreat to the city.

"Isn't it about time you went home for a weekend, or ..." Melody paused, and her face lit up, "Queen's Birthday long weekend's coming up. You could go then, and I could come with you."

"But why do you want to visit that place?" Christie could not understand how anyone could possibly *want* to visit the town where she had only ever known fear, and no freedom.

Melody shrugged her shoulders, "Seems like it would be a good lark."

"Listen you dodo, I never went there when I was a kid, when the dares and bribes were worth something and there was something to see. Now there is nothing to see, and you are not offering anything worthwhile." Christie stood up. "I'm late for a lecture, see you later," and she walked off.

Melody stared after her with a strange smile on her face. She flattened the magazine across her legs and tapped the cover. They would go to Hemlock for the Queen's Birthday long weekend. She stretched out her legs and leant back in the seat, closed her eyes and thought about what she would wear when she went exploring *Shangri-La*.

Chapter 12

Fletcher stood in the middle of the room. He was wearing fawn slacks with a white shirt and a loud blue and yellow Looney Tunes tie; his shoes were immaculate brown loafers. He'd left his brown sports jacket, along with his briefcase, in the car, but he still looked out of place. He could feel the agitation of the only other person there, a young woman. Ms Pamela Ellis was dressed in jeans with a tweed jacket, her dark hair tousled by the wind and unrestrained by the clasps valiantly trying to hold it in place. She wasn't very tall, and she clung to the clipboard like a frightened child clinging to a kick board as they learn to swim. He smiled to himself and slowly turned around, looking at the peeling newspapered walls where primitive drawings of stick figures were depicted sporadically across the pages.

He wondered whose hand had drawn them. Maybe that child was now a well-known artist demanding millions on commission, or had large, framed canvases hanging in the Tate, or maybe they were simply working a nine to five punching keys in front of a monitor, with these early aspirations well buried and forgotten. What a waste if that was the case.

He looked up at the ceiling, the central light a bare bulb at the end of a black electrical cord. It looked like it may have come with the house, originally. The windows were hazed with years of smoke, and spiders, followed by neglect. No curtains. He could imagine that in the prime of its being this would have been a very gracious room. But not now.

The place most certainly was an albatross. But it was a burden that suited him. Not so far out of the city that he couldn't access it quickly if the need arose, yet far enough away for his purposes. He turned to Ms Ellis, and she visibly jumped back, startled. That was good. She doesn't like being here. He strode past her and out of the room. She quickly followed him. He supposed that he should not get annoyed with her. She was only doing her job, but couldn't she leave him alone? Just for one minute, so that he could explore the rest of the house, by himself. He found it hard to concentrate with her there. She could stay in that front room. He'd find her when he needed her.

He walked into the spacious foyer and slowly mounted the angular stairway that led to the second floor. A hallway at the top of the stairs effectively bisected the house into two wings with bedrooms all in varying conditions either end. Most had moulding mattresses as floorcovering. They were more than reasonable in size, and all looked out on to the wide veranda which ran along three sides of the house. He walked to the back of the house, where the veranda had been closed in to provide for an ablution block, Ms Ellis his constant shadow.

There were two adequate bathrooms, though they would probably need to be modernized. He smiled and wondered about the old enamel bath in the one room. It sat, incongruously in the middle of the room on its clawed feet. That too, must have come with the original house. A veritable antique, and he wondered how it had come to reside in this house, here, virtually in the middle of nowhere when it belonged in the genteel homes of Europe.

Nodding his head in satisfaction he returned to the ground floor. Downstairs again he looked in every room and cupboard. This floor of the house had lost most of its original design, being now more a communal meeting place than family rooms. There was, of course, the main room, where he had first started the tour, but the dining room, and drawing room of old were now bare refractory issue straight from Dickens. Rubbish littered the floor and evidence of the rodent life was hard to miss. Miss-matched hard backed wooden chairs were pulled up to a couple of long tables standing end to end. Sentinels on duty, except for the errant ones which had fainted in the wait and lay, topsy-turvy, on the floor.

Fletcher picked his way through the detritus of decades and wandered through to the kitchen. It too, was a victim of a time warp. The old coal-range was a relic better suited to a museum, and the fridge was one of the old kerosene ones now only visible in the poorer third world countries. The bench, which ran along one wall, would once have been scrubbed wooden boards, but now was a scared mess of rotting timber. The sink could not be seen under the cobweb-glued residue of many past meals. Fletcher walked disdainfully around the room and left.

Other than being putridly filthy, the place was perfect. None of the rooms had curtains, or blinds, he noted, but that could be easily remedied, if required. A number of windows would need new glass. And the whole place would need a ..., well, it would need an army of chars to bring it up to the habitable standard he required. He sighed. That would be his next task. Otherwise, the place was perfect. He turned to Ms Ellis and smiled broadly; she gave a pale smile in return.

"Is that all you'll be wanting?" she asked tentatively. She really wanted to be elsewhere. Anywhere but here, the place gave her the willies – she was sure that she could feel unseen eyes following her, and, while this prospective purchaser had all the physical attributes necessary to keep her safe ... Well, she did not think that he would enact the role of deliverer, much in all as she would enjoy it if he did.

Fletcher could almost smell her fear. "Not quite," he said and was amused to see her blanche even further.

"Oh." She took a step back.

Fletcher laughed. "I want to take a look at what the outside offers. Come on, it won't hurt."

The woman, wide eyed, turned and walked quickly out of the room and exited the front door. Fletcher took one last look around the open foyer, and nodded his head. Yes. This place could well prove to be the perfect location for the assignment. He smiled to himself and followed her out of the house, admiring the view that she presented, and stepped down to what would have at one time been the front lawn.

He stood back and looked up at the old house. It would once have been magnificent. It would once have been loved, he supposed. If only it could talk, what tales it could no doubt tell. What mysteries it could reveal. Most of the left side of the house was obliterated by a tangle of convolvulus[1], ivy, and honeysuckle, it lent the house a lopsided appearance, as if something was definitely out of kilter. That figured and fitted, he thought wryly.

"Come on," he called to Ms Ellis. He and the others in the office had always laughed at the title 'Ms' suggesting it was favoured by women who were married and wished they weren't or those who were single and wished they were married. He wondered why she had chosen to go by that title.

Pamela Ellis clutched her clipboard tighter, then carefully negotiating the tall grass and uneven ground, reluctantly followed him around the side of the house to where the outbuildings lay. She knew what could possibly happen next, and her stomach started churning at the thought of encountering the man – referred to by everyone in town as The Hermit – with his knowing and challenging grin. She shuddered, fingered her neck, and sent a quick prayer skyward. Please, not again. It was always possible that The Hermit

---

1.   https://www.google.com/

search?client=firefox-b-d&q=convolvulus&spell=1&sa=X&ved=2ahUKEwiE_szVg6n3Ah

X0zjgGHcAbAMUQkeECKAB6BAgCEDI

and his flashing wouldn't appear and attempt to waylay her when she was in the presence of a man. She hoped that would be the case today. She also did not want to have to try and explain his presence on the property. It was going to be hard enough to explain the existence of the well-tended vegetable patch that she knew to be tucked in between two of the outhouses. Maybe this Mr Fletcher would not venture that far.

Fletcher felt, rather than saw her move closer to him. He raised his eyebrows wondering what could possibly have brought that familiarity about. Surely she was not trying to flirt with him? Until then he had been convinced that it was not just the property that had the wind up her, but that there was something about his own persona that had her walking on eggshells.

Chapter 13

Bradley Gentian peeked out from behind the tangle of blackberries that his vegetable garden backed onto to make sure that the interlopers had left, then waited some more before he felt secure enough to resurface. Scrabbling out from his hidey-hole he stretched, then dusted down his clothes of their mantle of leaves and dirt. He knew the property was for sale, but he always hoped that knowledge of his presence and the legend of the maldape would deter any potential buyers. He glared in the direction taken by That Man and Prissy Miss Goody-Goody—oh, he may not have ever known her name, but even without her caressing her neck as he had seen her do, he well remembered her and her prudish response. An involuntary shiver coursed through him, an omen that his illegal tenancy was about to end.

Slowly he made his way back into the house. He would have to come up with some plan. He was not prepared to lose the property. If he could not own it legally, as was his right, he would continue to squat here till his carcass fed the dingoes and his bones littered the place. He stopped. That was it. He would haunt the place for real, evidence of his occupancy would in future be accompanied by mournful moans and groans, noises and flutterings of dust. He smiled to himself. Yes, he could make that work. Bradley laughed. Easy enough to fabricate, didn't take a rocket scientist.

He knew that the locals all thought him a mad recluse, and he was happy that his ruse had worked, till now. The madman or the maldape, either worked to keep the rabble away. He was happy to live a life of solitude and concentrate on his own subsistence living,

67

the letters after his name had neither helped nor hindered him and out here there was no call for Doctors of Philosophy. How had he ever thought that a degree would pave his way to reclaim what his family had always maintained to be theirs by right, when all the others in the family over the years had never been able to reclaim the property? They had all run themselves dry and into their graves trying and there had never been any resolution to the contested will.

Yes. He smiled, and absentmindedly rubbed his hand across his crotch and felt the stirrings of excitement. He would come out of retirement, as it were. It was time to reintroduce the maldape to the area. But first, even though it wasn't scheduled, he would go into town and pay Ruby Street a visit.

Chapter 14

"What's that you're working on?" Paul asked as he walked into what should have been the formal dining room but had long since become Tim's study. Though 'study' was a misnomer. It was really wasted on Tim. He had covered every spare space, including the velvet-cushioned seat in the beautiful bay window that faced the side garden through diamond panes, with his paraphernalia. Periodicals and parts of planes graced the Persian carpet, and electronic trinketry jostled for space on a small bookcase. The table was the workbench and had a rat's nest of cords leading to and from any number of electrical gadgetry and appliances. A stack of papers from the extramural courses that Tim had enrolled in took up only a small corner of the table. Paul had long given up on any pretence to understand what it was that Tim did in here, but he was always interested.

Tim was bent over his Tandy Radio Shack TRS-80 computer, his fingers flashing over the keyboard in haste that would have done any professional operator proud. What looked like blueprints showed on the screen. White lines were radiating, growing and spreading like some disease across the decreasing expanse of the screen. Paul picked his way across the room and stood at Tim's shoulder. "What's all this then?"

Tim grinned, then punched some more buttons then leaned back in the chair and flexed his fingers.

"It's my new baby. Unlike the ELTs ..." Tim stopped when he saw Paul's eyes glaze and go blank. He rolled his eyes and sighed. "Sorry, of course you don't know what an ELT is, do you. It stands for

Emergency Locator Transmitter. They are mandatory in all aircraft and designed to help rescuers find aircraft following an a 5G impact with terrain."

He then went on to describe and explain the finer intricacies of his latest invention. His emergency locator transmitter was a manually activated personal portable transmitter. He saw it as a breakthrough in safety measures, not only if survivors of a downed plane wandered from the wreck, but it would also benefit boaties stranded because they had forgotten to fuel up their aluminium tinnies; and bushwalkers who had strayed off the beaten paths and ended up lost. If they had one of his ELTs on their person, then rescue teams homing in on the signal would be able to locate it to within ten metres.

Paul was totally confused by all the jargon, but he had picked up on the idea and was impressed. "You know, if I didn't already have the go ahead for a feature article, I'd be tempted to suggest doing a profile on you and this latest 'baby' of yours. When's it going to be ready for you to do a test run? Is that a thing? How would you test it without alerting the local Search and Rescue bods? They'd go ape-shit if they got called out on a false alarm."

"Well, I've got it all done here," Tim said, tapping the monitor, "and here." He tapped his head. "Then, it shouldn't take me more than a day or so to knock up a prototype. Haven't yet figured out how best to test it. I'd thought of maybe trying to fit it out with a personalised radio frequency, but I might get into trouble if I tried that. More trouble than a bogus call-out." He looked up at Paul and gave sheepish grin. "You said that you have an assignment?"

"Well, it's not exactly an 'assignment' as much as I went in to see Walt Hancock, my agent, today and asked if he could get me a buyer for an article on Demetrius Popolo."

Tim had returned to his keyboard briefly, then looked up again. "Who?" he pulled down a menu on the monitor, moved the cursor, and clicked on 'Print'.

"Demetrius Popolo. The author."

Tim looked at Paul blankly as the printer whirred into action and the continuous -feed pages started to slowly fold out onto the table.

"Oh." Tim cocked his head to try and read what was on each page before it folded over along the perforation.

"You *do* know who I'm talking about don't you?"

"No. Should I?" Tim stood up and moved over to the bookcase and surveyed the pieces of equipment there.

"Of course you should!" Paul sounded deflated, and he felt that way too. Here he was, full of his great news and his flatmate was more interested in metal beetles and miniature Lego.

"Why?" Tim picked up a capacitor and turned it over in his fingers, before discarding it and letting his hand hover over another piece of metal and plastic.

"Because he is one of the most controversial writers of today. Every time he has a book published, he makes more enemies." Paul looked around the room for somewhere to sit but gave up. Instead, he lowered the plastic bag he was holding onto the floor and placed his hands on the back of one of the chairs stacked with file boxes.

Tim picked up a conglomerate of electronic componentry and stretched his hand out to Paul, "Here, can you put this on the table over there?"

Paul took the proffered piece and raised his eyebrows, "Where?"

"Over beside the mouse."

Paul carefully placed it on the mouse pad.

"No, not there, to the left. Your left. That's right. Thanks. Then why does he write?"

"Because he has something to say." Paul played with the piece he'd just put down. Moving it first one way, then the other, with his finger.

"So why does he make enemies?" Tim picked up a circuit board and passed it to Paul, "Same place, please."

Paul put the circuit board down beside the first piece and used it as a bulldozer. "Because of what he has to say."

"What does he have to say, then, that makes him enemies every time he says it?"

A capacitor and a couple of transistors joined the train beside the mouse pad. A pencil got caught up in the earth works and fell to the floor. Paul quickly put his hands in his pockets. "Do you honestly not know who Demetrius Popolo is?"

Tim turned towards the table, his hands full of bits and pieces. "Would I be having this banal conversation if I did?"

"I guess not."

Tim put the bits and pieces on the table, pulled out the chair next to where Paul was standing and stared, mystified, at the collection of papers on the seat. He picked them up and stood, hesitantly, looking for open space to deposit them. Finally, he simply dumped them on the floor where he stood. "Then please put me out of my misery so that I can continue this in peace," he said as he sat down.

Paul followed his example and transferred the things from the chair he was leaning against to the floor and sat down too.

"Demetrius Popolo writes novels, fiction, that includes such thinly veiled criticism of his native country's corruptness, government immorality, child abuse and discrimination against its women, it is all but a blatant attack on the government. His government doesn't like it, and neither do their allies, trading partners and the governments of like-minded countries. He is now virtually a man without a home. Actually, his last book caused him to be kicked out of Italy. That doesn't leave many countries where he is safe to live. In fact, his latest book is said to be so defamatory that it is rumoured that no country wants him as a resident, far less as a citizen. Oh, they will all have him as a visitor, especially if it is to promote his profitable books, but he is only ever issued with a short stay visa."

"So why does he continue?" Tim had laid out the plans which he had formulated and was starting to disassemble the pieces which Paul had helped him to collect next to the mouse pad. "I mean, if he knows that he isn't safe anywhere, why bother to write? What good will it do?"

"Well, he feels that it is the right thing to do, to write about the conditions in his country." Paul watched, mesmerised as Tim cut and soldered and wired. "He feels that someone has to alert the rest of the world to the atrocities in the hope that the rest of the world will force his government to reform."

Tim looked up from what he was doing, tweezers in one hand and soldering iron in the other. "Apparently it's not working, so why continue?"

Paul shrugged his shoulders. He didn't know. "I suppose he can't help it, any more than you can help tinkering with toys for your plane." He waved his arms over the table in a manner of derision. "Anyway," he said, changing the subject, only slightly, "I'm to do a feature on him when he comes here."

"I thought you said that he was not welcome anywhere anymore," Tim mumbled to his circuitry.

"Yes, he's not. As a resident. So, he intends to travel the world promoting his latest books. And as he is on his way here, I thought it would be a great opportunity to write an article on him."

"But if he's promoting his books, how is he going to have time to write another one? People will go stale on his old books if no future ones make an appearance. Have you read any of his work yourself?" Tim looked up and over to Paul who was stretched out on the chair, hands held together behind his head.

"Well, no, not actually." Paul hurriedly released his hands and dropped them onto the table where he started to finger the pieces of paper in front of him.

Tim reached over and removed them from Paul's grasp. "Then how can you possibly write a feature on him?"

"Well," Paul had the decency to look a little uncomfortable. "I did start to read one of his books, once."

"Damn!" Tim dropped the soldering iron, stuck his finger in his mouth, and raised his right eyebrow quizzingly at Paul. He took his finger out of his mouth and gave it a shake. "So what happened?"

Paul's discomfort increased. "I didn't like his style of writing."

"What?" laughed Tim. "Does your agent know that?"

What did Tim find funny in that, Paul wondered to himself, crestfallen. "No. Why?"

Tim continued to solder wire and metal onto the circuit board. "Well, if you haven't read his work, because you don't like his style, how can you produce a good-enough-for-publication piece of writing that is in depth and unbiased?"

"I'll make up for it with photographs. You know, I've only ever seen one photograph of him."

"Surely his photograph has appeared more than once?"

"Yes, but it's always the same one, he's leaning against a column somewhere, all dolled up like something out of *The Great Gatsby* or *Saturday Night Fever*. I know if given the chance, that I'll be able to improve on that one."

"If he always uses the same photo in publicity shots, don't you think he'll be rather reticent about getting new ones taken? Even if they are taken by you. I mean, there must be a reason why he still uses the same one."

"Vanity," said Paul smugly. He knew all about vanity, he was a past master at the game. Without shame he remembered the time that he had worn a patch in the rattan carpet square at a girlfriend's place. It wasn't his fault that the carpet square was directly in line with the hall mirror. The mirror that he had not been able to pass without several preens.

"You don't know that he is vain."

"What else could it be?" Paul ran his hands over his high forehead and through his hair. "He looks rather dashing in the photograph." He unconsciously turned side on to Tim, revealing a chiselled profile which went unnoticed.

"Well, maybe he simply wants his detractors to think that that is how he looks. Makes less of a target for assassins if no-one has an up-to-date photograph."

"Hmm, hadn't thought of that."

"So, what'll you do now?"

"Well, I've left it with Walt to arrange everything with the PR people. The paper didn't give details of his visit, just that he was coming out to promote his latest book."

"Do you know when that is to be?"

"No. But I expect that Walt will tell me soon."

Tim put his tools down and stretched. He had nearly finished for the day. "So you don't really know if you have a feature to write or not."

Paul pushed back his chair. "Oh, I've got the feature all right. It's just the details and nitty-gritty I don't have. Give me time. I only put the idea forward to Walt this morning. But he said to go ahead. I can still do an in depth without an interview. Or photograph. It just won't be as good."

"Then I suggest that you start to read some of his books."

"What do you think these are?" Paul produced, with a flourish, a plastic supermarket bag full of library books. He stood up and walked out of the room. "See you later, I've got some reading to do."

Chapter 15

Fletcher felt very pleased with himself, and Ms Pamela Ellis didn't look too disappointed either. They were sitting in a stale office, either side of a large, highly polished, old bank manager style desk, a copious surface supported by a tower of drawers on either side. He smiled and congratulated himself on a job well done. Everyone ought to be pleased, and he really hadn't lost any owed favours this time either; he'd found the property on his own. That was a bonus.

He opened his briefcase and counted out the money as her eyes grew larger. From the hungry expression on her face he figured, quite correctly, that she had never had a purchaser pay in full and in cash after only one viewing of a property, and he chuckled to himself. He must have made her day. He hoped that her boss would give her a bonus too. He was tempted to do so himself but felt that that would be contrary to convention. Plus, he would have to justify the dent in his budget to Maxwell. While he'd been given carte blanche, he still had to present documented evidence of his expenditure at the end. Still, he could extend a courtesy.

"Does this town sport a decent pub, or café, where I can offer you a drink?" he asked, hoping there was a pub, and hoping she wouldn't accept his offer. One afternoon in her company was really all that he wanted today when he was working to a deadline. He suddenly wondered if it was simply the courtesy which had made him make the offer; normally she was not his type but there was something about her that he found himself attracted to. Maybe it was the vulnerability, or was it simply the challenge of breaking though her furtive antagonism?

77

"Er, there is The Grand View Hotel on Main Street. We don't really have a café, not anymore."

"Well then, The Grand View Hotel it is. Would you care to join me?"

The escaped hair was further dishevelled, as she shook her head. "That's kind of you to offer." Despite the windfall that Fletcher had presented her with, she really didn't want to spend any more time with him. She had to admit that he was not unattractive. But he was male and because of that quirk of nature, the bottom line was that she didn't like him plus, she was afraid that if she did extend the time they spent together, he might sense her unease and wheedle out of her the infamous history of *Braedon* and the resident hermit, and renege on the deal. It had been the third time she had taken a potential client out to the old place, and while it had not been any easier this time, it had proved to be worthwhile. "But Mr Spratt will be back soon and I'm sure he would rather have me here. Thank you."

Must be losing my touch, he thought—in the past he had been able to entice even the most unresponsive women under his spell and so form profitable albeit transient relationships. Still, he was glad she had dropped her head to hide her face, as he was not convinced that he had been fully able to mask his relief. He frowned. He had always been able to disguise his emotions in the past. What had gone wrong this time?

"A pity," he said, and hoped that neither his voice nor his smile would reveal his relief. "A drink could have sealed our deal admirably; but Mr Spratt should not be disappointed." Fletcher stood up and watched as she blushed and stood up as well. Can't have lost the touch totally, he thought. "However, if you cannot escort me personally, would you please direct me to this hotel?" That won him another blush, and his ego rose again.

"Down Main Street, you can't miss it. It's right beside the Police Station."

"Thank you." He reached down for his briefcase. "And thank you for an interesting afternoon," he said as he turned and walked out the door, a receipt for the purchase of the safe house in his wallet.

She watched him as he walked down the street and pinched herself. This was the first time that she had taken a client beyond the house and not have them beat a hasty retreat. She had refused the offer of refreshment not only to rid herself of Fletcher, but more importantly she had not wanted to tempt fate. Sure, the papers had been signed, and deposit paid, but there was still a cooling off period that put the sale, and her commission, in jeopardy.

She turned back to her desk and wondered if maybe she ought to have warned him about *Braedon's* incumbent hermit.

She need not have worried. Fletcher was very aware that there was someone in residence at the property. It was hard to not notice—in among the decades of detritus was evidence of more recent activity and mess. But he considered that to be the least of his worries. The security team would soon sort that out.

Chapter 16

Fletcher whistled quietly to himself as he walked down Main Street towards the only hotel in town. It was a sad reflection on the prosperity of the area that it only sported one hotel, and that had to be conveniently located next to the Cop Shop.

Main Street was also a misnomer. The only thing that was main about it was that it happened to be a bit wider than the other streets in town, and that it contained most of the amenities. There was a small supermarket with two disgruntled trolleys angle-parked outside. He skirted around them, fearful that should he get too close they would gravitate to him and roll unceremoniously onto the road. Next to the supermarket was a greengrocer. 'Established 1897' was tarnished over the door, and the awning looked as though it had seen every year since. The produce did not appear much fresher. There was also a butcher, complete with sawdust on the floor and a blue and white aproned plump man behind the display. Fletcher smiled and raised his hand in greeting. The butcher glared glumly out the window. "Grumpy old fart," Fletcher muttered to the empty street. Across the road was *The Emporium*. This forerunner to the department store predated the greengrocer by one year. Its tired mannequins overworked gathering dust in the window displays along with bolts of brightly coloured material vying for viewer space with gardening tools and television sets. Lovely town this, very friendly and all inspiring.

He wondered what The Grand View Hotel would have to offer. It stood seemingly sandwiched between the Masonic Lodge and the Police Station. Despite its location, it had, by its outward appearance, the very makings of success. The hotel was a modern two-story brick edifice. Its dulcet tones were neither too garish that it stood out incongruously, nor too pallid that it blended with the environment. A small beer garden, of sorts, was secreted beside the building, behind a white picket fence and hawthorn hedge. Within were a couple of round, all-weather plastic tables each with its own mushrooming umbrella. Trade was brisk in the quiet courtyard. Both tables were full.

Fletcher walked up three steps and through the front door of the hotel to be greeted by a palatial foyer, an unattended reception area to one side with the staircase to the second floor beside it. A small plastic and plaster fountain draped in foliage of dubious origin was strategically placed in the middle of the foyer with a direction pointer, growing out from the centre. Surprisingly it did not look out of place.

He had the choice of the Beer Garden on the right, which he had seen from outside, the Eatery and the Bistro straight ahead, along with the choice of three bars—three rooms on the left, decorated and named for the occasion—the Snuggery, Boozer and Den. The Snuggery sported deep red velvet curtains and cushions with candles on tables in alcoves for those who were clandestinely romantically inclined. The Boozer was simply a bar with stools for those who needed a quick drink on the run, and it was empty except for the obvious town soak, and a bored barman. Then there was the Den for the serious drinkers. This was the one that Fletcher entered.

Simple dark-stained oak tables each hosting two revamped cottage kitchen chairs with thin padded checked cushions were strategically scattered around the room. The lighting was subdued, but you could see who you were sitting with. A small bar was situated in the corner, discouraging guests from sitting anywhere but at the tables. Table service was affected by a young barman. Fletcher sat down at a table by one of the two windows in the room. His briefcase he set on the chair beside him. He looked out. All he could see was the cellblock of the Police Station next door. He hoped that that was not the view referred to in the name of the premises.

Chapter 17

With a tall lime, bitters and soda and a bowl of salted peanuts on the table in front of him, Fletcher was ready to review the situation.

He leant over and opened his briefcase then and pulled out a pad of paper and a spiralbound notebook, along with the biro from the real estate agent's. He lined them up on the table in front of him, the notebook taking centre place, with the pad of paper on his right. He twirled the biro between his fingers and thought of the task before him, and the people he had employed to help him carry out this assignment. They had been brought together from all parts of the country. They did not know each other, and, until the time came when the teams arrived together on the property, they would not.

Now that he had the safehouse he could start installing the teams. No, correction. First, he needed to get the place cleaned up. He scratched his head with the end of the biro.

He opened the notebook and looked at the label 'Catering'. Originally, he had lumped catering and cleaning under the one category, thinking that whoever was cooking could, when they weren't cooking, also clean. Now he was starting to doubt his earlier assumption.

Fletcher took hold of the label and flipped it over. He shook his head. No, the people listed here may be coerced into maintaining the cleanliness of the house, but they could not be expected to clean it up from its present state. The place was a mess. Not just the house, but the outbuildings as well, and some of those would be needed for accommodation. All the buildings would need to be totally swept, scrubbed, sanitized and debugged.

He smiled. Debugging. Not the usual debugging that his line of work called for.

The only part of the property that was not in need of attention was the unexplained, and well-tended, vegetable patch he had noticed on the whirlwind tour around the outbuildings. He dropped his hand with the biro down on the pad of paper and started doodling, while he rubbed his left hand through his hair and across the back of his neck. Why had she been reticent to spend time outside? When she had caught up with him, he had had a hard time keeping up with her as she scurried along the overgrown path, shooting furtive glances between the buildings till they were back, almost panting, at the front of the house and the real estate agent's car. He had been surprised that Ms Ellis had not made mention of the vegetable garden as it was such an obvious bonus to the property, but then again, maybe she was too out of breath. That vegetable plot was an enigma. Surely whoever was squatting in the house, could not take such care of a garden yet live in such squaller. He screwed his eyes shut and shook his head and decided that he would leave well enough alone. Besides, the garden plot was now part of his property, and would provide a nice supplement to the provisions that were being brought in. The less interaction between his lot and the town's folk the better.

He looked down at his doodling, squirls of circles, and frowned. "Fat lot of good you are," he muttered as he turned his attention back to the open pages of the notebook. Catering and cleaning could no longer be combined. Leastways, not initially. Maybe he could hire some of the locals to clean the place up before he moved the teams in.

Fletcher flipped over the pages of the notebook until he came to a blank page. It was still in the catering section, but what the heck? With deliberation he wrote a heading 'Initial Clean-Up', underlined it, three times, and put a forceful full stop at the end, then tapped the biro tip up and down on the page.

A dreary town like this must have some lay-abouts looking for an easy handout. He wrote down 'church' and 'school' on the sheet. He would talk to the people involved and see if they could recommend any needy, yet able youth or 'oldie'. The work would not be hard, only tedious. There was no security risk involved in the general 'let's get this place habitable' clean-up. So it was probably better to employ locals. Let them come and clean. Being local they would no doubt regale the townsfolk with embellished tales of the state of the place, but they could also relate that nothing unusual was going on, just general cleaning before the new owners moved in. Less chance for speculation that way. It was only natural to get the place cleaned up after being vacant for so long.

He made a note on the pad to remind himself to get local cleaners organized before he returned home. He wouldn't bother with cleaning up the surrounds, at least for now.

Fletcher took a long draught of his drink and picked up a handful of nuts. What would he be required to provide for the clean-up? He spent a couple of minutes jotting down what he considered to be the essentials—industrial brooms, litres of disinfectant. He chewed the end of the biro, he'd need a skip, or two no doubt. He wrote 'skip' on the pad and mentally cursed himself for not thinking of that earlier when he'd been with the real estate agent. Then he smirked—yeah, he'd go and see her again, see if she could be of some guidance on that score.

He turned back to the section labelled 'Catering'. This was a small, but vital area to be covered. Keeping the teams fed was a sure way of keeping them happy, especially if they were going to be confined to the property without the normal diversions sought for by normal men. He needed good cooks, chefs even, to provide meals that were a cut or four above the usual bland offerings of cafeteria or main street cafes.

In his experience those in the catering professions had been notorious for their mobile mouths so he had to be careful in his selection of the two cooks and two kitchen hands that he needed for the catering team. He needed people who were both good at their job and who would epitomize the three wise monkeys. He knew that he would be unable to stop them from seeing or hearing things, but he needed to be able to ensure that they did not say anything.

Finally they had been found for him. Dave Strother was a chef who had had his tongue so severely cancered that he no longer had one, and a kitchen hand that had been born mute. Of course they could both write, but the persuasive powers that Fletcher had at his command were adequate. The other kitchen hand was a political refugee who would never want to return to his home country, and the second cook, worthy of being a sous chef, as an illegal immigrant was in no position to talk.

Their list of requirements was horrendous. The shopping list was something the likes of which Fletcher had never seen. He really did not think that they would require all that had been requested, but Dave Strother had been adamant. Fletcher smiled at the recollection of the large tongueless chef, thumping his stubby forefinger onto the list that he had written. Fletcher could only imagine the words that he himself would have applied to the gesticular tirade. He did not really want to have to go shopping once they were all in place, nor did he know, exactly, for how long they would be there. So he had acquiesced and ordered in an industrial sized fridge and a couple of freezers.

He now looked down at the shopping list in front of him and felt sure that it was one which Napoleon would have been proud of when preparing for Waterloo.

He flipped to the next section of the notebook; it was labelled 'Medical'. He took a deep breath and let it out with relief – he had the medical team all lined up. There, on the first page of the Medical section the team was listed. Names, addresses, contact numbers, profiles. Three scrub nurses, and two doctors all with postgraduate specialties. They all had histories—both doctors had been struck off and the nurses all had dubious pasts—but that did not deter him; what concerned him was that they were all good at their job and were available to work for him and to ask no questions, nor tell any tales. Having a shady past made for easier compliance with the need for secrecy. There was no room for any squealers on his watch. But he did wonder at the nurses' lack of major criminal convictions. Was that because they were lucky or because they had had good representation? Whatever, all he was interested in was that they were good at their job and at keeping their mouths shut.

He turned the pages of their profiles to the list of required equipment. He had acquired the list through careful research, and consultation with Dr. Nigel Hartwell who would be the leader of the team. A lot of it meant nothing to him. Not that that mattered. Most of it had been ticked off, meaning that it had been purchased, or at least ordered. He had not realized how great a drain this part of the operation would be on his finances. The basic First Aid kit alone was nearly $100, no wonder he didn't have one in the car or in the house. He managed to get by with a box of Band-Aids and a tube of antiseptic. But Dr Hartwell ... no, it was the head nurse, David Lapaine who had insisted on a fully comprehensive kit.

The barman looked up from his nook in the corner of the room as Fletcher laughed.

What a name for a nurse! Nurse Lapaine. Looking at the photo of David Lapaine in the dossier Fletcher was convinced that if anyone dared cross Nurse Lapaine then he would not be averse to inflicting some real pain. To his way of thinking nurses were either female, or, if they had to be men, then gay, and epitomized the traditional image of caring people filled with empathy for their fellow beings, especially those afflicted with health problems. David Lapaine, Fletcher scanned the report in front of him, was all brute macho, dwarfing the average human in stature and demeanour. Not the image Fletcher would attribute to a male nurse. Still, he only had himself to blame, he wanted no females. Not on his work force. Women were too much trouble and a distraction. And distractions were something that had no place on this mission.

He really must go and spend some time with his mother, he supposed, puckering his brow at the intrusion to his thoughts. She had been entering his mind quite a bit lately. Little tendrils of conscience. A prickle. Maybe someone was trying to tell him something. He shook his head to clear the niggle. At the moment he had more important things to think about than his mother.

He looked again at the long list that Nurse Lapaine had presented him with, demanding that everything on it be included. He could not imagine why they would require such a large selection of bandages, plasters and other paraphernalia.

He shrugged his shoulders and flipped through the remaining pages of the 'Medical' section. He smiled, pleased with himself, that seemed to be under control. Once the place was clean, the catering and medical teams could move in.

Chapter 18

Move in. He snapped his fingers, and the barman came running. Fletcher waved him away. That was what he had forgotten. Moving in. The place would need to be furnished! Why had he not realized that before? He hurriedly turned the pages of the book over to the back where he labelled a new section, 'Furbishing', but then concentrated on the pad of paper beside him. Funny that he hadn't thought about it earlier. He had the larger bits and pieces that Dr. Hartwell had requested—operating tables, trolleys, stretchers, beds, high powered lamps, sterilizers and God knows what else, the list seemed to be pages long. And the industrial sized kitchen appliances and paraphernalia. How did he manage to forget about regular furniture, beds, sofas, tables and chairs just because no one had handed him a list of requirements? Probably because usually a safehouse is already furnished, and with this one he was on his own working from a blank slate.

He scratched the back of his neck in irritation and pulled the pad closer. He drew a line under the doodlings about cleaners and started to list the large items that would be required, some of which were already at the house. Would they remain? He needed to ask the real estate agent. He made a note. And beds. He shuddered as he remembered the rat-haven of mattresses back at the house. Definitely beds, whether the previous owner was leaving them or not. And toilet paper. He didn't remember seeing that on Dave Strother's list. But then cooks don't normally have much use, other than personal, for toilet paper. What else did he have to add to the shopping list?

91

Disinfectant definitely, but that was already on this list for cleaning. Washing up liquid? He flipped back to the section for catering. It was not listed under 'W'. He found it under 'D', for detergent.

He placed his elbows on the table and lowered his head into cupped hands and he sighed. He had thought that it was all sorted; yet now the gremlins were surfacing. The little things. He used his hands to raise his head back, and he stretched. He saw the light fittings on the ceiling and sighed. Light bulbs. Bet they weren't on the list.

Life had been so much easier ... well, maybe not always easier in the broad sense, but as far as he was concerned this was in the province of the desk jockeys. He was more suited to working in the field where there was the adrenalin rush that accompanied being given a task, going in and executing it, then the thrill of watching the ramifications unfold, generally on the television screen when he was safely back home. Whyever did Maxwell think he was capable of overseeing this escapade? The only danger here was him not only losing his job but his career. If this went belly up, then his creds would be deleted. What would his mother think, an Amway agent being given the old heave-ho? Maxwell certainly had a lot to answer.

He turned to the security section in the book. There were twenty men, and one woman listed. Most of them he had handpicked. Men that he had either worked with before, or had seen in action, or knew by reputation alone. He had had to call in a few, specialists, though. And that had cost him more favours. Nikki had been one of those.

Fletcher had not liked the idea of a woman on the security team. Certainly not a single woman out in the bush surrounded by virile men—there were no poncers on his watch thank you very much—was just asking for friction and trouble. But McFadden had insisted that she was the best for the job, and she could keep her mouth shut.

Rumours were often more deadly than the truth, so Fletcher had to be sure that the people he was employing were totally trustworthy to not talk even among themselves, about anything they saw or heard while on the job. And they would be on the job, constantly, night and day.

Maybe trustworthy was too strong a word, but he didn't like to think that he was buying silence. That made it all sound simply too under worldish and, well, illegal. He had stopped and thought about that one. What he was doing was essentially illegal. Maxwell had virtually told him that at the beginning. If it were legal then the company would have had no problem openly supporting him. No, what he had embarked on had put him beyond the pale. He was as bad as the baddies now. The realization did not sit well with him. Maybe that was why his mother kept crawling into his thoughts.

He stood up and leant against the windowsill. The Grand View Hotel. He wondered whether the other windows offered a better view than this one, and tried to imagine what the view would have been without the police station in the way—the main street sweeping away and up into the mountains? Or another building? Either way it didn't really matter to him. He turned back to the table and his papers, sighed and sat down. He needed to find someone to clean up the place, and he needed to go over the shopping list again, for the mundane things. He wondered if bath soap had been thought of.

The security team was the one that worried him the most. Comprising three symbiotic sub teams – electronics, surveillance and now robotics, it was the biggest team, and therefore would be the hardest to keep tabs on. He hadn't yet decided whom he would select as team leader. It needed to be someone he could trust, a good leader of men, then, as a mental afterthought he added, and woman. Nikki was destined to be a bone of contention. But, after overhearing the cleaning crew talk about the hauntings and bogeyman, he had come up with the idea of empowering the legends as part of the security. So he needed her, if she was the best. She had better be. It was costing him dearly.

But he still needed to get back to who could be the security team leader. He scanned the list of members in the security team. There was really none with whom he felt totally comfortable as leader. They were all good men, and he could see a couple who would make good seconds-in-command, but no outright leader. Maybe that would have to wait until he had them all together, and they had met and filtered into a natural pecking order.

He was so tired. How he wished it were all over. He had enjoyed the challenge of every other assignment. But this one? This seemed to be a lot of bother over nothing. Well, at least it was nothing for him as he had been told nothing, really. All this legwork was for rookies. He was used to being there, in the thick of the action, not being the busboy who built the background. Still, there was no sense in grumbling, only he would hear him, and he was not a good listener. There was nothing for it but to get back to work. He looked at his watch and rubbed his eyes. After lunch.

Chapter 19

He turned around and looked for the barman. The young man had his back to him, busy polishing glasses. Fletcher smiled to himself, polishing glasses seemed to be the universal time filler for barmen, and he had seen quite a number over the years. Men, and women, of all ages and persuasions, sponges soaking up snippets of information as they polished glasses. What a life. But was it really any better than his, he wondered? Even the lowest lives had a purpose, be they snakes or barmen. Yes, they had a purpose, and he had used them too. He only hoped that he had never been as free with supply as many of them had been.

This barman was cut from the same mould as so many barmen. He could imagine the graduating class photos of bartending schools—rows of black and white penguins with silver salvers at the ready and plastered smiles. The picture of congeniality and anonymity. The barman saw Fletcher looking at him in the mirror and turned, smiling, to face him, his eyebrows raised in a universal query. Fletcher gave his head a slight incline and the barman responded by putting the glass and tea towel down before scurrying across the room, beaming.

Fletcher was reminded of a dog he had once had when he'd been a boy. Scamp was the epitome of a Heinz 57'er—a little bit of everything thrown together and a dog came out at the end. All he needed to do was look at Scamp and he would come running, stumpy tail conducting a treat and tongue dredging the ground, hardly able to see through the thick mane of matted hair that hung as a fringe over his face. Always anxious to please. That had been the case until he had met his destiny with a Pit-bull. Fletcher shuddered at the memory, and the barman's stride faltered.

They had been taught a lot of things when Gareth had attended bartending school, but he had yet to learn how to fully, and with ease, put theory into practice and to recognize the full portfolio of human foibles. The sole occupant of The Den had been quite undemanding, until now. He had come in, sat down, ordered a drink, and had proceeded to engross himself in paperwork. He'd only called for one refill and had been quite content to work away on his own. He was definitely a stranger to these parts, and had, as yet, not displayed any curiosity about the town.

Most first timers to The Grand View Hotel had engaged him in conversation, asking about the name of the hotel, and were more than anxious to plumb him for information about the old, haunted house. Not that he had much to tell them. It had been haunted since long before he had come to work here. He knew nothing about it other than what he had picked up from the locals. Not that they had talked about it much when he'd first come. Simply warned him away from the area. Suited him fine. He wasn't into the macabre or supernatural. He sought his thrills behind sordid closed doors.

But there had been a buzz around town that the place was going on the market again. Rumours had it that the old codger who owned the place, and was said to still live there, not that anyone ever saw him, was going into a retirement home in the city. Then there had been a bit about it in some publication and the rubbernecks had started to trickle into town asking about the place. He'd had to learn a bit then to keep the customers satisfied.

Still, this man didn't appear to be a rubbernecker, nor really a travelling salesman. Now that was a dying breed. No, there was something funny about this guy, and the way he looked at him. Gareth was quite perturbed. Especially when the man shuddered like that, and his face took on a sad yet vicious expression.

Fletcher noticed the young barman blanche slightly, his freckles popping into relief, and his smile became mechanical. A real poncer, Fletcher thought, and wondered where he would get his kicks in this way-out place in the middle of nowhere. Surely there would not be too many to entertain him here? He shrugged his thoughts aside and smiled benignly at the barman, the nametag said 'Gareth', and Fletcher wondered at what sort of woman would call her son Gareth. That name conjured up little wizened men living solitary lives in dark sod houses in Wales, surely? He looked at the barman again and saw Gareth as such a sad man in thirty year's time. Life could be cruel.

"Tell me, Gareth," Fletcher arrested him before he came close enough to fully observe what Fletcher had spread over the table, "where is the best place to eat here?"

Gareth stood and tried to gather his thoughts. If only he could see past the man and get a look at what the pieces of paper were on the table, he might be able to categorize him and be in a better position to gauge what he was.

"Um," he took a step forward, to remove the glass from the table, but Fletcher pre-empted him by handing it to him. Damn, the man was good. Gareth took another, good, look at him. Was he an undercover cop? He frantically thought about what he could be wanting. He felt that he was in the clear, whatever it was. He had done no wrong. Not really. They always said that what you did behind your own doors was your business. Besides, he always made sure that he was never doing anything, strictly, illegal. He tried to smile the way he had been taught to when dealing with difficult customers. The effect created a lopsided grin which emphasized a dimple on his left cheek and exposed yellowed teeth typical of redheads, and Gareth was definitely a redhead—very short back and sides undercut a thatch of red unruly hair on top, cascading down over his eyes. No wonder he reminds me of Scamp, thought Fletcher. And just as useless, having to repeat everything to get anything.

"Where is the best place to eat here? The Eatery or the Bistro? Can I get a counter meal served here? Or am I too late altogether?"

Gareth thought about this. If the man was asking about meals, at this time, then he still had business to do. Maybe he would leave his things on the table if he directed the man to the Bistro, and he could get a sneak at the papers. Then again, probably not. He'd take his briefcase with him, for sure, all the tantalizing papers stacked neatly inside. But, if the man was to have something here, then he could wait on the table and maybe then get a look.

"The Eatery is closed now, and the Bistro, well ..." How could he encourage the man to stay here? Somewhere he had read that it was always a good move to make the customer feel that you were doing them a favour. "I can go and get a menu for you to look at here. I'm sure that the chef won't mind. We don't normally serve counter meals in here, but ... Seeing as how it's quiet in here at the moment, and you are in the middle of something, I'm sure management won't mind."

Fletcher felt irritated at the ingratiating manner of the young pup, but it really would be easier if he could eat here. He had the measure of the barman, and his own work was set out in front of him. It made sense to stay here. And he didn't believe for one moment that any favours were being extended to him. Of course management would not object, if they would, then Gareth would not jeopardize his job for such an infringement. "Show me a menu," Fletcher growled, hoping that the barman would be suitably intimidated.

Gareth beamed and quickly walked over to the bar and deposited the glass on the bench top. There were menus under the bench, but he was not going to let Fletcher know that. He looked back at Fletcher to confirm that he was being observed, which he wasn't, and left The Den to procure a menu.

Fletcher took the opportunity to straighten out his papers so that when Gareth returned and presented him with a menu—and Fletcher knew that it would be a theatrical presentation—there would be no incriminating material visible. Then, on second thoughts ...

Gareth returned happy. He had a menu, and he'd had a chat with the lunch waitress. He had regaled her with tales of the ferocious drunkard in the Den, and had told her that he did not want to expose sweet Juliet to this reprobate and his tongue, so he, Gareth, would lower himself to wait table and so preserve her innocence.

Juliet had laughed to herself. As if she needed saving, but she understood Gareth's need for importance, so allowed herself to be 'saved' and agreed that Gareth could substitute for her this once, thank you. Juliet had acquiesced with such humility and gratitude that Gareth began to wonder if maybe he should quit his games and settle for stable normality, she would certainly be a suitable catch and substitute.

Fletcher looked up from his doodlings as Gareth approached with the menu and smiled to himself as he made a point of trying to hide the papers in front of him. Gareth was solicitude itself as he handed the menu over, his eyes never leaving the papers with their scrawled diagrams of debauchery and the jotted names of men. It was all that Fletcher could do to stop himself from laughing as he chose the mixed grill and salad.

It was all that Gareth could do to drag himself away. He felt sure that in Fletcher he had found a kindred spirit, someone with whom he could have an enjoyable time, if not relationship. He left the room to place the order with the chef, wondering how he could best approach Fletcher. Getting another look at the papers would be easy, now that he would be waiting on him. He smiled gleefully as he came back into the Den and walked, light-footed, over to Fletcher's table, and stood opposite him. Fletcher's papers were in full view.

"Can I get you another drink?" Gareth's eyes scanned the papers on the table, taking in, even if they were upside down, the intricate illustrations which Fletcher had hastily drawn. Obvious nude figures, male, entwined together. Nothing lurid, that was beyond Fletcher's ability, but suggestive enough to make the tamest of imaginations run rampart. Gareth ran his tongue over his lips and could feel the familiar prickling of sweat in his armpits. Not here, not yet he couldn't. It was too soon, too public. It had to be behind closed doors. He tried to drag his eyes away from the drawings. It had never been this bad before, but then he'd never encountered anything like this before. 'Please, dear God, help me' he thought to himself, only there was no god, was there? There couldn't be. Otherwise, he wouldn't be like this, would he?

Fletcher watched him from under guarded eyes and was amused by the emotions that flashed across the face in front of him. It really was too mean, he knew it. Knew that he should not be playing with the boy like this, but ... He shuffled the pages into a pile and could feel the release of tension and the relief that Gareth was experiencing. "Yes please." It was really pitiful. A young man like Gareth to be so afflicted, but then, it was probably his parent's fault, calling him Gareth in the first place.

Gareth returned with Fletcher's drink, and another dish of salted nuts.

It really was too bad, too sad, too something, Fletcher thought, and his mother came to mind. She'd tell him not to tease or taunt him. So what if the guy was gay? So long as it didn't affect his work, or interfere with him personally, Fletcher was happy. So why was he baiting the boy now? Because he was frustrated, although not sexually. Frustrated with work. This damn assignment. He ran his fingers through his hair; it would be grey before this assignment was done with, he felt sure.

Gareth, hovering on the boundary of personal space, polishing the adjoining tables and fluffing up their cushions, watched and wished that he could be the one running his fingers through Fletcher's hair. Maybe that could be a start, offer to relieve some of the obvious tension with a shoulder or neck massage? He made a move towards Fletcher, then thought better of it as Fletcher stretched and stood up. Gareth, unnerved, rushed across the room and out to the kitchen.

Fletcher laughed quietly in the empty room. Damn the assignment. He needed to get away from here. He would go and visit his mother for a few days. Well, for a day anyway. Everything was nearly in place and what wasn't he could work on just as easily at his mother's as anywhere. He reverently removed the offensive pages and put them to the side. He then gathered up the rest of his pages and books and carefully put them away in his briefcase. He pulled the pages that had held Gareth's attention towards him and frowned. Little better than stick figures entwined around men's names. He hadn't really meant to lead Gareth on, or to make fun of him. Not really. He had simply not wanted to be obvious about removing his work from view. He knew that Gareth would be curious, anyone would be. It was natural to wonder what another was doing and try to find out. So he had substituted his work doodlings with cryptic ones. It had merely been a calculated whim that Gareth was homosexual.

Gareth re-entered the room, bearing down on him with all the aplomb of a ceremonial servant rather like the handmaiden who had borne John the Baptist's head into Herod.

Gareth was nearly there, not only in delivering Fletcher's meal, but he had masterminded his attack. He placed the tray on Fletcher's table, and with a flourish presented the mixed grill to him for inspection. Fletcher unthinkingly crushed the papers that Gareth was so adoringly looking at into a ball.

Gareth's countenance crumbled. He dropped the napkin-wrapped cutlery on the floor and tipped over Fletcher's half empty glass on his way down to pick the bundle up. Fletcher had crushed the papers up and discarded them, along with Gareth's dreams. Tossed aside as so much detritus, but with less thought. He ran from the room, leaving Fletcher to sit down, bewildered, staring after him. Fletcher shook his head, bent down and picked up his cutlery and started in on his lunch.

Chapter 20

Tim McNaulty sat facing the door, eyes glazed, thoughts far away. His visitors, Richard Ibraham and Harry Harris, sat opposite him, a contrast in appearance, relaxed and confident. They did not seem to be in any hurry. They were representatives of some medical conference that was to be held in May, they had said what it was, but Tim couldn't remember the name, medical was medical and of no interest to him. They had asked if he would be amenable to hiring out his Cessna 172. The organisers of the conference wanted to take three of the overseas delegates on a short air tour of the more scenic sights of the state.

Tim saw no problems. He often chartered out his plane; in fact, he'd rather it be flying than picketed on the ground waiting for him to use it. But these people were wanting more than his plane. He still couldn't believe it. He shook his head and tried to come to terms with what these people were offering him. They wanted him as well. Exclusively. For an indefinite period of time. They were prepared to compensate him, handsomely.

But he didn't know. Didn't know if he wanted to have his liberty dictated to. Apart from the fact that, legally, he was not in a position to accept payment if he was the pilot, after all, he only had a private pilot's license, not a commercial one. Such a license, he would tell his friends, was on the backburner for when he had the finances to undertake the training. If his friends had bothered to ask Paul Edgar, they would have been told the problem was not solely the money, but that procrastination played a major role in most aspects of Tim's life.

Tim refocused on his visitors. They sat either end of the sofa. Precise yet pedantic. He'd felt like laughing when he'd been introduced to Harry Harris. What a name! Somehow though, it suited the man. Besides, Tim had no preconceived idea as to what a Harry or a Harris was supposed to look like. The only Harris he had ever come across before was Paul Gallico's Mrs 'arris, the London char. And Harry kind of looked like how he imagined her, only masculine. All roly poly and frumpy. He could imagine Harry relaxing in a Hawaiian shirt, Tom Sawyer hat and Bermuda shorts, a blonde Danny DeVito, that's who Harry Harris reminded Tim of. The image brought a crinkle to his face. It was so in contrast to the man in the well-worn suit across the room from him. Waiting.

"Well, what can I say?" Tim heard his own voice, "I mean, money's money, isn't it? What's a life without money?" he ventured a laugh, but inwardly was hoping his euphoria over the amount of money on offer would not show. "You need it to live, right? But can't you give me any idea of how long you'll be hiring me for? I mean, I'd kinda like to know, so that I can arrange things. You know, things like other engagements." Tim didn't have that many future engagements, flying or social, but they didn't need to know that.

"I think that you will find that you will be suitably employed and that the period of time will not affect your commercial enterprises, too onerously," Richard Ibraham said loftily. They had already investigated Tim's schedule for the next four months and had found it somewhat lacking. They knew that he would accept the post.

Tim's financial situation was even more desperate than his employment status. The debts that he had acquired as he tried to create a niche and a name, build up an ailing business, support and fend off a soon to be ex-wife, as well as live a bachelor life were catastrophically insurmountable. What was being offered would be his saviour.

Richard mentally tut-tutted. It certainly could not be easy, being Tim McNaulty these days. It had been a sheer stroke of luck, or genius, to have found a pilot of such a persuasion. It had been the stumbling block all along. Trying to find the right man for the job. And now they had.

Tim knew that he had no choice but to take the position. But he did not like to feel that he was being manipulated or dictated to. He didn't know which it was, but there was something that didn't sit quite right with these men. He wanted to think about it, but they had been adamant that they required an answer, a positive answer, before they left. He wondered if he could haggle for more time to think about it, or more money. What he really wanted, was a timeline. A schedule. He really did not like not knowing what the next day would entail.

"Can't you be more specific about the length of time you would require me?" Tim tried, unsuccessfully, to appear nonchalant, resting his elbows on the arm of the armchair— Paul's favourite chair, which gave him some comfort—and holding his head up with his fingertips, legs crossed in true English gentleman style. However, in blue jeans torn at the knees and an unironed tee-shirt proclaiming the worth of some foreign beerhall, the effect was somewhat less than he had hoped for.

Richard Ibraham looked across at Harry Harris, this is what they had been waiting for. The opportunity to negotiate on safe ground. They needed Tim McNaulty, and he needed them. Only he needed to feel that he had some control over the situation. It was all part of the plan. Get him hankering after the money, scared of being controlled, then allow him to seem to gain control. They smiled at each other. A smile which Tim failed to interpret. Rather, he saw it and it unlocked the key to what had been unsettling him since the two men had entered the house. They were twins! Not the run of the mill twins, but twins, as in *Twins*, Danny DeVito and Arnold

Schwarzenegger. Richard Ibraham was a tall dark Adonis to Harry Harris' Danny. Tim sat back and relaxed. No problem now. He had it all sussed.

Richard and Harry both missed the moment of relaxation but felt the atmosphere change. It didn't concern them why it had changed, just that it had. They beamed at Tim.

"Well, we can't really be specific,"

"At this stage," Harry interrupted.

"When, in fact, your services will first be required."

The two men once again exchanged glances, glances that Tim thought looked remarkably similar to smirks and he wondered if there was a hidden agenda somewhere, and if so, what it could possibly be, and if knowing what it was would make any difference to his decision.

Harris looked to Ibraham before speaking. "It all depends on which delegates attend which elements of the conference, and how many will wish to take part in which of the activities that are being planned for their enjoyment."

Richard Ibraham nodded sagely. "It is all, still, in the final planning stages. We are simply inquiring if you, and your plane would be interested, and available, for hire, in May."

Tim thought it a bit strange that the organisers of the conference did not have it all down pat. May was only, what, three, four, weeks away? He didn't know how these things ran, but surely ... "Well, I'm certainly interested, and the plane is available for *charter.*" He was pleased to see Richard wince and realize that he had been using the wrong terminology, "but it would make things a lot easier if I knew when and for how long."

"I'm sure that we can come to some equitable arrangement over that. As soon as things are finalised with the conference and delegates. Nothing has been fully decided as yet. In all probability it would not be for more than three mid-week days spaced over a couple of weeks." Harry looked at Richard for confirmation, and received it. Richard was grinning fit to burst.

"Of course, we would want you to be available..." Richard hesitated, unsure of what the correct term was, he looked to Harry for help.

"On stand-by."

"On stand-by prior to that," Richard finished proudly.

"Of course." Harry applied the full stop. They sat back and waited.

They could see Tim's mind working. He was frantically doing mental gymnastics. Three days flying with what they were offering him would calculate out to quite a tidy dent in the debts. Now if he could tie them down to a specific week. Surely they could do that. He could afford one week, or even two if it came to that, away from what really mattered. He looked across the room at the opaque double doors, which separated the living room from the room where his electronic paraphernalia waited. Yes, he could afford to be away for a couple of weeks, especially if that time was occupied in making money. He succeeded in not showing his pleasure too much.

"Naturally. But I should like to know when, precisely, in May, you would be chartering my plane and hiring me. So I can make arrangements."

"That is totally understandable, but we cannot be precise at the moment, so may we suggest that you work on it being the first of May?" Harry smiled and rose from the chair. Richard followed him and they shook hands with Tim and let themselves out.

Chapter 21

Fletcher looked out his kitchen window and watched white triangles battle it out on the bay. It was a glorious day to be sailing, only his sailing was in another dimension. His whole life was sailing at the moment. Things could not be better. The weekend with his mother had been great. A godsend in fact. She had pampered him and bullied him. Mollycoddled and berated him. It was just what he needed. A weekend of little old ladies was more than enough to get his mind off work. And then his mother had even had a few wise words of wisdom to help him on his errand. Not that she was ever privy to his work.

She thought that he was an accident prone, yet successful, Amway agent. Well, she got the agent part right at least, but he never enlightened her. She would ask him about his work, and he would talk about the personnel altercations that cropped up and she would inundate him with old wives' remedies. The funny thing was that they often worked, where sophisticated psychology didn't. No wonder he needed periodic 'top-ups' of advice from his mother.

This time round she had cajoled out of him that he needed a team leader, but he didn't know whom to choose. She had asked him to list the qualities that he needed for his leader—charisma, trust, authority, honour, courage, intelligence, perseverance. She had said 'yes', unconvincingly, then added that, to sell something well all you needed was someone who had kissed the Blarney stone in Ireland. He had laughed at the suggestion at the time, to himself of course as he tried never to upset his mother.

He turned from the view and thoughts of his mother. The next phase of his plan was about to come to fruition. Everything was finally in place. He had initially experienced resistance to his offer of short-term casual employment for cleaners. The schools and churches had both been reticent to make suggestions, giving obtuse reasons for their reservations. Then, when he was making his way back to the real estate agents to add workers to the request for assistance locating a skip, he passed a couple of young men sitting on a low brick fence scuffing their feet on the footpath. Maybe he was looking in the wrong place.

Turns out he had been. While there had been a distinct lack of interest among the female population of Hemlock, there was no such reticence among the young men. To be paid to be out at *Braedon*, legitimately, had been like a magnet, and the tedious, manual cleaning had been accomplished a lot sooner than Fletcher had anticipated.

The house had been scrubbed so clean that it was almost as though it had just been built, except of course the exterior had not been touched—peeling paint and clinging vines presented a totally different picture to the interior and no doubt the male cleaners had happily filled the gossip coffers to overflowing with spurious suggestions about what was going on at 'Braedon'. But that could not be helped. With what he had in mind for the security team, coupled with discovering from the cleaners the existence of a local bogeyman, he felt confident that the locals would stay well away from the property. Let the tongues wag. He walked into his bedroom and gave a chuckle thinking about Gareth and what he would make of rumours. He was probably wondering how he could get an invite to the risqué bordello—one of the tales fabricated by the young cleaners.

The catering and medical teams were already up in Hemlock, settling in and getting themselves sorted. That just left the security team, and they ought to be on their way there now, so he had better get moving himself.

He picked up his case before checking that he had not forgotten anything, and that he had everything that he needed for the month or so. Fletcher stood at the open front door and gave the place he called home a mental adieu then shut the door and left.

Chapter 22

Fletcher had slipped up. Only it would not become apparent immediately. Admittedly the slip-up could not have been helped as when he was looking for the security team, he had not known the location of the safe house. Even if he had, he probably would not have thought it expedient to include it among his criteria for recruitment. He was interested in their abilities, expertise, honesty, trustworthiness and most importantly their ability to maintain confidentiality, not where they had been born.

Fletcher had thought it too cloak-and-dagger to black out the windows of the bus that delivered the security team to *Braedon*, though he had had the presence of mind to temporarily cover the welcome sign announcing arrival to Hemlock. So he was not to know that even without that aid two of his security team readily recognized where they were.

The qualities which he had listed as requirements for the security team had sounded and looked good at the planning stage. Yet now that he was here, he was beginning to have second thoughts. The team, his security team upon which so much depended, would be inside waiting for him. Would they be up to the task? Would they be good enough? Could he have chosen better if he had selected the team himself? Could one of his other contacts have done better?

Fletcher rubbed his hand over his eyes, and slowly walked up the front steps and entered the house.

The security team were waiting for him. Twenty-one people stood self-consciously distanced from each other in such a fashion that they seemed to fill the room. He was fully aware that they only knew that they were part of a security team, and that they were pretty much meeting each other for the first time, despite having spent the travel time from Melbourne together. It was only natural that they would be wary and eyeing each other up in an attempt to determine where they themselves fitted into the hierarchy. Who was going to be the alpha?

Fletcher wanted to laugh at the absurdity but was afraid that the tension which he could feel sparking in the air might ignite. It never was a good idea to keep so many wanna-be alpha males in a constrained environment for a long period of time.

He looked down at the clipboard he held in his hand and shook his head in despair. From their names they could well have been a United Nations delegation. There would never be peace until politicians understood that simply speaking another's language did not make for good bedfellows. It was the centuries of culture and history that separated people. It was the way in which people thought and reacted to situations that divided them. Until you could get inside another, thoroughly, there was no hope. But that was easier said than done. Culture could not be learned from a Stotts Correspondence College course. Even living a lifetime in another country did not always open all the doors to another's thinking. He looked around the room. And where was the woman Nikki? He could see neither her person, nor her name on the list on the clipboard. Would his unease with this whole security detail never end?

He looked up again and scanned the room for a second time, this time effecting a head count. Everyone was present. Where was the woman? He sincerely hoped that he would not need to call a roll. That would simply be too childish, especially when he already knew many of the faces looking expectantly at him. He mentally chided himself and brushed the confusion away.

"Gentlemen, and, er ..." Fletcher looked around the room again, trying to locate the woman Nikki.

Nikki was standing at the back of the room, not exactly quaking in her boots as that was not a characteristic that she held. But she was being very circumspect, trying not to look at her surroundings—she did not need the reminding. She never thought, nor wished to ever see this place again, and if she had known that in accepting this job she would be placed in this position she would never have been tempted by the promised vast remuneration.

Then he spied her. He had not seen her earlier because she was not what he expected to be looking for. She stood at the back of the room, half hidden and miniscule in comparison to the macho men exuding testosterone. She certainly would not be cast as the femme fatale in a James Bond movie. There was no hint of femininity in her stance—feet apart, arms akimbo across her chest, with her sunnies nestled in her close-cropped dark hair. She was more the epitome of a mother or, at a stetch, grandmother than the pin-up girls and models that would attract the notice of these men.

He looked again at the list of names, this time running his finger down them, one at a time. There definitely was no Nikki listed, and there was only one non-specific name on the list. That had to be her. Jamie McDonnell. But where had Nikki got to? And why had no one told him that there had been a substitution made?

A thread of unease snaked down his spine as his finger tapped on the name Jamie McDonnell, and a faint smile tugged at his mouth as he thought 'Good on you mum'. An Irish name. This could be his team leader, if his mother's intuition was accurate.

But did this Jamie McDonnell have the makings of leadership? And would the men accept her leadership? He would be very surprised if they would. None of the men appeared to even be aware of her standing at the back. He nodded in her direction; she inclined her head and he started again.

"Men, welcome to your home for the next however long. You will have noticed in your approach that there is a small town nearby." Fletcher stared across the team in front of him and hoped that his expression met with the desired effect of intimidating each and every one of them. "I can promise you that that will be all you will see of the town during your time here. For which I make no apology. I'm assured that you have all been made aware of, and have agreed to, the need for confidentiality in this er, shall we say 'project' and that you are prepared to remain here for the duration, without outside communication. Should the need arise for you to reach out beyond the boundary of this property, then you are to approach me before doing anything. Is that understood?"

He looked around the men, and Jamie, and was pleased to see that everyone was silent, still, and attentive.

"You have been selected and approached to provide a security team for a highly clandestine operation, and while you may not be privy to its nature, it is my desire that you do not speculate. Not among yourselves, nor among other staff that you will encounter while you are here. In fact, you are not even to speculate to yourself. Just believe me, and accept, that the very nature of this project is of paramount importance to the nation, if not the world." Though he was not convinced of his hypothesis, he hoped that by framing the importance of secrecy in such a manner these professionals would be, if not intimidated by their task, at least mindful of the need for complying with his directive.

"I am not going to ask, at this juncture, if there are any questions. They may be voiced to me later, in private. I am confident that by now you will have familiarized yourselves with your accommodation and the general layout of the house, mealtimes etc., and its surrounds so for now I shall point you to where you can start in on your specialized operations. Yes, you all have areas in which you individually excel but you are to work as a team. Collectively you are

The Security Team for this, er, project and I am relying on you to maintain this location as one of maximum security. The security base will be the room next to my office, you should all know where that is, if not, it is well labelled. I will appoint a team leader in due course.

Now, those, and you know who you are, with surveillance expertise can meet together in the room across the foyer from here and plan your strategy, I will check in on your progress and proposals shortly. Those with a panache for electronics will share the same room, it is big enough to accommodate both. IT is in the room down the hall. There is a sign to that effect on the door as well, and I shall be with you later. That just leaves, well, the rest of you. If you will follow me."

Chapter 23

Fletcher looked at the diary open on his desk. There was a large red circle three days hence. D-Day. Everything, and everyone were settled and in place. The catering cum daily cleaning team as well as the medical team, each under their own leader would be autonomous and he expected no issues with either of them.

But the Security team. He shuddered, shook his head and took a deep breath. He still had to assign a leader. Someone whom he could comfortably leave to oversee the daily running of what he considered to be the most important aspect of the mission. It was imperative that there be no breach of confidentiality with regard to the operation. There was no room for a leak, of any description. No one was to leave the property. No one was to talk to anyone, not even in their own team, unless it was to do with the work of that team. No one was to know the full nature of the operation. And the security team was to ensure that this did not happen. For sure he was in charge, the ultimate 'the buck stops here', but logistics was his prime concern.

Applying his mother's tactics, which he had taken to mean looking for an Irishman had not resulted in success. None of the team were Irish. The closest had been Jamie McDonnell. Or was that Nikki? He scratched his head. He needed to get to the bottom of that conundrum sometime soon. As for finding the Security Team's leader, he would have to take another look at each member of the team. Watch them in action. Yes. He would do the rounds. Again. He did so every day, but in the past he had been more concerned in what they were doing rather than how they were doing it.

Fletcher stood outside the room where Bazza Blake and Josh Membry were to be found. There was silence. They were either asleep, which didn't bode well for their vigilance ability, nor for leadership finesse, or they were busy doing what they had been employed to do, which was to work their magic with the cache of techno gadgetry. Would it even be realistic to contemplate that a computer nerd would have the charisma to be a leader? He thought not, and turned from the door, instead walking across to the room where the men responsible for the electronics and routine surveillance were to be found.

He was not surprised that no head turned as he entered the room. He had heard the noise of voices raised in contention long before he had arrived. His eyes were drawn to the cluster of tables that had been brought together in the centre of the room to create a large work surface—he was reminded of the large plotting tables that featured in the war movies. But instead of pert WAAFs moving pieces across maps, six of his security team—Johno Wheeler, Cliff Hunt, Spiro Salmucci, Gunner Jones, Max Knight, Vic Kirby—were in heated debate over the hand-drawn map of the property and loose papers that were spread out in front of them. Fletcher surmised that Dave Preston and Bruno Dolfi, the other two non-specialist surveillance team members, must be patrolling outside.

He'd catch up with them later. He watched the slanging match at the table for a couple of minutes, and despaired, none of them looked contenders. He shook his head woefully and turned to observe where the electronics men had set up a bank of monitors along one wall of the room.

Images of the surrounding grounds flickered across some of the screens, others portrayed aspects of the house, inside and out, and others again were receiving images from the strategically placed cameras that were 'patrolling' the outbuildings. He was pleased to see that all areas were under observation. Doug Beecham and Sam Cochrane sat in front of the monitors while Alex Daniels stood between them, then leant forward and pointed to one of the screens and swore. Doug and Sam just looked at each other and shrugged. Fletcher could see some jiggling on the screen so assumed that either Phil Anderson, Lou Vaughan or Arti Eitzen—the other electronics experts—were outside manipulating the cameras.

He watched silently as the scenes stabilized. A shadow moved across the corner of one of the screens which showed the pathway to the building where the rest of the security team—his high-tech team, those working on what he hoped would be the central component to the place's security—were housed. Neither Doug nor Sam watching the screens reacted.

"What was that?" Fletcher demanded. The three turned and looked at him, puzzled.

"What? That flickering?" Alex asked. "We're still experiencing teething problems; it happens all the time in the initial stages of setting up the system. Once the others have the cameras sorted and connected it won't be an issue."

He swore and mentally ticked them, and Alex standing over them, off his list. Along with just about everyone else in the room. That just left the five working in the outbuildings. He didn't hold much store in them either. They were specialists and brainboxes. No one looked up to brainboxes and so he doubted very much that any of them would prove to be leadership material, but what did he have to lose? He turned to go seek out the remaining five contenders when something on one of the monitors caught his eye. He turned back, leaned in over Doug's shoulder and pointed at the screen.

"There was someone, or something there, and it wasn't one of our men," Fletcher muttered as he ran his fingers through his hair and turned to glare at the men either side of him. Doug and Sam looked across to each other then up at Alex, who had moved away from the bank of monitors, and shrugged.

Fletcher looked back at the screens. "I tell you, there was something there." He could feel his ire starting to bubble within his chest. Damn it. These men, the best that money could buy, were next to useless if all they could do was sit there like stuffed monkeys. With a snort he wondered if stuffed monkeys would have been a better use of money, they, he felt sure, would have at least pretended to be interested in what he had seen, and not waffled on about teething problems.

There had been a figure walk past one of the cameras. He was sure of it. Even though it was only a brief sighting and blurred, it had not resembled any member of his teams. There was an intruder on the property and despite there being three of his security team inside at the monitors, and five wandering around outside it appeared that no one else had seen it. What was he paying these men for? He needed to get outside.

Inwardly fuming at the apparent incompetence of his men he crossed the foyer. As he reached the front door he heard a ruckus coming from outside. While the voices around the table back in the surveillance room were heated, what he was hearing now was that intensified several-fold and sounded serious.

He crossed the veranda in two steps and hoped that the peeling wooden banister was secure as he grabbed hold and vaulted over it. It was not as secure as he would have liked, and he momentarily overbalanced on landing before quickly righting himself and heading off towards where he could hear the raised voices and some serious scuffling. He turned the corner of the house and could see, further along the path towards one of the outbuildings Lex and Ben roughing up another person. As he hurried towards them dual thoughts plagued him: Where were Dave and Bruno? They were meant to be out here on surveillance; and, could this be the squatter, evidence of whom he had seen when first inspecting the property? And, if that was the case, then why was he still hanging around the place? Why hadn't the real estate agent woman done something about getting rid of him?

Chapter 24

In the outbuilding that was being used as a workshop Jamie McDonnell (Nikki to her friends, one of whom was the contact that had recommended her to Fletcher, and now her team members) was kneeling, head down eyeballing the insides of what she hoped would be the last prototype. Each of the previous attempts to bring the automatons up to standard had not met with her approval. There was always something that she felt could be tweaked.

"Lex? Ben? Hand me the soldering iron." She reached her arm behind her, but no instrument touched her fluttering fingers. "Damn it, I need it now, not tomorrow." She sat back on her heels and turned around. Where had the oafs got to? She let go of the wires she had pinched between two fingers and stood up. She dusted her hands down the sides of her trousers and was about to yell out to her assistants when she heard the noise of a heated fracas outside.

"What the hell?" she muttered, striding to the open door of the workshop. If those two were playing at fisty-cuffs when they were meant to be helping her, she'd give them what for. At least they had had the decency to take their altercation outside. Still, she wondered what had brought on the mêlée.

Once outside she followed the raised voices. She could see Fletcher hurrying in her direction, with Alex not far behind. Between them were Lex and Ben, and another person. She hesitated. There was something ever so vaguely familiar about the third person. Though she could not quite equate her memory with the figure being buffeted between her two assistants. The intruder, as indeed he could not be called anything but, resembled the homeless drunks, druggies

125

and vagabonds that languished around the less salubrious haunts of Melbourne. His matted beard reached to the middle of his chest and what was left of his hair was caught back in a tangled ponytail. The grey gabardine coat had certainly seen better days, which was not surprising as it reminded her of those that her father had discarded in the early 60's. Tattered trousers and dirty trainers completed the picture.

Nikki shook her head. It couldn't be the same person. She hurried towards them. Fuming that not only were the two men under her jurisdiction AWOL, but where the hell were the men who were meant to be out here, walking around the place on surveillance? Talk about a Mickey Mouse operation. Nothing about the whole set up made any sense. Except maybe the money. But she had begun to wonder if that was sufficient compensation for the secrecy, and restrictions on their personal movement? For one thing, not being allowed to go into town. Not that the town held any great enthrallment for her, but it still might have been nice to walk the streets once more, see if the locals would remember her and keep their distance. Nikki mentally shook her head to clear it of a past she struggled to forget. But right at the moment none of that mattered, she had other matters to attend to right now, like Lex and Ben.

The confrontation was becoming quite heated. Ben was slapping his hands against the man's chest in time with the verbal outbursts from Lex, each push causing the man to take a step back, his with fists raised in defence.

"What do you think you are doing?" Nikki demanded, coming to a stop a short distance away from the fighting men. She caught herself staring at the stranger as flashbacks unwillingly played in her mind.

Fletcher stopped in his tracks when he saw Nikki barrelling down on the fracas, then standing legs akimbo, hands on hips, not exactly yelling, but she was certainly making herself heard. He watched as Lex and Ben stepped back from the other man and hung their heads. Apparently not all his team were slackers. Maybe here was his team leader.

Fletcher quickly covered the intervening distance. "What's all this about, then?" he demanded between breaths, coming to a halt a few metres from the others. Once he had their attention, he took a step closer.

The third man, who was taking the opportunity to dust himself down and shrug himself back into his coat, was the first to respond to Fletcher.

He was a big man, in his mid-forties Fletcher guessed, well-built, but very scruffy in dress and appearance. Not anyone Fletcher would want to associate with. Once again he wondered if he was the squatter, and if he was, where was he living now? It couldn't be anywhere on the property. He, and his security team had been over the entire property and, other than the house and outbuildings, there was nowhere that would provide accommodation. So, where had he come from, and why he was here? And more importantly how had he come to be here undetected? What was his security team doing if some vagrant could simply stroll onto the premises? He would have to call a meeting later and have words. They certainly needed to tighten their act. There was no stopping the deadline, it was only three days away for goodness' sake, and everything had to be tight before then. His own job, and reputation was riding on the secrecy and success of this mission. Slack security would not do.

Shaking his head and shoulders, shedding dust and leaf detritus, the intruder straightened up, glared at his erstwhile assailants who fidgeted nearby, clenching and unclenching their fists ready to defend their boss if needs be, and took a step towards Fletcher. "They jumped me," he growled, not taking his eyes off Fletcher. "I wasn't doing anything."

Ben dusted himself down and looked first at Lex, then Fletcher. "We'd gone outside for a smoke and found him creeping around the back of the house." He did not think it the right time to mention that they had watched as the man relieved himself against the house, apparently taking delight in the pattern that he played across the boards.

"I was walking home. That's all. It's not a crime, is it?" The man's anger was evident in his tone as well as the set of his face.

"It is if you are on private property, and that is what this is. Where's home?"

The man waved his arm vaguely in the direction of the lake. "Over there."

Fletcher wondered at the venom in his voice. Another person might have found that, along with his posturing, unnerving and threatening, but it took more than that for Fletcher to be fazed. He was more interested in how the man had managed to escape detection and what he was doing here. Had he been conducting his own investigation of the property? Fletcher knew that speculation in the town would be rampant. Anyone would be curious, after all who wouldn't be? Maybe if he could engage this stranger in conversation, he could allay the locals' curiosity and at the same time learn what the stranger knew of the activities at the property.

"Then I had better accompany you. Make sure that no one else molests you." Fletcher was interested in the flinch that flashed across the man's face and wondered what was behind it. He had only meant it as a light-hearted reference to the physical altercation with Lex and Ben. He looked at his two men, a query in his raised eyebrow. Their blank expressions were sufficient for him to assume that there had been no excessive force used in the confrontation with the interloper. But there had been a fracas and that was something that he had to be dealt with, but right now he needed to get this interloper off the property. He scowled at Lex and Ben before giving Nikki a nod. Dealing with the security team could wait until he returned.

Fletcher gave a mental shrug and extended his hand to the man.

The two walked off together towards a visible gap in the tangle of blackberries along the boundary of *Braedon*, while Lex and Ben, grumbling, ambled back to the workshop.

Alex, who had stood back observing the activity from a safe distance, looked over to Nikki and cocked his head to the side. There was something vaguely familiar about her, as there had been with the man now disappearing into the tangle of vegetation. He had experienced niggles of recognition before, but having watched her now, in the presence of the odd stranger, memories were starting to filter through his mind.

Nikki had been experiencing similar mental nudges when in Alex's vicinity, but it was only in the context of the unkept man's apprehension that they were fully registering. Nikki gave Alex the briefest of nods, and Alex walked tentatively towards her. She met him halfway, then looked around to see if Lex and Ben were still around.

"Did you see who that was?" she asked in a cautious whisper.

Alex nodded. He did remember. "I thought he'd been run out of town."

Chapter 25

Over the years Fletcher had found that people who live a solitary life, when confronted with company, either clam up or talk nonstop. The man he was accompanying off the property fell into the latter category. What Fletcher didn't know was that the stranger's one-sided conversation was more a reaction to who he had seen, than taking the opportunity of having an audience to his vocalisations. But from those vocalisations Fletcher not only learned a lot about the area, but also the mysteries that shrouded Hemlock, and the man himself.

Fletcher was not overly concerned about the reasons why the stranger chose to live an almost hermit existence as he foraged or stole supplies. He was more interested in the fact that the locals labelled him *The* Hermit and considered him a pariah; that they saw him as a bit of a bogeyman, or, to use the local terminology, a maldape.

That admission had really caught Fletcher's ear, and his mind raced with possibilities. He smiled, thinking how a real live bogeyman or, in this case, maldape, would bring verisimilitude to the security that he had already factored in.

Then there was the old boathouse that the stranger had talked about. When Fletcher had been formulating the logistics of the project he had not taken into consideration that the drop would be any other than that – a simple one day deliver-and-go. But the thought that there could be somewhere to house and hide the plane

131

that was due to arrive with its precious cargo in three days' time, should that prove to be necessary, sounded attractive. He would have to look into that.

By the time the two men had come to the stranger's ramshackle abode further around the lake Fletcher had been able to negotiate a deal with him. In return for actively endorsing the existence of the maldape—how he proposed to do that was of little or no concern to Fletcher, so long as the man ensured that the curious were kept away from the property, as well as allowing the boathouse to be used for housing the plane—Fletcher would make certain that on the completion of the project, the property would legally find its way into the hermit's possession.

Fletcher had seen no need to disclose his own reasons for the negotiations as he had not wanted to go into the reasons for the secrecy. Besides, the hermit himself had made it perfectly clear that he had no notion, need or interest in knowing what was happening on *Braedon*.

For his own part, Bradley did not want it known that there was no one he was even remotely interested in sharing any information, and he had his own secrets to shield. Besides, he would be happy to do just about anything if it meant getting his hands on what he had always considered to be rightfully his.

Gary Fletcher was feeling very pleased with himself and the outcome of the day as he made his way back to *Braedon*. Oh, admittedly he would need to give Dave and Bruno, as well as the rest of the security team a rark-up later, but in a way their ineffectiveness, while showing where improvement was needed, had inadvertently assisted in the scheme of things. He had also found the team leader for the security team, and yes, his mother, and McFadden had been correct, Jamie McDonnell, or was that Nikki, was what he needed.

Chapter 26

Nikki couldn't keep her mind on the task at hand, instead she kept thinking back to the encounter with the intruder. Not so much who he was, oh, she knew who he was, he was The Hermit from her youth, the pariah, as some had called him. But what was he doing here? And then there was Alex's reaction. It appeared that, like her, he had recognised the man.

All this introspection was affecting her work, and she could not allow that to happen. She went looking for Alex in the house.

Nikki entered the house and made her way to the room where the surveillance team was headquartered. She stopped outside the door and took a deep breath. As team leader of security Nikki had every right to enter, but she still hesitated. What reason could she fabricate to justify calling Alex out of the room when he was working?

She straightened her shoulders, turned the handle and walked in. Doug, Bruno and Sam, who were manning the monitors, didn't look up. Vic, Jonno and Spiro were too busy shrugging themselves into their jackets to notice her entrance. Not so Lou and Alex sitting in deep discussion at the central table. They both looked up, and Alex rose to his feet.

"Ah, Nikki. Can I see you for a moment? Unless you were wanting ..." He looked around the room.

"No, no. It was you I came looking for in fact. If I'm not disturbing anything important?"

Alex turned to Lou, "'Scuse us."

133

Lou nodded. "Take your time, I'm not going anywhere, and neither is this," he tapped his finger on the pile of papers in front of him.

Nikki and Alex made their way to the room that served as a common room for the security teams and sat either side of a small table; the top of which housed a stagnating game of chess which meant they had to hold their mugs of coffee, acquired from the kitchen, cupped in their hands.

Alex was surprised that he was feeling slightly uncomfortable. He was certain that he had done nothing to warrant a reprimand that could not be given in the presence of his colleagues. He only hoped that by being brought into the common room the summons was of a more personal nature, and one that he himself had wanted to initiate – their commonality. He took a sip of his coffee and grimaced as he scolded his tongue. Ought he be the one to speak first?

"You wanted to see me?"

"Yes. It's about ... him. You know. Him. The man that Fletcher accompanied off the property the other day. You know who, or what he is? You said that you thought he had been run out of town."

Alex relaxed slightly; he wasn't here for a dressing-down. But that did nothing to relieve him of the dread that the alternative topic of discussion filled him with. He was still unsure if he was ready to confront what he had spent years trying to dispel from his memory. He wished that he had been able to initiate that particular conversation and so control its route. After all, he wasn't certain that his recollections were as accurate as they could be – the intervening years might well have distorted fact from fiction. He brought his mug of coffee up to his mouth and this time blew on it before looking across at Nikki. He took a sip of his drink and spoke into the mug, not answering her question directly. "It looked like you also knew who he was."

Nikki nodded, gazing into the emptiness of the room where they were sitting, happy to see that it, like the rest of the house had been freshly painted. There were no hints of who had occupied the rooms in the past. She didn't know whether to be glad or sad that the history had been obliterated.

"You do look vaguely familiar, but it can't be from Hemlock, or I'd remember you. So, what's your connection with that man?"

Nikki smiled and turned back to look at Alex. "Oh, it was from here, but no, you would not have known me. But I think it is possible that you knew of my sister. Tess."

Alex felt as though he had been gut-punched. He slumped back into the chair with such a force that even though his mug was now nearly empty, coffee still sloshed out and a damp patch appeared on his shirt. He leant down and placed his mug on the floor, hoping that he remembered to pick it up again when they were done.

"Tess?" Alex's mind flew back to his Uncle Ray. How could Nikki here be Tess's sister? Ray had said that Tess only had one sister, a younger sister, called Jamie after her older brother who had died as a newborn.

He had only been a kid himself at the time, but he had adored his father's younger brother. Followed him everywhere. Well, at least everywhere that Ray would allow him, and sometimes even when Ray had told him not to. It had been those times that Ray and Tess had unknowingly taught him about the birds and the bees. Alex squirmed at the memory, then looked across at Nikki, her hand hovered over the bishop, and Alex wondered if she would pick it up and move it. But she didn't.

Instead, she brought her hand up, ran it through her hair and looked quizzically at him and gave a discrete cough.

That was enough to break into Alex's thoughts.

"So, that is why I thought I'd seen you before. You resemble your sister!" Alex made it sound as though it was a eureka moment, and Nikki slumped. How many times had she heard the comparison made by people that knew the two of them?

"Probably."

"But your name is Nikki, and Tess's sister ..."

"Was Jamie. That's the name I went by, back then. I don't like the associations that it brings to mind, so I use my middle name with my friends, but Jamie is still my legal name and the name I go by in my work. But why do I feel that I know you? I didn't have much to do with anyone from Hemlock."

"Well, the man that she, Tess, was, um, friends with, he was my uncle."

"Ray Daniels? He's your uncle?" It was Nikki's turn to have the wind kicked out of her and she didn't notice the wince Alex made when she used the present tense.

"Of course. Ray Daniels ... Alex Daniels, and you recognised The Hermit. You do look remarkably like him, I mean Ray, you know. Why didn't I make that connection?"

"But how do you know what he looked like?"

"Ah, that would be telling, wouldn't it?" Nikki laughed as she sat back and remembered the times that she had silently followed Tess, who thought she had safely avoided detection, and had seen who she was meeting. But it was all past history now, so sharing couldn't hurt anybody, could it? Nikki then proceeded to tell Alex her story.

"I used to follow my sister when she would go to meet Ray."

"Snap!" Alex guffawed, and Nikki stopped talking and stared at him.

"Sorry, it's just that I used to follow my Uncle Ray! It's a wonder that we didn't see each other back then as we spied across the cavorting couple."

Nikki shook her head, and thought back to the time she had watched her sister. "I guess we were both too engrossed in what we were seeing between us to notice anything beyond that action."

"Sorry, I should not have interrupted, continue, please."

"To start with I never told her, but after a while she'd share with me, when we found any quiet, private moments that life in the commune rarely provided. You know, she really did love him. Ray Daniels was going to show Tess what life in the Big Smoke, away from commune life, was like."

"Did you know that he wanted to marry Tess? He'd asked her to elope with him," Alex asked quietly.

Nikki nodded and remembered how excited Tess was to be a wife and a mother, and live a 'normal life', one where she only had to share with one other adult. Where she would be the centre of another's life.

"Tess had shared with me the plans that were in place, so I took particular note to watch her every movement that day. And, when I saw her slip away and head towards the outbuildings, I made sure that I followed her.

"You see, I wanted, if not to be a part of the excitement, to at least see my sister meet up with the father of her child and say a silent farewell.

"But then, a ways into the bush, I heard Tess laugh, and say something. I couldn't hear clearly what she said, so I crept closer and that is when I saw him, The Hermit. He was exposing himself. We'd all seen that before. He was often spied about the place, and whenever he saw that we were watching, he'd get a grin on his face and flash. It never phased us kids, we knew all about the body. Couldn't help it being on a commune where privacy was not a commodity to be valued," Nikki laughed.

"But when Tess walked off laughing, I saw the man reach for his knife and I followed Tess. I didn't know what to do. I guess, in a way, I knew what I ought to have done, but I didn't. I should have raced back to the house and told them what I had seen. But if I had done so, then I would have been in deep trouble. Not only for venturing into the bush so late in the day by myself, but for allowing my sister to violate the commune rule. And then, if they found out that I had kept quiet about Tess's dalliances and plans ... well, there was no knowing what punishment I would have had to endure. So I returned to the house, found a quiet corner to hide myself and hope that The Hermit would not harm Tess, that she would meet her Ray and live happily ever after. I promised myself that when I was old enough, I would leave and find Tess, and my own happily ever after in the Big Smoke. That night has haunted me ever since. If I had physically intervened there and then would my sister still be alive? You know, I am positive that it was he who killed Tess. I saw him in the bush, and who else would be in there at that time?"

"But what about when your sister's body was found, why didn't you tell anybody then what you had seen, and was convinced of?"

Once again Nikki laughed sardonically. "And who would have believed me? The commune members maybe, but even if I did tell them, they would not have gone to the police with that theory. The police were generally as antagonistic towards the free-thinking people who formed communes as they were of communists. They would never have believed me, a mere child, nor the word of members of the commune. No, I kept what I had seen, and surmised, to myself. But I did decide to make good my dream to leave the commune as soon as I was old enough, and work towards finding a way to ensure that people, especially females, would be safe from the likes of that man. That's how I ended up here."

Alex closed his eyes. It was ironic that, despite having completely different experiences from living in Hemlock—she on the commune and he in a traditional nuclear family—they should share such similarities. He looked at Nikki and wondered what her story was. If it was half as bad as his, and he could only imaging that it was a lot worse, he admired her for where she is now. But he was still baffled - how did wanting to keep females safe explain why she was here building robots? He shook his head in confusion. "I'm sorry. I can't make the connection between building machines and saving the female population. How does that work?"

Nikki laughed again, this time with humour. "Robotics might be what I'm qualified in, and it certainly helped qualify me for this job, but I was recruited because of my reputation as a part time-vigilante."

Alex raised his eyebrows in surprise. That certainly was unexpected.

Nikki, almost affronted at the non-verbal interruption, frowned. "It was a means to assuage my guilt and anger. Fletcher wanted people with dual capabilities, and, shall we say, a mutual friend saw in me what Fletcher was after."

The two sat silently for several minutes, both caught up in their own thoughts. Nikki was the first to break the silence.

"Back then, when Fletcher was leading the man away, you said that you thought he'd been run out of town ...? What made you think that?"

Alex looked into the distance, then brought his clenched hands to his face and, with a bowed head and eyes closed as though in prayer, he gently pummelled his forehead with them.

"He was never liked. Everyone female I knew dreaded seeing him, and parents the town over were tired of trying to keep us kids on a short lead and scaring us with tales of the maldape and bogeymen. When, and after a number of years there had been no leads as to your sister's killer, the town turned their frustration and anger towards those in the community with the least means to defend themselves. The one remaining distant branch of the Gentian family that was still in town were barely tolerated, so they became the obvious target.

It took less than a year for the smear campaign to wear them down sufficiently for them to up sticks and leave. Their place down the road from the police station was simply abandoned. To my knowledge it was never put on the market, just left to revert to nature."

"And what about Ray? What happened to him?"

Alex let his arms flop down either side of him and he sighed. "Uncle Ray. That was terrible. Of course the family suspected that he was seeing a girl from the commune, and they hoped that she wouldn't influence him to join their lifestyle. And, because I was his virtual shadow, I had an inkling that they were planning something, but as a young kid I was not versed in reading the signs that would have alerted others. But he did not know that she was pregnant until after it came out publicly. He was mortified. Well, he was mortified well before finding out about the baby, that was the final mortification.

"I remember the night that she didn't show. I was there. Well, not exactly with him, I was in the bush further up the road, watching as he waited, and paced, and waited for her. Only she never showed up. But I did see The Hermit come out of the bush hitching his pants up and with a smirk on his face."

"And you didn't find that strange? You knew Ray was waiting for my sister, and The Hermit appeared instead?"

Alex looked sheepish. "I didn't take any notice of it. As kids we were used to seeing him around acting strange, besides, I was concentrating on watching my uncle Ray."

"But surely if you were watching your uncle Ray, you could see that he was upset. You said that he was pacing. You must have realised that something was up."

Alex shrugged. "Yeah, well hindsight is a great thing. I was just a kid, and I was where I wasn't meant to be, doing something that I should not have been doing. Guess I didn't manage to make any connection at the time."

He looked down at his hands and then up at Nikki. "But thinking about it now, I'm not sure if it would have made any difference to the outcome if I had. Sorry."

Nikki raised her eyebrows. "As you say, no matter now. Continue."

Alex took a breath, "Well, when Ray finally left their rendezvous point, I snuck out from my hidey-hole and trailed him back to his place. He was as dejected as I had ever seen him. I tried to engage him in trivial conversation, though in all probability he saw it as a badgering of inane questions. Whichever it was, I could not fathom the utterances he made. But he sure as heck was upset."

"But you must have suspected something. Why didn't you say something?"

"Like you, I figured that if I said anything then I'd be in trouble being out late at night by myself, and who would believe me? So I kept it all to myself. I have lived with the guilt all these years. Then when she was found ... he was as mad as a cut snake. With the police, with the people out at the commune, but mostly with himself."

"Himself? Why?"

Alex shrugged. "He never really did explain it to anyone. His garbled conversations with me were just that, garbled, and my young brain didn't really comprehend the anguish that he must have been going through. I don't know. Maybe he was already suffering from some mental instability – who would have known back then? But when it was revealed that she was pregnant he went right off his rocker. Right do-lally. So much so that my dad had to call an ambulance.

"That was the last time I saw him, until some years later when I was looking down at him in his coffin. And that was the impetus, I guess a bit like you, that has brought me to where I am now. Seeing what the events of that night did to Ray, made me determined that no one would get the better of me. So yes, I work in electronics, but I moonlight as a personal security guard."

"Funny how things work out in life isn't it?"

Chapter 27

Over the years Demetrius Popolo had refined enemy-making into an unenviable artform. His ancestry was enough to incite an ethnic revolution, he didn't need his writing to do it for him. Armenian, Italian, Greek, Lebanese, there was supposed to be a bit of Spanish in there somewhere too, a real melting pot, and an endless source for material for his books. His books were all fiction, it was just that most countries took exception to them. His style cut into too many quicks. His last, much acclaimed, novel was a simple love story, set against a backdrop of political espionage. He'd set it in South-East Asia, named it *Shalam,* meaning hello, so was then very surprised when both Israel and Lebanon banned it.

It was after this episode that he seriously started to think of retirement, or at least looking for some occupation which would not attract such unwanted, potentially dangerous attention. He slipped his minders and took himself to what he hoped would be an unassuming village on Tenerife. It was there that he was happened upon by Edward Maxwell, or Teddy-Max as Edward had insisted on being called, after many shared days of copious alcoholic indulgences.

Demetrius was tired, he confided in Teddy-Max. Tired of fighting. Tired of running. Even tired of writing. He wanted what he perceived others to have – a peaceful existence with no problems. To live in a place where his presence did not necessitate a menagerie of minders. A place where his presence did not upset the locals. A place where he could be himself, in anonymity.

Maxwell was on his own soul-searching retreat. He was looking for a salve, or a saviour. He was never too sure what it was that he felt was missing from his life. But he had an inner feeling that maybe he had found it in Demetrius. Here was a man whose sole presence brought out feelings that Maxwell had never known before. And he wanted it to continue beyond what many would have simply called a holiday romance.

Listening to Demetrius bemoan his good fortune, and his desire for a new life, Maxwell started to formulate an idea which he thought might assuage both their yearnings. Maxwell could not wait to share his idea, and after he had, Demetrius could not wait to start. Just one more press conference and he, Demetrius Popolo would be no more.

Chapter 28

Paul Edgar, pleased that he had scored a pass to this press conference, was among the reporters and photographers scrabbling to get in a good position to record Demetrius Popolo before he departed for his next promotion location. Even if he had not managed to secure a one-on-one interview, he felt certain he would have sufficient material to satisfy Walt Hancock.

With this much media attention he was not surprised that Demetrius Popolo was taking a charter rather than a commercial flight. What had come as a surprise was that it was Tim's plane providing the service, and he wondered why there had been the need for secrecy. He and Tim had laughed about the clandestine manner in which Tim had been approached and pretty much conscripted into his latest engagement. A charter which Tim had called his 'super-duper secret mission' as no details had been shared with him. In fact, up until yesterday Tim had not even known what day he and his plane were to report for duty.

Squashed among the melee of clicking cameras and shouted questions, Paul was torn between the need to make his own notes and photographs, and puzzling over how Tim fitted in an event that had no semblance of secrecy. He flinched as he felt a firm hand clasp his shoulder.

"What do you think you are doing here?" A deep and authoritarian voice boomed in his ear.

Paul's heart jumped as his stomach dropped, and his mind frantically scrolled though all the possible misdemeanours he'd notched up that would warrant such an accusation. Petrified, he turned around wondering who he would encounter.

Tim stood there, grinning, and Paul felt himself almost collapse with relief.

"I could ask you the same," he almost spat. "Me? I'm here doing my job—taking photos, taking notes."

"Yeah, me too," Tim laughed. "Not the photos and notes bit, but the doing my job bit. Good turnout you have here, huh? I didn't expect to have my photo taken when I signed up for this caper." Tim's eyes flitted over the gaggle of reporters, and beyond.

"If I remember correctly, you didn't know what you were signing up for. You only needed to hear the dollars you were going to get from it." Paul laughed.

"Yeah, you're dead right on that one."

Paul noticed that Tim's eyes never settled on anyone or thing, but were constantly roving, and he found that he was wanting to do the same but didn't know what he was meant to looking for.

Tim continued, "Still not too sure what is going on, but I can tell you, something is." He started to move away, then stopped, leant in close to Paul and almost whispered.

"I suggest you get reacquainted with the old B and B; and you might find it useful to take the Black Book with you."

Paul pulled back and looked down at his friend, his head angled to one side in query.

Tim's eyes were still roving. "I'd like to think that someone has my back. Best be off before they start looking for me."

Paul grabbed Tim's arm as he turned to go. "Be careful out there mate, and keep an ear and eye open for any entertaining gossip on your passenger that may help me with my article." He grinned.

Demetrius stood beside the light aircraft and turned to face the mass of reporters and photographers clustered behind the barrier to the apron. There would be no more interviews. It was with a pang of regret that there would be no more books, but then again ... He smiled and the cameras went clicking and some even flashed. He stood for another minute then silently climbed into the plane.

Paul and the other reporters and photographers waited till the plane in which Demetrius Popolo and his entourage of two was on the runway and cleared for take-off. Paul leant against the metal and mesh barrier to the apron, his hand shielding the sun from his eyes and watched Tim's plane take off. He was puzzled by what Tim had said about watching his back and that something was going on. Tim was not one to romanticise, or panic. And Tim referencing the B and B? Paul wondered what that had been about. It had been some years since either of them had visited the B and B or had a need for the Black Book. He found himself smiling as he recalled the various 'occupations' that the B and B had fulfilled.

The sleep-out at the back of his parents' home had started out as just that, a sleep-out. A place he and his mates had more or less made into a cubbyhouse. A place to hang out, swear to be 'blood brothers', camp out overnight and tell ghost stories until one or another of his friends would get too scared to stay. When he was about ten his grandfather had given him a crystal set and his interest in amateur radio was sparked, and the sleep-out became his 'radio-shack'. Then, when he was fourteen and his other grandfather introduced him to photography, the 'radio-shack' shared the space with his darkroom. It was not long before a bar fridge sat convenient to the bunk beds and 'come up and see my etchings' became 'come and help me in the darkroom'. That phrase soon became the nudge-nudge, wink-wink mantra of the two young men. It was a natural progression for the sleep-out to become known as the B and B – Bordello and Bar, a place that Tim and Paul were happy to share. The Black Book by then served two purposes – book of contacts, but also, which is what Tim had been referring to earlier at the airport, it was where the two of them kept a copy of the Morse code and recorded transmissions.

Paul was one of the last to leave the airport. He had stood and waited until the speck in the sky could no longer be seen. Tim obviously thought that he would have a need to communicate with him, but Paul could see nothing untoward. Still, when he got back home, he would go and dust off the cobwebs. Literal and mental.

Chapter 29

Tim was sitting with his legs stretched out in front of him and his back up against a lone coolabah, the only tree that was in his line of vision, whichever way he looked, and he wondered how it came to be there, and how it had survived. There was nothing but sparse red dirt pocked with patches of native grass, and rocky areas harbouring various saltbushes and spinifex for as far as he could see.

He was beginning to think that he ought not to have been so eager to take on this job when Ibraham and Harris had approached him. But at the time it had seemed to be manna from heaven—a job and good money to boot. Now he was not so sure. For one thing, it turned out that this was not an entertaining joyride for conference delegates. In fact, there was no conference. Instead, he was flying the author Paul was so keen on writing about, along with his old friends Ibraham and Harris, around the country.

Ostensibly Demetrius Popolo was on a publicity tour, but now it appeared that even that was a misnomer. Scenic tour of the state be damned! This whole charter thing was turning out to be a right fiasco. Tim wasn't too sure what the caper was, and he wasn't being paid to ask, he was simply paid to fly the plane. But from what he could see, there had been little interest from the media, and Demetrius himself appeared disinclined to enthusiasm. It was almost as if Demetrius was only present physically, that he had something else of import on his mind. Normally when Tim was piloting sightseers or commuters his passengers were more than happy to engage in conversation, if not with him, then with their fellow passengers. Yet here was a man who supposedly had never visited

Australia before, who was too preoccupied with staring at his hands clasped in his lap to even acknowledge when something interesting on the ground was pointed out. Tim had even started to speculate that Demetrius was here against his will and wondered if he should find out. Not that he had any idea what he'd do, or how he could help, if Popolo was the victim of a highly visible kidnapping. It would certainly be foolish to even contemplate grilling either Harris or Ibraham. And as for asking Demetrius himself, even if he were given a private opportunity ... Tim had given up trying to glean anything from the man that could be of worth to Paul. Idle conversation was in short supply. But it was near impossible to engage him in any form of conversation at all.

Tim had definitely been right in thinking that something was amiss and was glad that he had had the brief opportunity to share that concern with Paul back at the airport in Melbourne and hoped that Paul had understood the veiled inuendo, and was monitoring his communications in the B&B.

And why the hell had he been told this morning to fly out here with a mechanic? Just for he and some other dubious grease monkeys to tinker with *his* plane. And then be threatened with bodily harm when he started to question the directive.

He could hear the mechanics in the shed behind him working on his Cessna, and he could only hope that they knew what they were doing. He sure didn't know what he was doing. While Popolo and company were enjoying a book signing event he was out here in the wops on a long-abandoned airstrip quite some distance from Adelaide, or from anywhere for that matter. Though he supposed that the people in the cluster of buildings which constituted the miniscule settlement he had flown over shortly before landing, would debate that with him.

Everyone, Ibraham, Harris and these mechanics, even Popolo, they were all a fishy lot. He fingered the key in his pocket and felt a modicum of reassurance – he still had to fly Demetrius Popolo, busy in Adelaide promoting his book, back to Melbourne. So whatever they were doing in that shed he would still have a plane to fly. He crossed his fingers, pleased to have had the opportunity to pass on the cryptic message to Paul. It was a comfort to know that Paul would have his back. He only hoped that Paul had picked up on it, and had been receiving the morse messages that he'd been sending – a record of the travels of Demetrius Popolo and his two-man entourage.

He looked behind him, trying to see into the shed. But the interior was too dark for his eyes, pupils constricted against the sun, to see. He hoped that they were not interfering with any of his custom features, especially his latest addition. The further into this junket the more inclined he was to think that it might be needed. He'd have to remember to remove it from where he'd stashed it in his overnight bag and carry it on his body instead. But that could also be a problem. It might be portable, but it was still big. Big enough to create an unseemly bulge, and what with always having either Ibraham or Harris beside him up front ... he didn't like the idea of being questioned. He wasn't ready to share his invention with the public just yet, and certainly not with his passengers.

The sun was past the zenith, and Tim was tired of swatting the ever-present sticky flies away from the moist corners of his eyes and mouth. The insect repellent that he had fortuitously included in the first aid kit in the Cessna was proving ineffectual against the annoying insects fabled for their perseverance.

The only respite from the monotony was when a lizard would skittle past, or when a flock of cockatoos made their presence heard, squawking as they intermittently settled in the tree above. He had long given up on reading the literature that Harris had handed him when he had departed Adelaide early in the morning. He'd already read it twice, and without actually practising, the theory was just that, theory. And why the hell he would be wanting to know how to fly a floatplane was beyond him. But he supposed that gaining knowledge was never a bad thing.

It was late afternoon before there was a lull in the noise from the shed.

"She's ready to go now mate," the mechanic he had brought with him called out. He was standing by the door, rubbing his hands on a grubby rag which he then stuffed into the back pocket of his overalls, before heading back inside. Tim winced and hoped that the overalls were staying in the shed. He did not want grease or any other foreign object making its way into the interior of his plane. The mechanic was bad enough.

Tim scrambled to his feet and dusting down the seat of his pants, walked over to the shed and stepped inside. It took a few moments for his eyes to adjust, but when they did, all he could do was stare.

"What the hell have you done?"

Tim went over to the Cessna and slowly walked around it. The literature now made sense. It was bad enough that he was being paid to fly passengers around the country when he didn't have a commercial license. Not that he had ever lost any sleep over that, he'd always made sure that he was paid in cash. If questioned he'd always said that the passengers were friends, and he was taking them on a joy flight. But now he was being expected to fly a plane that not only had been modified, but that he was no longer rated to fly. He took some deep breaths in an attempt to quell the fury that he could feel building inside him. He turned to one of the other mechanics who was tossing tools into a hessian bag on the floor beside the plane. "You've put floats on the plane. *My* plane," the venom barely concealed.

"Yep. That's what we were asked to do." The mechanic now standing beside him answered as he took off his glasses and wiped them with a grubby cloth. He was pleased with the work they had done and couldn't understand Tim's reaction.

"What the heck do I need floats for?" Tim slowly circled the plane again, this time checking for any other eccentricities that might have been added without his knowledge.

"You never know when you might need them." The mechanic stooped down and picked up the hessian bag ready to carry it to a dust covered Land Rover parked beside the Cessna.

"I'm flying over the outback for cripes' sake. There's no bloody water in the there."

"Oh, wouldn't be too sure about that. Once the rains come it gets pretty damp out there." The mechanic grinned cheerfully, throwing the bag through the open rear side window of the Land Rover. The tools inside clattered against each other as the bag settled onto the floor behind the passenger seat. The mechanic slapped his hands together to dislodge any residual dirt to waft into the hot and still air.

Tim stared at the man. "I would not imagine that to be the case in May."

The mechanic shrugged his shoulders. "You got a point there, but we just did what was asked of us."

Tim looked back at his plane; there really wasn't much he could do about the adjustments that had been made. He only hoped that Ibraham and Harris did not expect him to fork out for them. For one thing, he didn't have the kind of money that these jackasses would be asking for. And they would be asking for a heap. He didn't doubt the mechanics' ability – from what he could see they had done a top-notch job, but still, to come all the way out here to get the job done just added to his unease about the whole set up.

"You'll be needing a hand getting this thing outta here and ready to fly then?"

The mechanic asked, stuffing his hands into his overall pockets. He gave a piercing one-note whistle, to draw the attention to the other two men at the back of the shed. They looked up and he gave them a side nod of his head to let them know that they were wanted.

Tim looked at the bespectacled man who was now standing beside him, and mentally sighed in relief to see his mechanic passenger had scrubbed up and was clean once more.

Tim nodded his head and watched as the three mechanics pushed the plane out of the shed. Then he did a quick pre-flight check, which included another stealthy message to the B and B. He laughed silently to himself, wondering what Paul would be making of the convoluted route that the tour was taking. He sure as heck didn't know what to make of it. Tim circled the shed and saw the Land Rover speeding towards the isolated settlement. No doubt for a beer or two. That was something that he was looking forward to once they got back to Adelaide. He would have appreciated a beer with his lunch – sandwiches, fruitcake and tea. A right disappointment. Being out in the wops, he had been looking forward to billy tea, the water boiled up over an outdoor fire, loose tea leaves thrown in and the billy twirled expertly at arm's length in a circle then drunk from enamel pannikins. It had been letdown not to relive his childhood camping memories. He certainly had not imagined that the tea would be made with the aid of an electric jug and poured from a china, albeit with a chipped spout, teapot, into mismatched china cups, with saucers!

He was more than happy when the lights of Adelaide finally appeared in front of him. It would not be long before he would be in his hotel room. He'd have a shower to rid himself of the sandy grit, get into clothes that were not sweat stained and then relax with a cold beer. Tomorrow he would take the opportunity of a day off to see the sights of Adelaide. Before the next leg when he was to fly the plane to Alice Springs. He shook his head, wondering what possible interest there could be there for Popolo.

Plans for his relaxing evening had gone awry when he'd been met at the airport by Harry Harris, all businesslike and full of bonhomie with the delightful news that the itinerary had changed, again, and they were to fly out in the morning. Would he please lodge the flight plan for Sydney.

"Two out of three ain't bad, so they tell me." Tim scowled at his reflection in the window of his hotel room and drank out of a can of Coke. It was a poor substitute for the beer that he had been dreaming of all day, but it was better than tap water or tea.

He turned from the window and crushed the can in his hand then tossed it in the general direction of the rubbish bin sat by the modular piece of furniture which constituted a desk cum TV stand. He turned on the TV before collapsing onto the double bed. Tim stretched his arms up towards the pillows and took a deep breath before cupping the back of his head with his hands. Sydney. In the morning. First thing. He was too tired to wonder what had brought about the change in plans. Besides, it was not his place to question what was happening. His sole purpose was to fly the plane and the passengers. He sighed, ran his hands through his hair and stared at the ceiling above him. A trill of canned laughter burst from the TV rousing him from his ruminations, and he looked at his watch. He needed to get to bed and sleep.

Chapter 30

Everything went according to plan the next morning. Ibraham sat up front with Tim who had given up inviting Demetrius to sit up the front for a better view. They took off from Adelaide and headed into the rising sun on their way to Sydney with scheduled refuelling stops in Mildura and Wagga Wagga.

It wasn't long after taking off from Mildura that Ibraham leant towards Tim and looking to the front, waved his arm erratically towards the front cockpit window. "See that?"

Tim looked at the man sitting beside him, then at the vista in front, and back at Ibraham. What the hell was Ibraham looking at that required his attention?

"See what? There's nothing there. It's desolate for as far as you can see, and it will be pretty much like that till we get closer to the Dividing Range.

"Exactly." It was all Richard Ibraham could do to stop himself from rubbing his hands together in glee, but he could not keep the euphoria from his voice.

"So, what am I supposed to be looking at?

"Like you said, there is nothing there. That's what makes it so perfect. When you get a bit further into that nothingness there, I need you to descend, rapidly, till you are flying below the radar. He looked across at Tim. "Fake a stall or something. You can do that, can't you?"

'What the hell?' Tim thought, looking aghast at the man beside him. He then turned back to look at the terrain. How much did Ibraham know about aviation? Did he understand the risks of

157

low-level flying? If the worst was to happen the terrain that the plane was fast approaching did not offer ease of rescue. Tim tried to formulate the words in his mind so that his automatic reaction would be tempered. He did not want to antagonize the man who was employing him by questioning the directive, but it was *his* plane and his responsibility to maintain the safety of all on board. And flying below the radar was not the best way of doing that. Especially when he was not familiar with this part of the country.

"You want me to fly at low level, over *that*?" It was Tim's turn to point out the window.

"No, I *need* you to fly as low as you can so that the plane's flight is no longer detected. I want you to make your descent such that for anyone observing, either in real time or on radar, will assume that the plane has, if not crashed, had to make an emergency landing."

Tim felt a shiver of apprehension prickle down his back. Had he been correct earlier, in thinking that Popolo was the victim of a kidnap? Or was there something more going on?

"What the ...?" Tim shook his head. "I thought you said Mr Popolo was due in Sydney this evening?"

"Oh, he is *due* to make a public appearance, but he is not going to be able to make that appointment. He has another one scheduled. One that he cannot afford to miss. And I am relying on you to help him get to that one on time." Ibraham smiled at Tim.

Tim took a quick look behind him at Demetrius. If he was the victim of an abduction, he was concealing it remarkably well. This whole caper was going from mysterious to downright creepy. Why would Ibraham be wanting to only fake a fatal crash? Was Harris in on it a well? Whatever scheme they were planning there was no way that he was going to endanger himself, his plane or his passengers on the whim of Richard Ibraham. He took a deep breath and opened his mouth, determined to refuse, but Ibraham cut him off.

"You are to make the descent appear involuntary, and then, after flying at that height for, oh, whatever you deem appropriate for a deception, you are to follow this heading and make for these co-ordinates." He thrust an opened notebook in front of Tim. "And stay under the radar," he continued, his voice carrying the unspoken threat that boded no argument.

Tim shut his mouth, took hold of the notebook and refocused his eyes from the horizon to the page. The co-ordinates meant nothing to him as to the actual location of the destination, but at least he knew that they would be heading south-west back to Victoria. Maybe?

"And when I get there? What then? Is there an airfield, or are you all going to jump out?"

"Funny. No, when we get there, I'll tell you what you are going to do."

"But..." Tim might not always do things 'by the book', but the safely of his plane and passengers, not to mention himself, he always took into consideration, and when it came to landing the plane, he needed to know all the details of what to expect.

Ibraham was not about to enter into an argument. His orders were sacrosanct.

"But no buts. I know what you are going to say, and I don't want to hear it. You can be assured that everything has been taken care of. After all, you know as well as I do, that we are not where we meant to be, so just do your job, and fly this crate."

Tim's knuckles clenched the joystick. He would have thought that being in control of the aircraft gave him some leniency in following protocol. Such a barrage of injustice reminded him of the tormenting that he, and other junior boys had had exacted out to them when they were at school, and with that in mind he kept his lips firmly together and started to think about what he was going to do next, he would work on the landing later.

He glanced again at Ibraham and smiled sardonically. A stall be damned. If that was what the smug bastard beside him was expecting, then he was going to be in for a surprise. Fed up with all the changes that were happening Tim had decided to make some of his own. If Ibraham wanted the appearance of a stall to persuade any onlooker that the plane was losing altitude, then he would give them something else to enjoy. He mentally ran through the procedure that he was going to implement and hoped that he could carry it off now that he had the extra drag of the floats.

Ibraham, having, in his mind, put Tim in his place, turned around in his seat and gave his partner Harris a thumbs up. Harris in turn nudged Demetrius and indicated that he should tighten his seat belt and hold on.

Demetrius, despite being thought of as a jet-setter, was not particularly fond of the 'jetting', blanched and looked first at Harris, then up to the two men in front of him and then out the window as the ground appeared to race towards them, even though Tim had not done anything yet to alter their altitude. Demetrius was the only one of the four who did not know that what was about to happen was a ruse, all he knew was that this flying around was part of the bigger plan that Teddy-Max had orchestrated for his benefit. When Harris gave a chuckle, it did little to improve Demetrius' composure. He was already filled with a mixture of euphoria and trepidation thinking about what was ahead of him without his added dislike, almost fear, of flying.

Tim, aware of the dangers, and concentrating on his forced and involuntary manoeuvre, was unaware of how Demetrius' consternation was entertaining his minders, but Harris and Ibraham were taking delight in their charge's pallor and handwringing.

Oh yes, you'll need those seatbelts real tight, and you should probably locate the sickbags while you are at it. Tim thought smugly then winced as he thought of having to clean the interior once he'd landed. But what the heck, it would be worth it just to have Ibraham get his comeuppance.

Tim concentrated on the sparce landscape below and then, feeling sweat break out in his armpits, and with a grin on his face, he pushed the nose of the plane into a spiral dive. He gleefully heard gasps from his passengers, along with some choice expletives as their chests were flung against their seat belts, and their fingers grappled to cling onto anything they could grasp as the ground rushed up to meet them. No sooner had they adjusted to sitting at an almost 45-degree angle than Tim banked the plane about 30 degrees into a steep turn. He pulled back on the controls increasing the angle of the bank, tightening the turn, and increasing the rate of descent. Tim's enjoyment was inversely proportional to the discomfort of his passengers, and he took a perverse delight in imagining their pallor, knuckles white as they hung on to whatever it was that they were grasping.

Once the plane had reached what he considered to be the desired altitude to avoid any radar detection, he closed the throttle and banked the plane till the wings were level. He then slowly raised the nose, watching the airspeed indicator to know when he could add power, and resume flying on the new heading that was written down in the notebook which he had by now clipped onto his clipboard for safe keeping and quick referral.

Swathed in sweat that he would vehemently deny if ever questioned, Tim breathed a sigh of relief and mentally congratulated himself on the success of his aerial manoeuvre.

"How was that for an adrenalin rush?" Tim laughed and took a quick look at his passengers. He laughed again. The exhilaration he felt was further buoyed when he took in their lack of composure. All three were hyperventilating and looking decidedly green, but at least the sickbags, held tightly in their laps, were still empty.

Now he had to think about how he was going to alert Paul to the changes. If it was Ibraham's intent for the public to assume the worst, then he needed to at least get the new co-ordinates to Paul even if he was not able to inform him of the subterfuge that would no doubt soon feature on the news.

His communique earlier this morning in Adelaide had been easy, he simply made the twiddling with the knobs and tapping out the morse code part of the take-off procedure. To now fiddle with dials on the instrument panel could arouse suspicion and precipitate an inquisition. But it was imperative that he send those co-ordinates to Paul. He smiled as he recalled a friend of his who was a tour operator in Africa and had once taken his light aircraft up to a level where the decrease in oxygen sent his garrulous passengers into slumber. Unfortunately for him not only would the others in the plane notice if there was an increase in altitude, but it would also generate an unidentified ping on the radar, which Ibraham would not want. He sighed and hoped that an opportunity would present itself.

And it did. Exhaustion from the aerobatic manoeuvre had set in. Tim noticed that the man beside him had slumped towards the side of the plane, his head resting on the side window. A quiet snoring purr was coming from behind him. He turned around and sure enough both Harris and Demetrius were relaxed in their seats, heads back, eyes closed and mouths open. Tim held his breath for a couple of seconds, then checking the notebook, sent the co-ordinates. However, with his fingers shaking and flying the plane now requiring his full attention, he was not able to send anything more.

Whatever happened, whatever was reported, he could only hope that Paul would realise, without his beacon being activated, that any reports of a crash were a fabrication. And that the co-ordinates he had just sent would work as breadcrumbs for him. He also wondered what the authorities and Search and Rescue would make of the lack of an ELT transmission, but that could not be helped. Unless ... he thought of his prototype. If he activated that and jettisoned it out the window ... But doing that would no doubt generate confusion when it was found without any wreckage nearby.

He laughed quietly to himself as he imagined the suggestions that such a find could generate – UFOs and alien abductions; or massive sink holes which, once engulfing the plane, sealed themselves up again like an anemone feeding. No, it had probably been for the best that he had forgotten to remove the prototype from his bag and stash it in one of his pockets. Besides, be might yet need it for real.

Tim looked at the instrument panel and checked his watch. No mention had been made as to the next leg of the journey, and with dusk not far off he hoped that he would not be expected to continue today, and that wherever he landed there would be provision for him to refuel. He had been looking for an airfield but all he could see ahead of him were the mountains which made up this segment of the Great Dividing Range, with the fading sun glistening on the higher snow-dappled peaks. Between the mountains, the snow and all the trees there was scant indication of habitation, far less any suggestion of an airfield or even an area of land cleared sufficiently to provide a landing spot. The only indication of habitation was one random narrow road, mostly hemmed in with trees, carving a solitary path through the vegetation below. He hoped that if it led to where he was to land his plane, there would also be some sort of accommodation for he and his passengers. He laughed to himself. If he was expected to land here, then of course there would be something or someone to meet them. It didn't make sense for him to fake a multiple fatality only for them all to disappear in the bush. Though survival in the bush would be preferable to in the inhospitable environment surrounding the locale designated by Ibraham to stage a crash. This whole exercise had been like flying by the seat of his pants.

He hated not knowing anything. Other than he in a couple of hours he'd be approaching their target area.

Two hours later Richard Ibraham roused himself and once again leant over to Tim and waved his arm about.

"There. That's where you are to land."

Tim already knew that he was in the general area, but for the life of him, he couldn't see any airfield or even an airstrip where he was meant to land.

Then he remembered the floats that had been added to his plane, without consultation, and he bristled at the memory. Damn it! He should never have agreed to take on this job. But the renumeration had been so enticingly mind boggling that he had not been able to help himself.

Of course. Floats. Perversely pleased that he had taken a look, and he was glad that it was a relatively in-depth look—with nothing else to do under the coolabah tree—at the literature yesterday, he started to look around for a body of water. Then he saw what Ibraham was busy pointing to. A lake. He lined the plane up for landing and hoped like heck that he would be able to apply what he had read without too much difficulty, or damage to the plane.

Tim felt like letting out a jubilant shout as the floats finally settled on the surface of the lake. The landing had not been the smoothest, but heck, they were down, in one piece, and not sinking. Now he needed to determine where best to stop – on the shore and possibly cause his passengers to get their shoes wet during the transition from plane to sand, or to gamble with what looked like the remnants of a jetty. Taking a quick look at Ibraham beside him with his smart, highly polished, and no doubt expensive and handmade shoes, he was tempted to aim for the beach, but decided on taking a chance that the jetty was not as flimsy as it appeared was preferable to the inevitable wrath if precious shoes were ruined. Gauging his approach with surprising accuracy, Tim brought the plane to a gentle stop, relaxed back into his seat and let out a sigh. He had done it. Flown a floatplane, at low level, across the state of Victoria. With a chuckle he wondered if that was worthy of the *Guinness Book of Records.*

He looked across at Ibraham, anxious to know what was to happen next. Ibraham was turned around busy talking with Harris. Both men were looking refreshed from their tension-induced slumber while Demetrius Popolo, sweating and rumpled, was not exactly a radiant model of composure. None of them were interested in enlightening Tim as to what was expected next, so he turned back to look out the cockpit window. There wasn't much to be seen. Just a small beach and beyond that bush. There certainly wasn't anything to indicate that a plane was expected. No fuel pump, not even a drum that might contain fuel. No hanger, no anchor, not even a rope with which to secure the plane to the jetty. He then looked to the jetty. It was doubtful that the jetty could secure anything other than a remote-controlled boat of minimum dimensions.

Two men, standing at a distance apart, were waiting. The one on the shore was shabby-looking and skulked near what would possibly have once been a boat house. A rusting corrugated iron roof barely visible under a collection of creepers was valiantly fighting gravity with the support of a single land-based but lopsided wall. The other wall was missing, except for a few upright supports. It was definitely a sad building that had seen better days. The man was signalling Tim to steer the plane in that direction. Tim frowned and shook his head. Surely that dilapidated boathouse wasn't meant for his plane? Neither Ibraham nor Harris had said anything about this being an overnight stop. Then again, they hadn't said it wasn't to be. He certainly wasn't expecting the need for the plane to be accommodated. Tim thought that he would prefer to find something to which he could secure the plane, out in the open. He'd prefer to leave the plane exposed to the elements than risk spending the night under the inadequate shelter of that structure. He chose to ignore the man, for the moment at least.

He looked to the other man, standing halfway down the jetty. He was more presentable. He stood, legs apart with hands on hips, and had an air of authority which Tim found disconcerting. Tim shook his head and tried to dredge up where he had seen that stance before. It was certainly one that he was familiar with, but the cues to memory were being stifled as he went through the shutdown procedure of the plane.

Smiling, and feeling utterly exhausted from the demands of the earlier death-dive manoeuvre coupled with hours of concentrated low-level flying, as well as the euphoria of having successfully manhandled the unfamiliarity of the plane now that it had been converted, he reached over the joystick and patted the top of the instrument panel as though it was a living thing. He looked up again at the man standing on the jetty. Tim's smile faded, and his gut caught in a tight squeeze as his teeth clenched. He remembered, with bitter hatred, who the man was, and he pounded the panel which he had so recently been caressing.

Chapter 31

A week after watching Tim's plane take off, Paul was tired of going out to the B and B to only receive itineraries from Tim. Paul had hoped for something about the famous passenger that would pull him away from the photo-article about a recent men's fashion house launch he was working on. Anything would be better than that he thought as he collected his camera gear for yet another tedious photo shoot. The TV soap, which he had turned on for company, ceased its background chatter with a *Breaking News* announcement. Normally he would have been impervious to such an interruption, especially when he was getting ready to head out to work. But he looked up when he heard the name Tim McNaulty mentioned.

The news reader was reporting that the light aircraft with Demetrius Popolo on board was missing. There had been no emergency communication from the plane, and it was now thought to have crashed somewhere north of Mildura. Search parties were trying to determine exactly where it had come down.

The plane had crashed? Paul shook his head in disbelief. He had no idea what the reporter was talking about, but he was confident that Tim's plane had not crashed. Tim was a good pilot. He would have done everything to save the plane. Besides, he was positive that Tim would have taken his new emergency beacon with him, and, if anything untoward had happened on the flight, after sending out a mayday call, Tim would have activated it.

And search parties trying to determine where it had come down? Paul was confused. What did the reporter mean 'trying to determine where it had come down? He knew. 99.9%, that the plane had not crashed. Besides, with Tim's beacon thingie, there was no way that the plane could have come down and not let the world know about it.

Paul was utterly perplexed. What was the plane doing in New South Wales? According to the co-ordinates that Tim had last sent, this appeared to be a major deviation. The last place that Demetrius Popolo had promoted his book had been Adelaide, and according to Tim they were no longer flying to Sydney, but heading to somewhere in Victoria.

Something was definitely out of kilter.

Paul had been reluctant at first to contradict the reports of the lost plane. But after several days of intensive ground and air searching, with no sightings reported, and nothing from Tim over the ham radio not even in response to his own attempts to reach him. Paul had started to worry. He had to do something.

Finally, he went to the police with his thoughts on the inaccurate location of the search. But, knowing that Tim thought that there was something fishy about this charter, and, because he didn't want to get Tim into trouble, he had to be careful what he said. The local station was amiable and referred him to the search headquarters. There he received the usual platitudes and assurances. But nothing concrete eventuated, and it didn't take long for the media to lose interest. The search for Demetrius Popolo and the plane had been bumped off the front pages of the newspapers—the Falklands War and the AFL games now jostled for prime space.

Paul virtually moved into the B and B so he could keep an almost constant vigil. He cleared a space at the table for his Amstrad computer and tried to work from there, but ended up spending more time staring at the transceiver, willing it to activate. But no amount of mental persuasion brought dots and dashes to his ears. The only time he returned to the house proper was to quickly attend to his daily ablutions, change his clothes and prepare a quick meal to take back to the sleep-out.

After several weeks of radio silence Paul started to miss the creature comforts of his own bed and the amenities of the house. Although he was still convinced that Tim, and the plane, were out there, he reluctantly moved back inside, only venturing out to the B and B when he thought it most likely that Tim would make contact. Living back in the house rather than in the B and B meant that Paul heard the knock on the front door. It was a pleasant distraction from the banality of trying to complete his current magazine piece. He walked through the house, unsure who to expect. He opened the door. It was the police. Paul tried to read in their faces to see if he should be feeling euphoric or look for a chair to sit down on. But it was simply a courtesy call to let him know before the media release about Demetrius Popolo's probable death in a fatal aeroplane accident, that the search for the plane had been called off.

He felt like slamming his front door closed in response. He *knew* that the plane had not crashed. Why wouldn't the police, or Search and Rescue believe him? Did they think him a nutter like those people who responded to requests for help from the public when someone went missing simply because they wanted some notoriety?

Inwardly fuming and muttering to himself he returned to what had been occupying him before their interruption—another inane photo-article. Why couldn't he get his teeth into something gritty that would bring in the bucks and help him up the ladder of success? Walt's contact had not been interested in his article about Demetrius Popolo. Damn it. Now he was stuck with this photo-article about Princess Diana look-alikes. That could wait. He walked into the kitchen and helped himself to a can of beer from the fridge.

He turned on the TV as he came back into the living room and settled himself onto the sofa. He pulled the tab on the can, but before he could raise it to his mouth there was another knock on the front door.

"What do you want now? Did you forget something?" Paul took a swig of beer from the can before thumping it on to the floor and hauling himself up off the sofa.

Two men stood in the doorway when he opened the door. They weren't as friendly as the last lot. Nor were they the police. These two men looked like they meant business, and not of the white-collar variety. Hardly even a blue-collar either. These men were more like biker thugs. All brawn and little brain. Without offering any credentials they muscled Paul aside and pushed their way through the door.

"Nice spread you have here." The taller of the two nodded his head as he looked around the room. "Be a pity to waste it. Don't you reckon?" he addressed his companion who was making his way around the room, picking up the odd ornament and kicking books and socks aside as he went.

"Yeah, would be a real shame."

If their intention is to intimidate me, then they are succeeding Paul thought to himself as he followed them, straightening the ornaments as he went. His mind flashed back to Horse from school, and he tried to conjure up what he had done back then to overcome those feelings of intimidation so they would not be evident when he opened his mouth. He stuffed his hands into his pockets and clenched and released them in time with his breathing as he counted slowly to ten and formulated what he was going to say. Not that it needed much formulation.

"Who are you? And what are you doing here?" Paul hoped he sounded fearless and assertive.

As synchronized swimmers the two men turned and faced Paul. Their faces showed that they had not come in peace and that they had the means, power, and immunity to carry out the as yet unspoken personal physical threat.

Paul mentally quailed and hoped it was not reflected in either his face or his posture. He waited, using all his courage to stare the larger man in the eyes. It was his companion who finally broke the silence.

"You need to remember. The plane, the pilot, and the passengers are all lost. If you know what is good for you, forget about it. Capeesh?" he crunched his hands together, the knuckles cracking, as he walked to the still open front door.

"That is to say," the larger man smiled malevolently as he walked past Paul and followed his partner. "Don't interfere. Got it?" He was a man of few words. But he made sure that he delivered them in such a manner that there was no mistaking the malice behind them.

Paul stood facing the open door and watched as the two men ambled down the path. He expected them to mount large rumbling deep throttling Hondas, or at least a heavy-duty jeep, but instead they crossed the road and shoehorned themselves into a purple VW beetle.

He shook his head and slammed the door shut. Damn them! Who did they think they were? Who did they think he was? More to the point, how did they know that he was looking for the plane, and Tim? Who had sent them, and how did they know where to find him? He frowned. He'd spoken to no one other than the police, and then the Search and Rescue people. Someone somewhere had blabbed. There was definitely something dodgy going on. So what did they know that he didn't, and didn't want him finding out?

He knew that Tim's plane had made a normal touchdown, somewhere, and no one, not even those thugs, would stop him trying his darndest to find it. Tim had intimated that he was expecting trouble. That's why he'd maintained sporadic contact. At least until the last transmission. No doubt Tim was now trusting that he, Paul, would sort the problem out. And by God, come hell or high water he would not let his mate down.

He looked at this watch. Good God, it was three hours since the thugs had left. He had just spent three hours sitting, fuming and mulling over his options. But what had he accomplished in that time? Three hours of doing nothing while Tim was relying on him. He had to be constructive in his thinking. He reached for the opened can of beer. It would be flat by now, still, he picked it up and gave it a sideways shake before lifting it to his mouth. Flat, but not stale. Could have been worse. He quaffed down the remaining liquid then crushed the can and dropped it to the floor beside him, then picked it back up again as he stood up. What he needed right now was Tim's last transmission. Paul looked about him as he moved into the kitchen. The louts had ransacked the papers on the table. He had no idea what they had been looking for, but they had left emptyhanded. He looked at the mess and shrugged. The mess could wait. Thank goodness the Black Book, where he had jotted down those details, was still in the B and B. He threw the spent beer can into the rubbish bin and went out to the shed.

It was as he thought, and as he had told the police, and the Search and Rescue. The plane could not have crashed in NSW, Tim was flying to some location in Victoria. He had told the Search and Rescue people that Tim had given him the revised co-ordinates, but no one had been interested. Instead, in no uncertain terms, they had suggested he leave it to the professionals. "Huh! They call themselves professionals?" Paul laughed sardonically. "All they've been doing is wasting time looking in the wrong place. And now, having found nothing, they are giving up?"

At the time Paul had only taken a cursory look at where the co-ordinates actually met, sufficient to know that it was somewhere north of Melbourne. Now he felt that he had a vested need to know exactly where that point was, because even if the authorities had given up, he hadn't.

He raced to the bookshelf, heaved out the atlas and dropped it on the table. Not bothering to sit down, he leaned over the book and flipped the pages till he reached the appropriate one. Then, with the reference co-ordinates he traced his finger across the page and tapped on a spot on the map. Tim's plane ought to be only a couple of hours north-north-east of Melbourne.

Paul pulled out a chair and sat down. 'X' didn't exactly mark the spot, but he knew where he had to go, and with fortune on his side he would locate Tim's plane and Tim would not be too far from it. At least he hoped that would be the case. He looked at his watch. It was too late to set out now. Which was probably for the best as it gave him time to find out if there was accommodation to be had in, he pulled the Atlas closer and looked once again at where the co-ordinates met. Hemlock. He scratched his eyebrow in thought. He'd been there once. Some magazine had been doing an exposé of haunted houses or some such and he had gone out to Hemlock to do a piece. Had the article ever appeared in print? He couldn't even recall if his piece had been accepted. He remembered that the house was said to have been doubly haunted. He shook his head, frustrated that he could not remember any details – of the article, the house or Hemlock.

The next morning Paul was on the phone booking a room at The Grand View Hotel— it had proved to be the only establishment in Hemlock that offered accommodation *and* meals. He then spent some time on the phone ringing around his mates, no one was willing or able to lend him a vehicle. He had then turned to his other friends and ended up sweet talking Marion into lending him her car for a couple of days, as his was being cared for at the mechanics. Getting Marion to agree had proved more difficult than he had anticipated and it had required some time-consuming midday wining and dining before he was finally sorted. It was late afternoon before he was able to lock up the house and head off.

The day was closing in by the time he joined the Maroondah Highway and started to climb over the Black Spur. Paul drove past the turn-off to Fernshaw picnic ground, the locale of a small township in the mid-1800s, and if he hadn't been in such a hurry he would have pulled in and taken a walk around to see if he could find the oak tree said to have been cultivated from acorns taken from William the Conqueror's oak trees at Windsor Castle. Instead he continued on.

He could now understand Marion's reluctance to lend him her car. He owed her bigtime, and he was looking forward to fulfilling the bargain they had struck – from being casual friends in a crowd to intimate meals and time spent with her would be heaven. Compared to his ute, Marion's car was a dream to drive. He relished in how her Datsun Bluebird hugged the corners of the road as it twisted and turned through the tree ferns and towering mountain ash. His ute would have groaned and protested with each gear change, all the while emitting a symphony of clanks, grumbles, and probably would have been belching smoke before reaching the layby at the top. And as for the descent ... he hated to think what the brakes would have been like at the bottom. He mentally thanked Marion for trusting him with her car.

By the time he emerged from the rainforest of the Spur the late afternoon sun was no longer visible behind the mountain range to his left and the land about was clothed in a dull light. Paul was glad that and it was not long after turning off the highway onto the road that would lead him to Hemlock that it started to snow. That was all he needed. He didn't mind snow, normally. From a distance.

But driving in it? No. He could do without that, thank you very much. Now he'd have to be more cautious. And it would take longer to arrive at his destination. And it would not be pleasant trudging around looking for Tim and his plane if it continued to snow all weekend.

Rounding a sharp corner in the road, Paul was startled out of his lassitude with the appearance of two very agitated figures waving frantically by the shoulder of the road. Their obvious distress, coupled with the foul weather, prompted Paul to waive his usual policy of never stopping for strangers.

Chapter 32

C hristie wondered for the hundredth time why she had ever allowed Melody to drag her away from the warm fire to 'get some fresh air'. That had been the spiel that Melody had spun, and it *had* to be in front of Christie's mother.

"Oh, what a splendid idea! It will do you both the world of good after the long drive up here, but I suggest you hurry and don't go too far, it'll be dark soon. I don't understand why you'd rather hug the fire than go out for a walk. You never wanted to be such a homebody when you were young, Christie."

Christie had looked open-mouthed at her mother. "Mum! Do you hear what you are saying? Melody is wanting to go walking *in the bush* and you are encouraging her? I've always been a homebody because you never allowed me to venture off the property when I was young! And now you are encouraging me to go for a bushwalk and to take Melody with me? Have you looked at the sky mum? There is snow in the air, and, and ..." exasperation won the day and Christie ran out of words.

"Oh Christie love, that was when you were little. You're an adult now, and you know that the maldape is not real. And besides it's not going to snow for hours yet. Off the two of you go and enjoy yourselves." She laughed as she shooed the two out of the room, then muttered under her breath. "Even if there are some in town who are saying that he has returned."

Christie followed her friend out of the warm living room and into the entrance hall where their parkas, hats, gloves and boots all waited silently sentinel.

Melody *would* want to take a walk in the bush when the weather was packing in. Christie sighed and struggled into her boots. Well, she knew *why* Melody wanted to go for a walk and, being a city girl, she could have no idea what such a walk would be like, especially now that the weather was turning foul.

Rugged up against the cold, the two walked a short way down the street and cut across the empty children's playground—wise kids, thought Christie, even without the threat of the maldape they were astute enough to stay indoors on a day like this—and they were soon entombed on the bush path that led away from the town.

The only sound as they made their way further along the path was their footfall. Melody had stopped exclaiming about how beautiful the trees were, pointing out the tree ferns and bracken, and wondering at the smell of the damp earth and humus that covered all but the clay path they were on. Maybe she was finding it too cold to talk. But when even the birds were silent, knowing that bad weather was approaching, and Christie had suggested that they return home, the suggestion had been met with fervent objection.

So the two women continued to walk further into the bush, quickly losing track of time. Suddenly they were enshrouded in a white, damp world. Clusters of snowflakes sprinkled themselves against Christie and Melody as they hunched their shoulders and pulled their parkas closer to their bodies.

"I told you that it was going to snow. Come on Melody, we do really need to get back."

"Yes, please. I never knew that snow could be so cold, and wet."

"What?" Christie could not believe it. "Have you never seen snow before?"

"Well, not in real life I haven't."

Christie shook her head. "Well, welcome to winter in Hemlock. Now come on, it's only going to get worse."

Melody looked around and held her gloved hand out. Everything was blanketed white – the path, the leaves and now her glove. "Do you know where we are? Or where we are going?"

Christie's patience with Melody and her earlier exclamations of wonder at the tree ferns punctuating the stands of tall mountain ash and her delight at the snow, had long grown thin. She was fed up with this obsession of Melody's to visit Hemlock and see the haunted house that wasn't haunted.

"Well, we *were* going to take a look at that house, but now we are going to go home. If I can find the way."

"What do you mean, *if* you can find the way? Don't you know the way?"

"Well, I've never been in *this* bush, have I? I told you. The bush was out of bounds, remember? So how am I supposed to know the way, especially now that it is snowing?"

Melody gave an embarrassed giggle and shrugged. "What if we just turned around and walked back the way we came?" Her voice tapered off after seeing the exasperation on Christie's face.

"Can *you* see the path?" Christie waved her arms about. The trees all looked the same and the snow had obliterated their footprints.

"No, not really." Melody shook her head as she looked at the ground about her feet.

"Then shut up." Christie stared about them. A few metres ahead she could see what looked like an opening between the trees. It could well be the path, and if so it would hopefully lead them to someplace that she would recognise and she could then get them back to the warmth of her mother's house. "Come on, we'll try this way."

The snow continued to fall, and the wind that had picked up started to rage as the girls trudged on, gloved hands in their pockets. They didn't say much, too lost in their own thoughts to talk.

Christie was mentally grumbling about her own idiocy in letting Melody talk her into not only travelling up to Hemlock, but actually going out for a walk when she knew all along that the weather was going to turn foul. But here she was, trudging through the snow, hoping that she was leading Melody in the right direction. Hoping that soon they would be back in the warmth and comfort of her family home. Her home. She felt a warmth spread through her as she thought of what she had been missing in the years that she had avoided coming home to Hemlock. Yes, maybe she ought to take this opportunity to rid herself of the fears and resentment from her youth and renew her bonds with her heritage.

Melody was starting to question her desire to visit the haunted house. It had seemed a good idea in the warmth and familiarity of her own surrounds back in Melbourne, but, as a city-slicker, being out here in the cold and snow was not the adventure she had anticipated.

Melody squeaked, and Christie, startled, turned to her and between mouthfuls of snow asked, "What is it?"

Melody, wondering if she was hearing things, and not wanting to alarm her friend by admitting that she was scared, shook her head. "Nothing." She looked around to see if she could isolate where the faint rustling noise she had heard was coming from.

"It's not nothing, you've gone all pale, and you're shivering."

"Don't be silly. I'm just cold," Melody snapped. She already felt an idiot, so she didn't want to alert her friend to the noise, if in fact it was a noise and not her imagination. Christie would most likely embarrass her by telling her it was just some native animal that she should have known about. "How much further to the main road? Surely it's not much further now?"

Christie shrugged, and kept walking.

Suddenly the wind ceased, and white silence fell. Soft, gentle snowflakes made no noise as they landed on the leaves and the ground. Only the scrunch of boots compressing the newly fallen snow against mother earth, interspersed with frosty harshly caught breath, broke the air.

Quietly at first, a low moan rent the air. As it increased in volume so too did the women's heart rates. Melody knew she had heard something other than the wind and snow. If she had said something to Christie back then, any embarrassment would now be vindicated. The moan was soon followed by a cry of utter frustration stopping them in their tracks. Christie and Melody looked at each other.

"Is that a wild animal?" Melody asked.

Christie shook her head, thoughts of maldapes and bogeymen filling her head as she felt her heart further racing. She knew that such things were not real, but those cries were not from any animal or bird that she could identify. She also knew that whatever it was, she did not want to meet it.

"I don't know what it is, but that's *not* a native animal. Come on." She grabbed Melody's arm and they ran. Bracken ferns clawed at their legs, it no longer mattered whether it was a path they were on. They only wanted to get away from whatever was there in the bush with them, as quickly as possible. Christie tripped and fell into a tangle of bracken, pulling Melody down with her. Melody clambered off her friend and dragged Christie to her feet. Together they blindly stumbled forward, weaving around the scraggly bushes. Breathing hard, they had no idea where they were going, or that they were floundering in circles.

"Oomph!" Christie collided with something solid, almost knocking the wind out of her as she fell unceremoniously to the ground again.

Melody, hard on her heels, barrelled into her.

After spitting snow out of their mouths and shaking off what had cascaded down on top of them from the surrounding vegetation, they looked up from their nest in the snow to discover the cause of the unwelcome, ungraceful and abrupt cessation to their flight.

Christie gasped. Melody, always the one to quickly accept the paranormal and marvel at things supposedly extra-terrestrial or of an abnormal nature, was the first to recover. She giggled, "That's amazing. Do you think it could be what your mother was talking about?"

Christie was staring at the 'thing'. Could this *really* be the maldape? Seen close up, without the moaning, it was nothing to be alarmed at. She shook her head in disbelief. The dreaded maldape was not a living creature, it was a mechanical device. She laughed. "After all the years of terror, the maldape is a fake!"

"Sh! Listen."

They both listened. Through the softly falling snow they could hear footsteps scrunching nearby; quickly followed by a deep, and threatening voice.

"Where the hell is that robot?" Rocco stopped and glared at the men accompanying him.

The women looked at each other, and quietly moved away from the now silent maldape.

"It must be around here somewhere." Rocco almost screamed. He had to admit that it was a stroke of genius that Fletcher should piggy-back on the aboriginal legend and the town's reluctance to venture near the property by engineering a monster, but Rocco was fed up with the maldape. It was meant to frighten off the locals sufficiently for them to stay away from the property, but it only seemed capable of having 'chip' problems. Still, whatever, so far the locals were keeping well away.

"I keep telling you, it's *not* a robot it's a highly developed automaton. Or, if you prefer, a reprogrammable manipulator," Lex belligerently responded. He took exception to any criticism of what the team had created. Even if he did agree with their general consensus that setting up a sound system with speakers strategically placed in the trees around the boundary perimeter would have been easier to establish and maintain. And more reliable.

"I don't give a hoot what it is. Fletcher might think tall metal monsters bearing down on you are a necessary deterrent, but they're a nuisance, perpetually malfunctioning and now this one's gone haywire and taken it into its whatever of a brain to go walkabout. Now where is it?" Rocco asked.

Ben looked apologetically across at Lex, huddled in a huff the other side of Rocco. Lex gave him a half-hearted grin before Ben shuffled off into the bush to look for the automaton.

"But you must admit it was a good idea of Fletcher's to make the local aboriginal monster legend a reality," Lex said, hoping to soothe Rocco's mood. Rocco had been like a caged, he didn't know what, mumbling and grumbling all afternoon about them being the only ones who had to be out in this weather, and all because Nikki wanted them to test out yet another of the automatons.

No one at *Braedon* had been pleased to see the weather close in and bring snow. It was bad enough being stuck out here in the bush with only each other for company, and no distractions. A couple of the team had tried going into the town; they still bore the ramifications. And now this automaton had gone AWOL. Ben sighed and took off after Lex. The sooner the automaton was found and returned to workshop the better.

"Hey Rocco! I've found him! Over here!" Ben yelled.

Footsteps passed the girls in a flurry of snowflakes disturbed from their resting places on the overhanging branches. Christie and Melody held their breaths and waited, no longer aware of the snow and dark which had suddenly become their friend, as they stared after the disappearing figures.

"Yeah, and look what else you found. Someone's been here. You know what that means," Rocco continued. "Unless we apprehend them, our work for the past month will be wasted. And I don't want to be the one to tell Fletcher. He will be more than unhappy." Rocco grumbled, kicking at the disturbed snow about the robot's feet.

"Ballistic." It was almost a chuckle, as Lex, coming to an abrupt halt beside Rocco, imagined Fletcher's reaction. The man certainly had a temper. They had all seen that at various times—when progress had not been to his standard, or after the attempted breaches of the regulations.

Rocco was sick of baby-sitting Nikki's robot. No matter how much Lex said it wasn't a robot, the bottom line was that it was, and it had malfunctioned, yet again. He scowled, then hung his head and massaged his forehead with gloved fingers. He had to think. And fast. There would definitely be hell to pay if Fletcher heard about the breach in security. And it had to be on his watch, of course. Was it an incursion to be taken seriously? Or was it just a local youth out on a dare? Either way, the intrusion had to be kept from Fletcher. But maybe he'd have a talk with Nikki, and she could then yell at the surveillance team. Get them to sharpen their patrolling. That was one problem. The other was equally taxing – having to tell Nikki that one of her babies had spat the dummy, and this time with dire consequences. It had been discovered by intruders. Intruders! What did that say about the security of the place? He shook his head and kicked at the snow.

"We need to stop them."

"Stop them? We don't know who they are. They could be part of our team." Ben looked up from where he was squatting down beside the maldape.

Rocco stared at Ben, then let his breath hiss out in exasperation. "If they were one of us, do you think they would have run off like that? Bloody hell Ben. No, they need to be stopped. Permanently." His hand instinctively massaged the bulge under his arm.

"Permanently?"

Rocco shook his head, they called themselves part of the security team? His kid sister had more gumption than either of these men. Then again, they were not employed to provide active surveillance. They were merely robotic technicians.

"Yes. Permanently."

"But why permanently?"

"Why do you think? Maybe, once whoever has been here and seen the robot shares that with the press, you'd like to be the one to explain to Fletcher how his secret weapon against intruders is no longer secret? We need to find whoever has seen *that* thing." Rocco gesticulated wildly at the maldape.

To the women's ears, the venom in Rocco's voice, set alarm bells ringing. Whoever this Rocco fellow was, he, didn't sound like the kind of man either of them would like to meet. They looked at each other. Melody opened her mouth and Christie shook her head before putting her finger to her lips. She leant close to Melody's ear, "We'll have to move. Now! Before they see us! But quietly. Follow me and watch where you put your feet, even with the snow you could still make a noise. Step into my footprints if you can, then if anyone does follow, they will think that there is only one person. We might be safer that way."

Melody stared at her friend; her eyes wide in fright. "Do you know which way to go?" she whispered and slowly stood up.

"No, but any way is better than staying here." She grabbed hold of Melody's parka and as quickly and quietly as they could, trying not to disturb the snow laden branches that reached out for them, they set off through the bush. The voices of the men followed them.

"Unless, of course ... you never know, it might have been ... what's his name?" Ben interrupted Rocco's thoughts.

"You mean that silly old coot down by the lake?" Lex chuckled.

Rocco looked at Lex. He and Ben were bent over in front of the maldape. They had some sort of hatch open, and Lex was trying to fit his gloved hand inside.

Of course. The strange man at the lake. Fletcher had engaged him to add credibility to the deterrent maldape, though no one in the security team seemed to know how or what he did to earn his keep. But surely his movements were not restricted? So maybe it was him. He'd talk to Nikki, see what she thought. Maybe she'd give him permission to seek the man out and ask him.

"Yeah, don't know why Fletcher tolerates him," Ben continued.

"You reckon Fletcher has a thing for him?" Lex mumbled into the insides of the maldape.

"He'd have to be desperate, that's all I'll say."

"Which one?" Lex did laugh this time.

"Lex!" Rocco barked. He wasn't sure that he wanted to hear any more of the conversation.

Lex and Ben both looked up at Rocco, wondering where the aggro had come from.

"It's not your job to speculate on anyone's sexual preferences, certainly not in public."

"This ain't exactly Collins Street, Rocco."

Rocco took a deep breath as he rolled his eyes. "I know that Ben, but you can never be too careful, you don't know who could be listening."

"Out here?" Lex laughed.

"Tonight especially, we already know that someone was here, and they could still be out there in the dark. Now Lex, you had better stay here and do what you have to do to get him operational again. Failing that, lug him back to the workshop. Ben can help you once he has backtracked and found out where the intruder came from. I'll follow these tracks. See if I can catch up with whoever it was. Keep all this bally-hoo from Fletcher's ears. In fact, don't say anything to anyone. For the moment we will keep the intrusion to ourselves." He raised an eyebrow in query.

"Gotcha," Lex and Ben replied in unison,

But Rocco didn't hear, he was already thrashing his way through the wattle and bracken looking for where the intruder had gone. He found the flattened snow where Christie and Melody had been hiding after they'd moved away from the maldape. From there it was easy to follow where they had gone because of the path of disturbed snow. He was confident that he would catch up to the intruder – they had made no attempt to camouflage their retreat. As he pursued the tracks, he frantically tried to formulate what he would do when he found them. Should he confront them? Play the aggressor or stalk quietly? He once more fingered the outline of the pistol that nestled in his shoulder holster, a familiar weight that offered both security and threat. His mind danced with scenarios, contemplating when and how to brandish the weapon. Would he use it as a deterrent, or as a weapon? The uncertainty of the encounter weighed heavily. He supposed that all depended on the identity of the intruder – suppose he knew the person? He had no compunction about using it against another human, he'd done that before. He supposed the more haunting question was how to dispose of the body and escape the repercussions.

It didn't take long for Rocco to recognise that his target's tracks would inevitably lead to the main road, and it quickly became obvious that he knew the layout of the land better than the target.

The road would be their inevitable meeting point. He left off following their circuitous trail and, laughing, cut through the scrub towards the road. The purr of a vehicle in the distance urged him on. He increased his pace, ripping through the blackberries, disregarding the prickles pulling at his trousers. But, on arriving at the road, all he could see was two a pair of footprints in the snow at the edge of the road and set of taillights fading into the night. Cursing at the missed opportunity, he whipped out his pistol.

Chapter 33

Christie and Melody were lucky enough to reach the road just in time to see a car approaching, headed for the township. In their state of obvious anxiety, combined with the weather, it wasn't difficult to thumb a very timely lift.

"Please, hurry! Away from here. We'll explain in a minute." Christie said as she and Melody turned to look out the rear window.

Paul checked in his rearview mirror as he carefully accelerated. What he saw caused him to hit the accelerator and the car bucked.

"Sorry about that," he said as Melody gasped, and a ping sounded on the car.

The car responded with a further burst of speed. Paul sure as hell had no idea what was going on, all he knew was that he didn't want to have to explain to Marion how bullet holes came to be in her car. He looked in the rearview mirror at the two women who had flagged him down. They were huddled together, shivering. Automatically he turned the heater up, even though he suspected it was more a reaction to their recent ordeal, as an ordeal it must have been for someone to be shooting at them. They had some explaining to do, that was for sure, but maybe now was not the best time.

"So, where to?" That was not the question he wanted most to ask. But it seemed to be the one with the most immediate relevance. Not that it mattered as he received no reply.

He looked in the mirror again. "Ladies?" He knew he had to ask, but for his own reasons he did not want any further dealings with the constabulary. He was here on his own mission to find Tim and his plane. "Should I take you to the police?"

189

Big clear blue eyes met his. He could see alarm there. Had he done the right thing in stopping and letting them get into the car? Instead of rescuing damsels in distress was he aiding the escape of the perpetrators of some crime?

"Um," Christie shook her head. There was no way that *she* wanted to front up to the Police Sation, least ways, not right now. She turned to her companion.

"What do you think? Police station, or back to my mum's place? For me, I don't really feel like having mum see us like this. She'll only pull the 'I told you so' routine. Even though she was the one encouraging us to go for a walk." In reality, now that she was out of the weather and had caught her breath, and seen who had picked them up, what she was really thinking was that she was in a car with Paul Edgar. And she wanted to spend more time with him, quiz him about his career, get an autograph even. She felt like a giddy teenager with a front row position at a pop concert. And that feeling did not gel with the thought of time spent explaining to a country cop what she and Melody were doing in the bush during a snowstorm. For all she knew they might have been trespassing. It would be better to wait and find out what was what before making waves.

Melody sat up a bit straighter and looked out the back window again before nodding her head and mumbling something.

"Um, maybe you could drop us off somewhere ... somewhere warm and where we could catch our breath before we head home?" Christie smiled at the eyes looking at her in the rearview mirror.

"Then, how about we go to the bar at the hotel where I'm booked in?"

"You're staying at The Grand View?"

Paul wondered at the incredulous tone. "Yes. You got a problem with that?"

Christie shook her head. "No, it just didn't strike me that you would be overnighting in Hemlock. I mean, it's not on anyone's usual itinerary, especially in winter unless you are a skier, and you don't look as though you are." She sat back, embarrassed at her impudence. What must he think of her? Unless he had private accommodation then where else would he be going at this time of day? There was nothing but ski fields, and their lodges, beyond Hemlock. She sucked her bottom lip into her mouth. 'Stupid. Stupid. Stupid.' She thought to herself.

"Well, it's on my itinerary for this weekend, and you're right, I'm far from being a skier. Now, how about it? Come back to mine?" Paul looked back up at the mirror and grinned.

"Sure, why not?" Melody responded. "Anything will be better than being interrogated by your mother." She dug her elbow into Christie's side. "I guess we can get something to eat there? This snow has made me hungry."

Introductions on a first name basis having been made, the three sat at a table close to the potbelly stove set in one wall of the Bistro—the bars had been too busy, and the Eatery was closed, so the Bistro it was, even if they felt underdressed. Melody held the floor with idle chit-chat while Christie found herself overcome with a mixture of awe and embarrassment, wondering if she would have the courage to let it be known that she had recognized Paul and was a huge fan of his work, pretty much since the time he had spoken to her mother all those years ago."

"So, tell me what this is all about, and why my car was shot at," Paul said, after having decided that the time for superficial pleasantries was over.

Melody, aware of but not understanding her friend's reluctance to enter the conversation, launched into relating all she knew about Hemlock's mysteries, and how she had entreated Christie to show her *Braedon,* finishing with what had happened earlier in the evening.

While Melody was relating the story, Paul was thinking over his own reasons for coming to Hemlock. The co-ordinates of Hemlock matched those that Tim had last given him as his next destination, and unless something had happened to Tim, he and the plane should, in all probability be in the vicinity.

Now the women were telling him that strange things were happening in the area.

He wondered if there could be a connection, what with the strange goings on in town, and Tim going missing after intimating that his charter may not be as simple as first appeared. With Melody's enthusiasm and Christie's knowledge of the area, the two women would be able accomplices in his investigation if he could bring them on board.

"I have no idea why they would be shooting at us."

"Oh, for goodness' sake Melody. You can't be serious. They were shooting at us because we had seen the maldape. They know that we were there. What they don't know is what else we know. It's obvious that they are hiding something, and they don't want us to find out more. That shot was a serious warning to us."

Christie, blushing, turned to Paul, "And I'm jolly glad that you were there for us. Sorry if the car was shot, though. Do you know if there is much damage?"

"Haven't looked. Hope not, seeing as how it's not my car." Paul mentally grimaced. He'd best take a look at the car. If the damage was more than negligible then he would have some explaining to do. And now that he'd met Christie he was no longer looking forward to carrying through with the expensive bargain he'd made with Marion.

"What?" Christie exclaimed, "Then we will definitely have to pay for any repairs." She wondered how much the potential repairs would eat into her savings. Not that it really mattered, this was Paul Edgar that she was talking to. Paul Edgar!

Paul gave an embarrassed laugh, "Thank you, but I've got a better idea. Do you know of any place around here where a light aircraft could land?"

He then went on to obliquely explain his motivation for being in Hemlock – to try to locate a friend who had gone missing. What he didn't divulge was that he thought he had the beginnings of what was potentially a whistle-blowing article.

Melody shrugged her shoulders. "Don't look at me then, like I said, it's my first time here."

Paul glanced at Christie. She was looking down at her hands, twisting them in her lap as she continued to marvel over actually being in Paul Edgar's company.

Melody waved her hand in front of Christie's face, "Earth to Christie? Anyone home?"

Christie looked up and blushed again. "Sorry? Did you say something?"

"I didn't, but Paul did. He wants to know if there is anywhere handy that a plane can land."

"I might have grown up here, but I haven't been back for a while, so I don't know about now. But back then there was too much bush, and not much flat ground that was clear. So, I'd say no." Christie sat back in the chair, her brow creased, thinking.

Paul exhaled. He had been so hoping that the women could help him.

"Not unless it was a floatplane," Christie mused, half to herself, thinking of the lake. It was the only flat area anywhere near Hemlock.

Paul almost leapt across the table in his eagerness, instead he stood, hands on the table, leaning across towards Christie. "Floatplane?" He had no idea why Tim would be flying a floatplane, unless there'd been a change of planes, but if there was no ground nearby flat enough for a plane to land, and he had the right co-ordinates, then maybe water and a floatplane was the answer.

"Yes. You know, an amphibious aircraft."

"I know what a floatplane is, but why? Is there water here?"

Melody clapped her hands and laughed. "I knew you weren't listening to me!"

Paul looked at her blankly. "Pardon?"

"When I was telling you about what we are doing here. I was telling you about me reading an article in a magazine about ... wait!" She sat back in her chair and looked at Christie, then at Paul, she tilted her head. "You're ...?" Melody looked back at Christie, who nodded. "Oh, my God, no way! You're *that* Paul? Paul Edgar. No wonder Christie looks like someone who's been hit across the face with a wet fish." She laughed. "Christie, the stunned mullet!"

It was Paul's turn to be embarrassed. He had no idea what was going on. He searched Christie's face before he turned to Melody. "Er, you were saying?"

Melody composed herself, knowing that she would have ample opportunity to rib her friend once they had returned to Christie's house. "Yes, like I was saying, if you had been listening to me, you would have heard me mention people drowning in a lake. In fact, Paul Edgar, you ought to know that already, seeing as how you wrote the article that first made me want to come here."

Paul gaped at her. She'd read the article. It had been published. He screwed up his face as he tried to remember if he had ever been paid.

"That was you, wasn't it? Who wrote that article?"

He puckered his brow and tried to remember if any mention had ever been made of a lake. Had he even known of the existence of a lake?

"Yes. Some magazine was doing a series on haunted houses, there'd been a murder here in Hemlock and my girlfriend at the time had said something about a house here that was said to be haunted. I came here and wrote an article and submitted it to the magazine. Never heard back from them so never knew if it was published. Don't remember much about the article, or Hemlock for that matter." He looked at Christie. "Sorry."

Christie's opinion of Paul was starting to sour. She had read the article after Melody talking about it. The piece had been as brilliant as any of the other articles of his she had read in the quarterly magazines, and he had been most effulgent about the lake. Yet here he was, sitting opposite her denying any knowledge of the expanse of water that had claimed lives, and shrouded *Braedon* in mystery and spawned the maldape—the nemesis of her childhood and that of generations of children.

"Well, there is a lake, and if the plane you are looking for is a floatplane, then it might have landed here." The venom in Christie's voice was only thinly veiled.

Melody stared at Christie, puzzled by her behaviour. Paul, while unsure what had brought on the sudden outburst, could almost feel the sharp blades with which she was mentally skewering him. He could not understand why Christie would be looking at him with such rancour, so looked to Melody.

"Would you be able to take me there?"

Melody laughed. "Hey! I only got here this morning. You'll need to ask her."

He sighed and turned to Christie.

"What do you say? Will you show me the way to the lake?"

Christie did not respond immediately. She was trying to rationalize her feelings. The elation that she had felt when she realized who their knight in shining armour was, and then to be spending time with him, almost alone. She had even thought that there may have been a connection between the two of them. Then for all her fantasizing to come crashing down with one admission. She recalled the saying that pride comes before a fall, well if that was true, the esteem she had reverently placed at Paul Edgar's feet had certainly crashed down. Would her dignity now permit her to ignore his faults? 'Come on Christie,' she thought to herself, looking at the perplexed expression on Paul's face. It wasn't his fault that the blinkers have been lifted from her eyes. After all he didn't know how his lack of recollections of Hemlock, or of having seen and spoken to her at the time had shattered her crush.

"Come on Christie," Melody implored, then looked at Paul. "Maybe if you show him the lake, he'll accompany us as we take a look at *Braedon*."

"You still want to go there? After what we've just gone through? Being shot at? You must be mad!"

"Hey, it's what we've come here for. What's a gun shot or two between friends?" Melody tried to laugh, but seeing the expression on her friend's face, what her mouth produced was more like a strangled squawk.

"Paul's car could have been damaged, we could have been injured or worse, and they are *not* our friends. You may have come here to gawp at a derelict building but I'm only here under duress," Christie said.

Christie's sulking wasn't Melody's fault, but if it hadn't been for her, then she would not be sitting here at a table with Paul Edgar and there would be no need to sulk. How could she be so naïve as to carry a torch for a man she had never actually known? She ought to have realised that meeting your childhood crush was never a good idea.

"And to see your mum, don't forget."

"And to see my mum." Christie sighed. Yes, she probably was being selfish expecting her parents to always visit her.

Paul watched the interchange between the two women. He liked them, and would like to get to know Christie better. There was something about her that intrigued him, and there was a niggle that he had crossed paths with her before today. A rescue and an hour or so in the hotel hardly afforded him time to even scratch the surface of getting to know her. And the earlier snap change in attitude intrigued him. The beginnings of a smile played on his lips as an idea came to his mind.

"If you," he addressed Christie, "can point me in the right direction to the lake, maybe I could then escort Melody to wherever it is that she wants to see."

"Oh yes please." Melody beamed.

"Very well. Tomorrow, I'll show you to the lake, then you and Melody can go gadding about in the bush. But I don't want any part of that, thank you very much. My mother was right all those years ago. It's best to stay out of the bush."

"Oh Christie, you saw for yourself that the maldape is not real. Don't be such a wuss, with Paul here no harm will come to us."

Neither Paul nor Christie was as confident as Melody. They each had their own reservations. Christie's was rooted in a lifetime of brainwashing compounded by the earlier encounter. Paul's apprehension was fuelled not only by the shooting incident but also by the run-in with the thugs that warned him off looking for Tim and the plane. He still couldn't work out who would have had alerted them to his interest in the plane, and why anyone would not want the plane and people found? But after that encounter he felt he knew the type of people that he, and most likely Melody, could well be up against.

Chapter 34

Determined to reclaim the property, but wary of his past, Bruce Gentle had reinvented himself and he returned to Hemlock as Bradley Gentian. After all, his mother had been a Gentian. Not able to face his childhood home, more or less camped in the abandoned house that was *Braedon*. With possession being nine-tenths of the law, he hoped that he could acquire the property legitimately. That had been a laugh if ever there was one. And that is what the real estate agent had done. Laughed. The real estate agent had not told him the asking price, or even if there was one. All he had done was laugh in his face then propel him out the door, telling him not to bother calling again.

When it had become evident that the property had been sold to That Man that Miss Goody-Goody had brought out to the place, Bradley had reluctantly moved his belongings over to what had been, back in the day when the place had really been something to behold, the gardener's cottage over by the boathouse. The cottage had been in a far worse state than he had imagined, but there was no way that he was going to remove himself beyond there. Anyway, it was far enough away from the house that That Man probably wasn't even aware of its existence, and, with luck, he'd still be able to access the veggie garden for his own needs. Not that there would be much growing now with winter approaching.

He had kept tabs on the recent the comings and goings, watching perplexed as the intermittent convoy of crates and boxes were delivered. He had no idea what they contained, but there seemed to be quite a number of deliveries being made, and people

199

arriving. That all culminated in the arrival of a busload of people. After that That Man and his lot kept to themselves. They didn't even go into town. And there appeared to be an overabundance of security. It was all very intriguing, and he had taken to clandestinely creeping closer to the house and the outbuildings to see if he could fathom what their business was. Whenever he approached the house, he felt the compulsion to leave his mark, to stake his claim as it were. It gave him a sense of power or one-upmanship. That Man might have bought the place, but the house still belonged to the Gentian family.

Then there was the day that he had been caught marking his territory. He had tried to outrun the two men, but they were quicker and soon caught up with him. The melee that followed could have been brutal. He hadn't liked the prospect of taking on two younger men, so had been glad when the woman intervened. There had been something familiar about her, and another man who had appeared, but he'd been too het up with being caught to concentrate on dredging his memory. The arrival of That Man had not only thwarted the fracas but had provided a coup rather than a disaster. That Man had escorted him over what he had obviously assumed to be the property boundary, and an agreement had been reached. In exchange for providing That Man with security, That Man would hand over the property to him, once his business there was completed. Security? Bradley laughed. All he needed to do was return to his flashing to keep the locals away from *Braedon,* not that That Man needed to know his methods. All he need know was that the townspeople steered clear of him and wherever he frequented. It was a definite win-win as far as Bradley could see. Legitimising the maldape in return for *his* property.

He had been looking forward to finally bringing back ownership to the family. He thought the only thing that could hinder the outcome would be if the flicker of recognition he thought he had seen from the woman who had intervened in the punch-up, and the other man who had turned up, resulted in either of them saying anything detrimental to That Man. But to date they apparently had not said anything, so maybe the flick had just been his paranoia.

Back when all the arrangements had been made between he and That Man, he had not anticipated that he would have extra duties placed upon him. That Man's newest instructions had been both crystal clear and brutal. The pilot was to be stripped of his clothes and trussed up, and he himself was not to let him out of his sight. He'd smiled to himself at the stupidity of that directive. How he was to provide his extra security, and keep tabs on the pilot, at the same time? It was impossible for him to be in two places at once. Mind you, That Man didn't know what he had been doing to keep the locals at bay, and his recent flashings seemed to have reinstated the desired effect. He had actually lost interest, and no longer enjoyed the exposure. The challenge and thrill had gone once it had become an expected routine, especially when this new generation of targets seemed to find his performance all rather blasé. It was no longer the ego booster it had been in the past, so he didn't mind forgoing that part of the bargain.

Bradely glared across at Tim as he paced from one end of the room to the other. He had been more than happy to oblige That Man and flash his way into gaining *Braedon* but four weeks? He had had enough.

Other than the quick recces of the traps which he'd set about the surrounding bush, and forages for firewood, he had not ventured out of the place – just as That Man had instructed. If it hadn't been for the weekly delivery of food that would mysteriously appear at the edge of the clearing, the two of them would have gone hungry.

What he wanted to know was what was going on? If the pilot-man was so tied up, then why did he have to keep such a vigilant eye on him? Nothing made sense.

And as for the pilot! Bradley snorted. Things might have been different, or even more endurable, if his prisoner was better company. Or any company for that matter. All he did was lie there, trussed up as That Man had instructed. Bradley didn't know who he hated the more, That Man in *his* house, or this man cluttering up his space here. Not that he was actually 'cluttering', and it wasn't really his 'space'. The pilot had been foisted on him and he was having to eke out an existence in this place. It was all That Man's fault.

He looked over at the bed where the pilot lay dozing and shook his head. No, today was going to be different. The pilot was not going anywhere, and That Man was not going to come visiting. He never had, so why would he now? He rubbed his hand up and down over his crotch. Yes, he was going into town. It didn't matter that it was daylight. He *needed* to go to town. He needed Ruby Street. He smiled sardonically as he mentally relished in his disobedience. Nothing, and no one was going to stop him.

Bradley grabbed his old army surplus coat from a pile of clothes at the foot of his bed and struggled into it, before pulling leather motorcycle gauntlet gloves out of the deep pockets. He ambled over to the door, pulled it open and looked out, nose in the air as though he was a kangaroo sniffing for trouble, before turning back for another look at the pilot. He laughed and clutched his crotch. Poor bloody sod, if he hadn't been so prissy and scared of 'catching something', they could have had a good time. Just because he himself was unkempt, it didn't stand to reason that he did not know how to keep clean. Blame That Man for the current lack of hygiene. If it wasn't for him, he'd be able to luxuriate in a weekly bath. It was too cold to go out and bathe in the lake, and there was no way in hell that he was going to get buff naked and wash himself in the old tin tub by the fire. Exposing the delicate part of his anatomy to young girls and women was one thing, but his *whole* body to another male? He hadn't done that since the changing sheds at school after sport, and he wasn't going to start again now just for the sake of hygiene. Plus, there was no way he was going to bed-bathe the pilot. His personal hygiene would have to wait on the discretion of That Man. But as for himself, he was going to indulge in a deep bath in town. He smiled at the promise and gave his crotch an upward jerk, then laughed before jumping down to the ground and walking around to the chimney to make his ritual mark – a spiralling pattern, resembling a target on the granite brickwork.

He watched as the stream of urine sketched out a dark circle against the granite stones. He tried to remember when and why the habit had become a tradition when he was in the familiar surrounds of Hemlock. No doubt it was an ingrained reaction to the bitter tales of usurped ownership that he had grown up with and which flamed his obsession to occupy and own *Braedon*.

Once the routine was completed, he zipped up his trousers and strode purposefully away from the cottage, his feet squelching through the melting snow along the path that would take him into Hemlock. He smiled at the prospect of what awaited him there.

Chapter 35

The snow had settled when Christie and Melody ventured out the next morning, and there was a pale sun valiantly trying to infiltrate the layer of fog that was now clinging to the treetops. Christie looked down at her booted feet as they plodded along the slushy path that wove beneath the canopy, and quietly fumed. She did not like winter. Did not like the snow. Did not want to be out, this early, trudging through the melting snow, even if it was in the company of Paul Edgar. She didn't even know if she still had a crush on the man. Not now that she had met him. Egotist that he was.

The idea had been that she would show him the way to the lake, but no, he had to take the lead. For all the good she was doing she could still be snuggled up in her warm bed or having a leisurely breakfast with her mother. Why had she allowed Melody to goad her into coming home, and then expect her to venture outside this early?

"Oomph!" She had not seen Melody and Paul, walking in front of her, stop, and she barrelled into Melody who in turn collided with Paul. They both turned around.

"Watch it will you. I nearly tumbled," Melody giggled, righting herself.

Paul glared at both of them. "Shush up both of you." He turned and waved his arm in the direction slightly to their right.

The women looked at him in alarm, then followed his gesticulating arm. Through the thinning bush was a ramshackle building. It was hard to define it as a house, but it was too big and rambling to be called a hut or even a shack. The building appeared to be an agglomeration of bits haphazardly patched together, all

205

perched on a variety of stumps and concrete blocks. An undulating veranda under a roller-coaster tin roof partially held up by a couple of mismatched uprights fetched up along the front, no steps to be seen. The bleached timber walls were held together with a number of strategically placed *Pandoea* climbing over it and up onto the rusting corrugated iron roof. A granite chimney. Miss-matched windows, either side of an ill-fitting door that looked to have come from a church hall, stared blankly back at them. It looked unoccupied, except for the immediate surrounds—the ground was not only bare of vegetation but had recently been cleared of snow.

"Did you know this was here?" Paul asked, still keeping his voice low. He shepherded the women back along the path, simultaneously scrutinizing the surroundings. Despite the winter season, which would typically bring signs of habitation such as a warm fire and smoke rising from chimneys, the place remained eerily quiet. Even the currawongs, which the trio had observed settling in the trees earlier, were now notably silent.

Melody and Christie both shook their heads as they backed up along the path.

He looked directly at Christie, "I thought you lived in Hemlock?" Then he continued his surveillance of their surroundings.

"Yeah, she did, as a child."

Christie glared at her friend, then looked at Paul and nodded, then felt foolish as his head was turned away and he couldn't see her. "But I've never been *here*. No one ever came *here*, or into the bush."

"No one?"

"Well, none of my friends did. We kids all grew up with stories of the maldape catching us if we went into the bush by the lake. Guess, after the murder, our parents were just being overprotective. Some of the boys would dare each other, but not many followed through. We were all too scared.

Paul nodded. Back in his hotel room last night he had refreshed his memory on the article he had written and could understand how the townspeople back in the day would have feared for their children.

"What about the lake, then? You'd have been to the lake, wouldn't you? All that water on a hot summer's day?"

Again, Christie shook her head. "Not this part. The town side of the lake was all private property, and we would have had to walk through the bush to get to the lake. Sometimes families would drive around to the other side, to have a picnic or go fishing. My mum never did. I think I may have gone one or two times with friends, if my mum would let me. The water was too cold to go swimming, so there really wasn't any incentive."

Satisfied that he could detect no activity about the place he turned once more to face the women. "Well then, what do you reckon? Shall we go and take a look?"

"Oh yes. I'd love to take a closer look. I've never been this close to a haunted house before," Melody was almost jumping in her excitement.

Christie stared at her scornfully. "When have you ever been anywhere near a haunted anything?"

"Shush!" Paul had instinctively assumed a squatting position and waved at the women to do likewise. They looked at each other, shrugged and dropped down beside Paul.

"What?" Christie whispered.

"I thought I saw a movement across one of the windows."

"Where? Which one? Let me see." Melody leant closer, then quickly sat back on her heels. "Oof!"

The three watched silently as the door opened. A muffled, one-sided conversation drifted towards them.

"Quick! Move!" Paul grabbed an elbow of each of the women and hoisted them onto their feet. Then, as quietly as he could, one on each side of him, he quickly towed them along the path until the undergrowth thickened and he saw an opening where they could safely leave the path and hopefully hide. He looked back towards the building and was pleased to still see it, albeit obscured by foliage. They'd be able to observe what was happening but still reduce the chances of whoever was inside observing them in their concealment.

The three crouched down and watched.

A man emerged from the door. He was as unkept as the building. He wore a rumpled and filthy calf-length coat over an equally dirty sweater, and baggy trousers, which he now hitched up with gloved hands. He turned to look back into the building, his long, greying, greasy hair now visible, it matched his matted beard. He clutched his crotch, laughed, and gave it an upward jerk, before jumping down to the ground.

All three in the undergrowth gasped. Paul seethed to think that a man could be so uncouth; Melody felt sympathy for the apparent recipient inside, while Christie's gasp was one of recognition.

Despite the passage of years there was something about the man that she felt was familiar. Her mind went back to a man who would wander into town, a smirk on his face and a bulge in the front of his pants which puzzled her until she was older. Older girls would drop their eyes and hurriedly cross the road as he approached. He would saunter down the street that her mother told her to never go down and reappear sometime later beaming. She shuddered as memories flooded back, tales of the maldape that had terrorized her to such an extent that, like so many of her peers, she had fled Hemlock as soon as she could. Her mouth suddenly felt dry, and a sensation of warmth started to slowly seep through her and spread, but before the nausea took hold something else caught her attention. And she wished it hadn't.

The man was relieving himself against the chimney, making a swirling pattern, and he was smiling. The same smile that he would have when he had come into town back then. So, this was where he lived? Did anyone know? Surely not, because if they had, why was he still here?

Christie covered her mouth with one hand and clasped her other across her stomach. She could not be sick. Not here. Not with company. She took a deep breath and willed her stomach to stay put.

For the sake of everyone, her stomach obeyed. Ignoring the scrunching of bracken fronds she sank back on her heels, dropped her head between her knees and continued to breathe deeply. She was still breathing deeply when she felt a hand on her back and Paul whisper in her ear to be quiet or hold her breath.

Crouching as small as they could, with their heads held close to their knees, they all held their breath, hoping that they would not be spotted, as footsteps could be heard squelching along the path.

Bradley, pleased with himself and anxious to be on his way, passed by their hiding place without hesitation.

"Well, so much for the place being haunted, or empty. What do we do now?" Melody asked as she stood up and with hands on her hips, arched her back, then flexed her legs.

"Anything is better than further cramping my legs," Christie muttered as she too stood up and stretched.

Paul was busy looking at the building, a frown creasing his forehead. He rubbed his hand back and forth over his head, the knitted beanie meeting his eyebrows in time with the movement. "I'd like to know how long that oaf will be gone. I want to see what, or who, is inside. With that carry on I'm betting it's a woman. And if so, then I want to see if she is all right as I doubt after that display she would be."

"Oh, he'll be a while yet," Christie muttered angrily.

Paul looked at her. "Why do you say that? Do you know him?"

"No. Not personally. But I'm certain that I have seen him before. And if he is who I think he is, then I'm also pretty sure I know where he's off to."

The other two looked at her, waiting for her to continue. They both knew that there was more, Melody was sure that it was something gossipy or juicy, while Paul, having witnessed Christie's reaction to the appearance of the man and his activities, wondered why Christie's casual admission of knowledge was tainted with bitterness. He tilted his head and raised his eyebrows in query. Melody on the other hand, knowing Christie as she did, simply shook her head. There would be nothing more coming from Christie unless she chose to elaborate.

"He's off to finish what he didn't complete in there." She nodded her head in the direction of the building. "Or to repeat it elsewhere, where it will no doubt cost him."

"There's a brothel in Hemlock?" Paul, thinking of the size of the town, sounded shocked.

Melody looked at him in surprise. "Doesn't every town have one?" Then looked at her friend. "There's a brothel in Hemlock?" Melody repeated Paul's question and laughed. "Of course there would be. Skiers. Snow-bunny bonanza! What?" Melody looked at Christie who had choked back a laugh.

"I think you have the wrong terminology there. If there are snow-bunnies galore, then there would be no need for a brothel."

"Snow-bunnies, brothels, either way that, that creature is gone and I'm going in. You two better stay out here, and hidden, and cover for me. Whistle or something if he, or anyone else for that matter, comes near. I don't want to be caught ..." Paul stopped himself before saying 'with my pants down' and smiled as he thought it would have been a most inappropriate phrase to use in the present circumstances.

Chapter 36

Fletcher sat at the desk in his office, elbows on the papers strewn across its surface, head cupped in his hands and wondered what else could go wrong. He thought that he had covered all tangible glitches, but he had forgotten to factor in Murphy's Law and the unpredictability of human nature. God, he hated this job, and Maxwell. What he needed was the sage advice of his mother, plus her calming nature. For an ever so brief and fleeting moment he contemplated breaking his own rule and heading into town to phone her. Why in damnation had he not had the phone connected when he took possession of the property? The expense of the connection for such a short period of time was immaterial. Then he remembered the rationale behind the decision. He had not foreseen any emergency warranting a phone that could not be dealt with in situ. Of paramount importance had been the need for secrecy. It was bad enough that the people of Hemlock were aware of the sale and occupation of the property, he could not afford, even with an unlisted number, the risk of curious callers. And it was equally essential that there was no chance of communication with the outside world from any of the teams at *Braedon*. He could not afford for anyone to have the opportunity to talk about what had taken place, or what they might think had occurred. His future depended on total secrecy and nobody squealing, even after the operation had ended and everyone had left Hemlock, and *Braedon* had returned to its rightful owner.

He sighed and rubbed his hands over his face, up over his forehead and through his hair. His mother was not here, and he was a grown man. He had faced dilemmas in the past and not needed her input, so why was this time different? He slapped his hands down on the edge of the desk and pushed his chair back. Damn it! It was having to deal with all that went along with the administration. Daily checking with the individual team leaders that everything was as it ought to be. Ensuring that everyone was on task and not exhibiting any indications of 'cabin fever'. He was not used to being in command of all aspects of a project and the logistics that went along with that.

He stood up and walked over to the window. From there, beyond the tangle of bracken, wattle, tea trees and blackberries that fought to invade the area around the outbuildings, was a stand of mountain ash. Between the trees he could catch glimpses of the lake, and he was quickly reminded of another wasp in the honey. The plane and the pilot! That made the third chink in what he had prided himself as being his flawless planning.

Damn it! He thumped his fists against the windowsill, then lent his head against the cold pane. Nothing seemed to be unfolding as he had intended.

First there was when Dave and Bruno failed to detect that breach in security, leaving Lex and Ben to deal with the intruder.

Mind you, that had turned out to be to his advantage. He smiled as he recalled that particular coup.

He had walked the intruder back off the property to where he lived quite some distance from *Braedon*. And what a rundown place that proved to be. How anyone could willingly live in such conditions was beyond comprehension. Initially the man had been silent and taciturn. However, once the conversation changed from accusatory 'trespass' and 'violence' to expressing an interest in the property and its surrounds, the man had become remarkably eloquent. He had almost taken delight in sharing the somewhat grisly history of the property in great detail. How he had been diddled out of what had rightfully been his. The man had also said that he thought the notion of having a security team was ludicrous, as no one dared come near the place while he was known to be in the area. And he had laughed before going on to explain that 'for some reason' the locals liked to tell their kids that he was The Maldape – the local which kept the curious kids away, and the adults all avoided him, thinking him an unpleasant pariah, and best to be avoided.

That was when Fletcher had struck upon the idea of employing the man, and to date it had proved to be a most fortuitous investment, seeing as how his own versions of the maldape, despite all of Nikki and Lex's best efforts, were not proving to be as efficient as hoped.

Fletcher pushed himself away from the window, but remained there, surveying what he could see of the property. To have the recluse out on patrol and spreading fear in the town had been a good move. After all, handing over the deed for *Braedon* seemed small compensation when it was, according to the man, rightfully his in the first place.

He turned his back to the window and stared across the room. He ought to be doing something, only he could not get motivated as thoughts rotated though his mind like a carousel, the chinks hiccupping like the misplaced or disabled horses on the ride.

He had not become aware of the second chink until after the altercation between his security team and the recluse had been witnessed by Alex and Nikki. Since then, he had often seen the two of them, heads close, talking. And he had heard enough of their conversations to pick up on the fact that they both had connections with Hemlock. He had beaten himself up over that misdemeanour until he rationalized that he could not be held responsible for the error. In his efforts to keep the whole project clandestine, as had been required, he had not been at liberty to share information about the locale with his contacts when he was recruiting. When he had approached his various contacts not even he had known where they were going to be holed up.

But the pilot. That third chink. That was something that he could, and should have been able to circumvent, if Richard Ibraham had bothered to let him vet the candidates. Though, in all fairness, he had given Richard freedom on that score. What quirk of fate had brought that particular pilot into his sphere? It was funny that he could not remember the name of the little runt, but the face. Oh yes, the face, he well remembered the face and how he delighted in making the kid's life misery at every opportunity. Oh yes, he remembered the pilot. He had stood out from the beginning, so different to the other boys that he was all but begging to be taunted to the limit.

He recalled the moment of mutual recognition as the floatplane came to a gentle halt against the jetty. The smile faded from the face of the pilot, to be replaced with pure hatred in the set of his jaw and glowing in his eyes.

There was no denying that the pilot was not the same podgy kid that he had taken such glee in persecuting when they had both been at school. He had been in his last year when the kid, a junior, had arrived after the year had started. Initially the kid had been easy pickings and Fletcher had been able to take his own feelings of inferiority out on the new kid. That was until another new kid had championed for the pipsqueak. Fletcher screwed up his face, he couldn't remember his name either, but then, it was quite a number of years ago. He couldn't be expected to remember all the younger boys he tormented. Yes, the pilot was a potential squealer. He could only hope that he had not already done so. He would have to trust Harris and Ibraham on that one.

Fletcher clenched his fists, pushed himself away from the window and walked across the room to sit at his desk. The pilot may well have squealed, but if he had, he couldn't do any more damage now that he had been handed over to the hermit. It had been a stroke of luck that the man had been there when the plane had landed. He had happily handed the pilot over to him with explicit instructions, a nod and a wink, to look after him.

No, he only had himself to blame if anyone squealed. Maybe *that* was why Maxwell had given him this project. To test him. See if he still 'had it'. He wasn't too sure what 'it' was that he was meant to have, and he was beginning to doubt if he was even up to the job. Too late now.

Damn it! Maxwell had removed himself from the equation when he had given him the assignment. Telling him he was on his own. Well damn it, it was too bad, there was no denying it he needed his mother's words of wisdom. They had always served him well. And he decided that he needed them today. He looked at his watch, it was not yet midmorning. Everyone would be preoccupied with their own morning tasks. Catering would be preparing the midday meal for everyone, and what was left of the medical team would be doing whatever they needed to help Popolo recuperate and rehabilitate. He'd been informed just yesterday that progress was ahead of schedule and that soon 'the patient' would be ready to resume life 'outside'.

That thought alone made Fletcher perk up and feel justified in his truant decision. He would break his own rules and head into town. Once there he could phone his mother and then report the progress to Maxwell. With his vested interest in the operation, he might like to have an update – a bit of kudos coming his way might make him feel better. After that he would seek out some human company. Maybe drop into the real estate agent's and see if the woman that sold him *Braedon* was free to have a late morning tea with him at the Grand View. At this time of the day there ought not be too many people about. Failing that he could probably have some banter with the barman. Thinking about it, that would probably be the better idea – to needle someone would go some way towards salving to his injured ego.

Fletcher grabbed his jacket and gloves and left the office, slamming the door behind him, and stormed out of the house. He had to get away. He no longer cared if the whole place went to pot without him there. He would only be gone a short time. An hour at the most. Just a quick walk into town, a couple of phone calls and a social interlude then a brisk walk back. He dared anyone to comment on his absence. They all had each other to sound off to. He had no one. He was alone. He had no one to share the buck with. It stopped with him, and his shoulders no longer felt that they could bear that mantle of management without a kind word of support from his mother.

Chapter 37

Christie and Melody found a mountain ash just off the track and near the edge of the clearing that they could lean against while they waited. They watched Paul walk cautiously towards the building, keeping to the undergrowth as much as he could.

As he came to the edge of the clearing Paul stopped and turned slightly to his left. He raised a hand to shade his eyes and squinted.

"What's he doing?" Melody asked, straightening up.

"Dunno." Christie stared in the direction that Paul was looking. "Oh, I see. Look over there." She pointed. "That's another building, and Paul's going towards it."

"Shall we follow him?" Melody asked excitedly.

"What?"

"Let's follow Paul. We know what this building is, people are living here. I want to see what that one is."

Christie shook her head, once more exasperated with her friend. It was bad enough to be out here hanging around in the cold without courting more danger by following Paul when who knew what the other building was, or when the man who they had just watched leave, would be returning. Maybe he was not going to Ruby St, but just out for a short walk for wood, or something. He might not be away as long as she thought.

"No. we'd best stay here, Paul knows where we are, and he has asked us to be lookouts for him. That, that man is going to come back this way. If we follow Paul, then we might miss him if he returns."

Paul had indeed seen a building, even more dilapidated than the one from which the man had emerged. He stood silently for a couple of minutes, listening and watching. When he thought it was certain that there was no one about, he quickly scuttled in a half crouch around the edge of the clearing till he came to a narrow beach on the shore of the lake. He stepped back into the scraggly wattle trees and bracken and scanned the surrounds. To his left, further along, was another beach. This one was wider, and it was home to a jetty that looked, from where he stood, to have seen better days. To his right there was the remains of a building, no doubt it had once been a boathouse. Keeping to the tangle of scrub and undergrowth that fronted the sandy beach, he moved warily towards it.

As he got closer, he could see that along with the creepers encroaching on the walls and roof, it had been securely camouflaged with military-style webbing. He stopped, and faded back into the trees. Why was there a need, out here pretty much away from everywhere and everything, for hiding a dilapidated boathouse, if that was what the webbing was for? It certainly wasn't for weatherproofing. He pushed his beanie back and scratched his head.

He looked back towards the house and remembered his intent to rescue whoever was inside. But what was now in front of him was more tantalizing, and he felt sure that it would not take long to investigate. He was already here, after all, and all he needed to do was raise a corner of the webbing and peek inside for his curiosity to be satiated. Then he could go back to the 'rescue mission'.

Confident that the two women he had left back by the track would watch his back and alert him to any need to hide, he left the comfort of the trees and stealthily approached the boathouse.

He took a deep breath and reached for the webbing, half expecting to be accosted by some unseen watchman. But his advances went unimpeded. He looked back to where he could just make out Christie and Melody. They indicated that he should drop down to the ground. He frowned. Their gesticulations were not frenzied so they were not warning him of imminent danger, so what were they wanting him to do? Or rather, why were they wanting him to lower himself? He watched as Christie crouched down and mimicked opening the bottom edge, the corner, of the covering, while Melody aped an attack at chest height. That made sense. If there was some vigilante inside, then of course they would be prepared to attack an intruder entering in an upright position. He squatted down, took another deep breath and lifted the corner of the webbing.

The only thing that greeted him was silence. Light slatted in through the gaps in the timber wall and dappled through the webbing. Even though it was not entirely dark, it took his eyes a few moments to adjust to the interior; and then he saw what was hidden. A floatplane. It looked surprisingly familiar, but he couldn't be sure. Slowly he rose to his feet and stepped into the space, quietly walking toward the plane. As he got closer, he realized why the plane was familiar. It was Tim's plane. But with floats?

So, he had been right. Involuntarily a smug smile found a home on his face. The plane and passengers had not crashed. And the search parties had been looking in the wrong place.

But if Tim's plane was here, where was he? He wondered whether an inspection of the interior would hold any answers and stepped towards the door. But what would he be looking for? He could see that there was no body slumped in any of the seats, and it made no sense for whoever it was that had employed Tim to do away with him, so where was he? And why had Tim not contacted him? Or set off his beacon. That would have been the logical thing to do.

Paul turned and looked in the general direction of the building he had first set out to investigate. Was that where Tim was? But if he was, the scene that had been played out earlier with the stranger did not make sense. He shook his head. He needed to get out into the fresh air, maybe then his mind would function better.

Paul looked at the plane, ran his hand along the side of it and made his way outside. He looked across to see if the women were still in place. They were. He gave them a couple of 'thumbs-up' and pointed towards the house. They reciprocated.

Feeling more confident, and having confirmed with the women that the coast was clear, he quickly made his way to the house. Having earlier watched the man stride along the veranda he guessed that the boards were stable and so he jumped up. He had expected his arrival to produce a response from whoever was inside, but he was disappointed. All was quiet. Almost too quiet, and he paused, trying not to conjure unsavoury visons of what he might find inside.

He carefully stepped to the door and hesitated before reaching for the handle. He looked back to where Christie and Melody were waiting. They were no longer resting against the tree trunk but were almost leaning towards him in anticipation. He smiled, surprisingly comforted by their eager presence.

He closed his eyes, expecting that it would be dark inside once he opened the door, and he wanted to his eyes to adjust quickly. He then took a deep breath, and almost laughed, thinking of the work-out that he'd been giving his lungs with all the deep breathing to steady his nerves. The thought that he had nerves that needed steadying was enough to bring him up short. What was he afraid of? For all he knew the place was empty. After all, the strange man was just that, strange. His crotch antics could well have been part of a ritual, as no doubt, was the manner of his relieving himself. Just because Christie thought that the man was governed by his dick, they had all assumed that he had left someone, presumably a female, inside.

'Come on, man-up.' Paul told himself, conscious of both his heart racing and the passage of time. Who knew when the strange man might return, despite Christie's oblique timeframe. and he turned the handle and opened the door. The odour of living assailed Paul, and he was taken back to when he would be dragged along with his parents as they visited the elderly and destitute in binges of charitable noblesse oblige—boiled cabbage mingled with stale beer fighting for precedence over sweat and other bodily functions, not always human. stepping into this place was no different.

When Paul's eyes had acclimatized, he could see that he was in a large open room that constituted the interior of the building. It was furnished with what looked like the pickings from several years of the annual council kerbside dumpings. Not one piece of furniture matched another, and all manner of decades were represented. An old sofa and a couple of armchairs; a wooden table and three chairs. On one dresser was a small, galvanized tub with a selection of crockery haphazardly stacked beside it, happily inviting the local colony of blowflies, who were oblivious to it being the middle of winter, to come and feast. At one end of the room a sea truck serving as a wardrobe rested beside a rumpled and unmade wood-framed double bed that was sagging in the middle. On the opposite side of the room was another bed, with someone occupying it.

"Well, you bloody well took your time."

"Tim?"

"Yeah. What took you so long?"

"Why didn't you let me know you were here?"

"Oh, you know how it is when I get tied up on a project."

Yes, Paul knew all about how insular and absent-minded Tim became when he was concentrating on one of his projects. "Yeah. But four bloody weeks? I was almost camped out at the B&B waiting to hear from you. I knew that the plane hadn't crashed. But ... why didn't you use your new-fangled emergency beacon thingy? Then the authorities would not have wasted their resources looking for your plane in outback New South Wales while I was trying, unsuccessfully you might have noticed, to tell them where they needed to look. It was almost as though they did not want to know. Or does this just prove that your beacon thingy doesn't work?"

They had been looking in New South Wales for the plane? He had managed to successfully evade detection. That meant that the plan orchestrated by Ibraham, or had it been Harris, had worked. Not that he knew what it was all about, but their ruse had worked.

Tim chose to ignore the question about the beacon for the time being, and feigned annoyance. "Well, I could say the same for you. You've had four weeks to find me. If you were camped out at the B&B, who'd you have with you? Must have been some beauty for you to forget about me, huh?"

Paul strode over to where Tim lay unmoving under a haphazard pile of old grey army blankets then, horrified, stopped short when he saw what could only be tethers running out from under the blankets to the bedframe.

"You were being serious when you said you've been tied up?"

Tim chuckled and raised his hands, rope wound tightly around his wrists anchoring him to the bedframe, and shook his legs as best he could. They too were anchored by his ankles to the bedframe. "I kid you not. Been like this since pretty much landing the Cessna on the water. Boy that was a treat and a half. Never done that before. But it was fun. Until I saw who was waiting to receive us. Here, can you, sort of, kinda, well, release me, do you think?"

"So, what happened? And why are you here, like this?" Paul asked as he set to work freeing his friend, wishing that the restraints were of the hospital manacle variety with buckles rather than these of rope and knots that he was struggling to untie "If you couldn't send me a message to the B and B why didn't you activate your beacon thingy so that I'd know where to look for you? Co-ordinates are one thing, but then there was nothing more. I had to assume that this is where you were, but why didn't you send anything further? You had me haring around like a mad thing getting nowhere, blocked every time I tried to tell the authorities where to look for you, and even having heavies harassing me. You could have *told* me."

Tim looked sheepish. "Er, yes, my ELT. I didn't use it because, well, as you can see, it isn't on me."

"But what about before you got like this?"

"It wasn't on me then, either."

"It wasn't on you? I thought the whole purpose of having a personal, portable emergency beacon was that you would have it on your person?"

Tim looked embarrassed. He knew why he didn't have it on his person, but he didn't want to admit that to his friend. With the change of flight plans back in Adelaide thoughts of his beacon had been pushed out of his mind. And even though he had remembered it when *his* plane had undergone its transformation, he'd been fuming too much to think about retrieving his ELT till it was too late.

"Well, how was I to know that I'd need it? Not on land, with people around me. Didn't know that I would be needing it, did I?"

"So, what happened?"

I left my bag on the plane."

"You what?" Paul undid the last knots and dusting off his hands reached out to Tim's hands.

Slowly and carefully, Tim swung his legs over the side of the bed and sat up, rubbing his wrists, and waiting for his head to stop spinning.

"Not sure. One moment I was checking over the plane after landing and looking forward to a long hot shower and a good night's sleep; the next thing I'm here like you found me."

"What? Did you black out? But why tether you here?"

Tim shrugged his shoulders. "You remember a while back, we were talking about Horse, Gee-Gee, and wondering what had happened to him?"

"Yeah, we went through all those old school books and papers and what have you that you had squirrelled away for safekeeping."

"Well, I can tell you that he hasn't changed over the years. He's still a bully."

"How'd you know that?"

"He's why I'm here like this."

"You what?"

"Yeah. Like I said earlier. Landing the Cessna on water was, well, let's say exhilarating." Tim wasn't about to own up, even to his best mate, how shit-scared he had been. "Then when I came to a stop there was this man waiting to greet the goons that had engaged me for ferrying your friend Popolo around and orchestrated the transformation of the plane, and the subterfuge of the crash. Well, the pose of the greeter looked familiar."

"Pose?" Paul was unsure what Tim meant.

"Yeah, his stance – legs akimbo, hands on hips. Didn't take that long for the memories of torment at the hands of Gee-Gee to come crowding back. Only this time you were not, immediately, there to bat for me."

"Horse? Here?"

"Yeah. But more to the point, he recognized me. Took the two minders to task for employing me 'of all people'. There was quite the barny, until Gee-Gee pulled himself together and remembered what he was there for—to greet Demetrius Popolo. Now that was a horse show if ever there was. Fawning all over the big man, welcoming him to *Braedon* which is some big outfit that Gee-Gee enthused over at great length. Then this other man, he'd been double-handed waving at me like some marshaller with the paddle pops, I didn't know what he was about. Well anyway, Gee-Gee has some words to him, and tells me to follow him. He directs me to haul the plane to what could best be described as a wanna-be has-been boathouse."

"Yes, I've seen it. Been in there."

"Oh, is the plane still there? Is it in one piece?"

"From what I could tell it is all there."

"Well, that's something, I guess. I always hoped that it was being cared for better than I was."

"So how, or why, did you land up here, like this?"

Tim shrugged his shoulders. "Can't think of any other reason than Gee-Gee wanted to show me that he could still bully me."

"Seriously?"

"I don't know. And another thing I don't know, is where my clothes are. You wouldn't mind taking a look around for me, would you? Or failing that, there might be something salvageable and not too disgustingly dirty in that pile over by *his* bed."

Chapter 38

Alex and Nikki were once again sitting, heads close, in the room that served as a common room for the security team when they heard the door to Fletcher's office slam shut and his footsteps clump across the foyer and out the front door. They looked up and out the front window. Fletcher was making for the path that led off the property and into Hemlock. They turned to each other.

Fletcher was openly breaking the most important rule that he had imposed and had ensured that all those working for him had etched firmly into their brains.

"Do you know what that is about?"

Alex watched as Nikki shook her head, absently running her index finger around the collar of her shirt. Growing up he had seen other girls, and women, performing similar actions when anxious, scared or worried. Until he had left Hemlock to find work, he had thought that such a gesture was peculiar to females. Now he knew that it was endemic to his hometown and wondered if he had the courage to ask Nikki about it, but the expression of bitter hatred on her face dissuaded him.

"I have no idea."

"I wonder if it has anything to do with that man, The Hermit, that he escorted off the property the other week? You know that Fletcher's been having boxes of provisions taken out into the bush to be collected by him? And that there is always more than what would normally be required for one person."

227

She looked aghast at Alex. She did not know. Mixed thoughts raced through her mind. How would this lack of knowledge impact her position as the head of the security team here at *Braedon*, and her otherwise impeccable reputation in the wider field. "No. I did not know that. How do you know? And why wasn't I told? As team leader of security I need to know if there are any breaches to the ..."

"Like Fletcher's breach now?"

"Well, yes. That too." Nikki puckered her brow and scratched the back of her neck with her right hand. Why would Fletcher storm out of the house and head into the bush towards Hemlock, and not alert her? Why would food be left out for the man to collect? And there was no one that she could report any of this to. Maybe it would be best to wait till Fletcher returned and confront him as to why she, the security team was being left out in the dark?

It was hard for anyone to know what was happening beyond their own team's activities. Socializing with members of the other teams was discouraged, except for the symbiotic nature of the tasks of the robotics, electronics and surveillance teams which made that mandate pretty lenient for them. "What is going on Alex? Do you know?"

Alex shook his head. "Wish I could help you Nikki. All I know is that up until last week the medical team had been super busy and had kept very much to themselves. Even when I had Lou and Arti fabricate a couple of incidents requiring medical attention, they were fobbed off with Band-Aid cures. Then last week all but one of the medicos, a male nurse, left."

Nikki stared at him. "Can they do that? Leave us without medical assistance? What'll happen if there's a serious injury?"

"Guess it'll be a case of 'too bad, here's a band-aid.'"

"Oh do be serious Alex."

"I am."

"Whatever." Nikki's eyes took on a faraway look as she tapped her lips with the fingertips of her right hand. "Have you noticed that Fletcher's been on edge and anxious ever since we got here? But I think it's got worse since we saw The Hermit, here, fighting with Dave and Bruno and Fletcher took him off the property. I wonder where they went?"

"Do you want me to go and find out?"

Nikki sat up straighter and stared at him in alarm. "What? Find where they went, or find The Hermit? Why would you want to find him?" Her finger found its way to her throat.

"Well, if as you say, Fletcher's demeanour changed after that debacle, and there have been deliveries of food since then, it's got to be tied up somehow. Maybe The Hermit's blackmailing Fletcher."

"What could he possibly have on Fletcher to be blackmailing him with?"

Alex shrugged. "I don't know."

He watched as she marked her throat red with the friction of rubbing.

Alex reached out his hand to take her finger away from her neck. Nikki drew back with a gasp. He pulled back his hand.

"Why do you do that? Run your finger around your throat? Almost all the females in town do that. Nowhere else have I seen women do that."

"It's because of that man."

"What? Who? The Hermit? Is it some secret sign between women, instead of saying his name?"

She shook her head, her hand still resting on her neck. "No, it's because he would sometimes threaten us with a knife to the throat."

Alex sat back, silent for a while, thinking. "So why would he threaten you? What danger were any of you to him?"

Nikki laughed. "You mean we couldn't be a threat to him because we are the 'weaker sex'?"

"Well, no, not really, but surely what with him being bigger for a start, why would he need to threaten you with a knife?

"He's a flasher, and if we did not indulge him by at least looking, screaming or acknowledging his, er talisman as he would call it, then he would produce his knife and slowly draw it across his own neck, leering at us and all the while masturbating. And sometimes worse. Some necks have been scarred."

"He was never stopped? Parents? The police?"

Nikki shook her head. "Not to my knowledge. But even if we had spoken to anyone about it, would it have made any difference? Times were different back then, and still not much better now. Sexual assault and harassment were just something that we females had to ignore or tolerate. No one would have believed us if any of us had complained. It was just how things were. And still are."

"But what about your own parents? The adults on the commune? Wouldn't they believe you? Did you tell them?"

"Like all the kids in the commune, I was too scared to tell anyone because it always happened when we were places we had been told not to go. We grew up being told stories of how the maldape would get us if we went too far into the bush, or to the lake. The kids in Hemlock, when we mixed with them, used to tell us their parents had told them the same. You must remember."

Alex nodded his head, remembering. But he remembered more. He remembered his Uncle Ray's girlfriend, Nikki's sister Tess, being found by the roadside, with her throat slashed. And the murderer never being apprehended, and the theory that both he and Nikki shared about The Hermit.

"I for one would like to know what's going on around here – why all the restrictions and secrecy. I mean, those OTT non-disclosure agreements we had to sign. What was all that about? Not that I objected, the money I was offered negated any concerns I had about that. But how is that level of secrecy connected to The Hermit and the food deliveries? I don't care if I am about to contravene any of Fletcher's ludicrous mandates or agreements I've signed. I owe it to Ray, and I want to know what The Hermit knows. He *must* know something. I think we, or just I, need to pay The Hermit a visit."

Nikki wanted to know the answers to all the points that Alex was raising. But her heart and her head were conflicted. She had listened to her head from the time that she decided to leave the commune and Hemlock. It was through listening to her head that she was where she was now, and it was reminding her that she was the leader of the security teams and it was her responsibility therefore to stay at *Braedon*. Her heart, on the other hand, was calling out for vengeance, guiding her thoughts toward her own reasons for wanting to interrogate The Hermit, even if it meant beating the shit of him, which is what she felt would be needed. For her there was no room for polite conversation. The Hermit had in all probability killed her sister. She wanted him to pay.

"We are in this together, I don't care if I'm hauled over the coals for leaving the property. There's no way that you are going on your own, I have some questions for him too. Do you know where to find him?

"Oh, from where Sam and Spiro have said they leave the boxes of food, I think I know where." He looked at Nikki, "I was one of those boys who didn't believe in my parent's tales of the maldape. There is, or was, an old boathouse and cottage further around the lake. I'll wager that is where The Hermit is. Come on, Fletcher is not here to find out, it's not as far as a walk into town. You're off duty today, plenty of time for us."

Chapter 39

Fletcher stood in the phone booth, carefully stacking a collection of coins on top of the telephone while he ruminated as to whether he ought to phone his mother or Maxell first. He did not relish the thought of engaging in conversation with Maxwell, not when he was still to reconcile with what he considered to be his banishment. But if he rang his mother first then who knows how long she would keep him talking, and he might run out of coins before he could speak with Teddy-Max. Teddy-Max. He scratched his head. Why did they all call him that behind his back? When he was brought in from the field and given the hated desk job he had thought the nick-name had something to do with diminishing Maxwell's air of self-importance. But whatever the reason, it worked for him. The man was totally too full of himself. Too much the dictator.

Fletcher sighed and clinked the coins in their pile. He could always reverse the charges, he supposed, that would save his meagre pile of coins. But not to Maxwell he couldn't. A reverse charge call to him would leave a trail, and this mission was totally clandestine, completely off the record so that if anything went wrong then Maxwell would not be in the firing line. For the briefest of moments he relished the thought of the secrecy backfiring in Maxwell's face, but the thought was short lived. It would be his own butt that would be kicked. Kicked right out. Kaboom. No more job. A midlife career crisis of his own making, with no comeback. Well, that settled that.

233

Whatever had he done to deserve this? He was not cut out for all this responsibility. The welfare of others. He wanted to be back being a lone-wolf operator.

He may have preferred to talk to his mother first, get some clarity on the situation from her perspective. Not that he could share any of the details with her, he'd only make vague generalizations and hope that she would not see through his falsehoods. But no, he would phone Maxwell first, using all the coins if necessary and then he would phone his mother, reverse charges. She would chastise him, but she would be happy to hear from him. And without the prospect of a chewing out hanging over him he could relax and take on board the advice that his mother would impart. He smiled. In fact, if he phoned her after talking with Teddy-Max she would be able to smooth any ruffled feathers he might have gathered.

He wiped the palms of his hands down the sides of his trousers before picking up the handpiece. Slowly he dialled the office, his hand holding several coins above the slot waiting to receive them. Fletcher tapped his foot impatiently as he listened to the incessant chirping of the phone. Damn it, why didn't Maxwell pick up? The ringing stopped. He returned the handpiece to the cradle and beat the coin against one of the windowpanes on the side of the booth. A number of cars, skies firmly secured on roof racks, slowly snaked along Main Street and the proverbial penny dropped. Of course. Maxwell would not be at work. Or at least not in the office. It was Saturday. What an idiot he was. Tut-tutting, he corrected himself. He was not an idiot. He had been isolated from the rest of the world and lost track of the days. No problem. He would take delight in interrupting Teddy-Max at home.

Fletcher replaced the coin back onto the pile precariously balanced on top of the phone module and, gleefully grinning to himself, rummaged in his jacket pocket for his notebook. He then rifled through the pages until he found Maxwell's home phone number.

The STD pips sounded as Maxwell picked up the receiver at his end, and Fletcher inserted a number of 10 cent pieces into the phone as he gulped and took a deep breath.

"Sorry to disturb you at home," he hoped his voice didn't sound too syrupy, "but I happened to be near a phone and thought you might like an update."

He held the earpiece away from his ear as Maxwell remonstrated him for not only phoning him, but at home as well. Typical, he thought. Try to do the right thing and get a bollocking for your effort. The light flashed alerting him that the phone was hungry for more coins, which he fed in. The pile atop the phone was diminishing.

"No, no. Everything is going according to schedule. It is all working a charm. We should be ready to ..." A figure further up the road, probably heading towards The Grand View Hotel, caught Fletcher's attention. He leaned against the windows to get a better look.

"Sorry, gotta go." He dropped the handpiece and left it dangling as he pushed the door open and rushed outside. What the fangle-dangle was that man doing here in town? He was meant to be back at *Braedon*, making sure that no one came near the place. Yet here he was, bold as anything, for all to see. Fletcher crossed the road and chased after the man as he elbowed through the crowd of skiers outside The Grand View Hotel. Surely he wasn't going to enter, not dressed like that? But no, the man extricated himself from the jovial group and kept walking until he turned into the street the other side of the cop-shop.

Fletcher pushed his way through the group congregating around the hotel doorway and hurried past the police station. But when he got to the corner and looked down the street the man, who had assured him that he never came to town, was nowhere to be seen.

Another nod to Murphy. Would the chinks never cease to erode the operation? Fletcher could feel his blood pressure rising, along with his anger. What to do next? He didn't much feel like going back and phoning Maxwell again. Fuming, he looked at his watch. Neither could he phone his mother, it was nearly her lunchtime and she disliked being disturbed at mealtimes as much as Teddy-Max did at being phoned at home. He decided that the best solution to his quandary was to appease any prospect of an ulcer and get himself a feed at the hotel.

Berating himself over his bad luck and wishing that he had had the nerve to refuse the assignment in the first place, Fletcher turned around and with his head bent down against the biting wind that had picked up, he started back along Main Street, wondering if the gay barman would be there, and if bantering and baiting him would improve the day. He thought it might. The day was going so pear-shaped that anything would be an improvement.

Anything, that is, except what he saw when he looked up.

Chapter 40

It had not taken Paul long to retrieve Tim's clothing, which had been haphazardly bundled into a suitcase under the other bed, and once Tim was suitably attired Paul made haste getting the two of them out of the place.

Christie and Melody watched, dumbfounded, as the door opened, and Paul emerged supporting another man.

Tim leant against Paul and shaded his eyes with his hands, hoping that it would not take long before his eyes adjusted to the light.

"Easy does it Tim, there're no steps, we're going to have to jump. Think you're up to it?"

"I'm up for anything that gets me out and away from this place. Don't suppose there's any chance of visiting the plane? I'd like to check her over, grab some things. Don't think Gee-Gee bothered to bring my overnight bag to my suite."

"Not a chance. Not right now," Paul pulled at his friend, urging him forward.

"But ..." Tim baulked, pulling back from Paul and looking around as though he expected to see the boathouse and his plane sitting patiently at the end of the veranda.

"No. We need to get us all away from here as soon as. You can borrow my toothbrush if you're anxious for your pearly whites. Ready to jump?"

Tim took an unsteady step towards the edge of the boards and grabbed hold of Paul's sleeve. "Um, I think I might need a bit of a hand," he mumbled, ashamed of his weakness.

237

Paul jumped down from the veranda. He looked over to the women and was surprised to see them still standing where he had left them, and apparently disinclined to move, even now when he was with a person obviously in distress. Weren't women the inquisitive and compassionate ones, unable to leave things alone? He knew that if the positions had been reversed his curiosity would have won over the need for caution.

He shook his head and turned back to Tim. "Come on then," he held his hands out, "I'm ready to catch you when you're ready."

"Guess I'm not going to get to see the haunted house after all," Melody tried to sound flippant, but failed.

Christie stared at her friend. "I've told you already, the house is *not* haunted. Besides, isn't that place enough for you?" Christie waved her arm towards Paul and his friend as they staggered towards them.

"Well, I was expecting a bit more. Like maybe wandering around and looking the place over. Not standing out here in the cold while someone else does all the exploring."

"Well, sitting at mum's with a roaring fire would be my choice for spending a winter's morning. But no, you had to drag me out here, and you now say you are not happy with the outcome!"

"I thought you'd be happy to help me, and to spend time with your crush," Melody raised her eyebrow in a challenge.

"He's not my crush. In fact, I'm beginning to wonder why I ever admired him. He is not as impressive in person. Think I preferred him more when he was in print than in person."

"Come on, you like him. No matter what you say, I know that you like him."

"I admire his journalistic photographic essays. And yes, I admit I was enthralled to meet him. But really? I can honestly say that he has not pushed any buttons for me. Not my type."

"Oh, you have a 'type'? Can't say that I have noticed. It's quite an eclectic lot that you have gone out with, no 'type' to be cast there, not that I have ever seen. Other than they have all been male."

Christie and Melody's conversation was slowly climbing to contention when Paul, with Tim limping carefully behind him, reached them.

"Come on you two," Paul grabbed hold of Christie's arm and pushed her forward along the path that they had walked in on earlier.

"Lead on, and step on it ... you do know the way, don't you?"

Christie gave him a scathing look and stared beyond him at his companion. "What about ... but Paul shook his head and gave her another gentle push.

"Not the time for pleasantries. We gotta get out of here before that man returns. And I don't want to meet him on the way, or anyone else for that matter, we still don't know who was behind that gunshot. Introductions can wait."

"If you are in such a hurry, then why am I leading?" Christie mumbled as she stumbled forward.

"Oh great, and thanks a lot," Melody retorted as she too was pushed ahead of Paul. "You don't want to meet that wacko on the path, so you push the two of us ahead of you? That is so, so not chauvinistic of you."

She caught the muffled chuckle from behind Paul and glared at the man accompanying him. She was uneasy about how her subconscious responded to the dark eyes that observed her with humour. She harumphed, turned away, and followed Christie. She had come out here to look for a haunted house and instead she was being haunted by an unknown male who was obviously not dressed to impress.

The four progressed in silence as walking single file was not conducive to meaningful conversation. But once they were out of the bush and back on the road that led into Hemlock, they were able to walk in pairs, though Paul was yet to introduce his companion.

At the first intersection Paul bundled them off the main road. "Right then, even if he comes this way, he is not likely to see us down here."

Christie stopped and looked back at him. "How do you know that he is going to be using the main road, and not this one?"

"Er, right. Good point." Paul looked around him, there were only a few scattered houses on the street that he had led them into. He grabbed Tim's arm with one hand and with the other gave Christie a gentle shove. "We'd better move. You know this town. So lead us to somewhere innocuous. Preferably where we can sit a while and catch our breath."

Christie sighed, and with her hands in her pockets pulled her parka tighter to her. "There's a kid's playground near here," she said and headed down a lane between two houses that had seen better days. "By the look of these houses I reckon the playground won't have changed much from when I was a kid – it wasn't much back then."

Once at the playground they could all see what Christie had meant by 'not much'. There were the requisite two swings, one with the chains so twisted and tangled that the seat was balanced precariously on the horizontal beam from which they hung, the seat of the other one hung loose from one chain. There was a wooden seesaw with peeling paint—a refuge for copious splinters waiting for the unwary. The only thing that provided anything resembling safe and secure seating was the witch's hat carousel – a circular swing pivoted from a tall central pole. Other, smaller, metal poles radiated from this, supporting a circular wooden seat about child waist height. The whole thing resembled a witch's hat. It would provide somewhere to sit, so they made their way there. Christie was the only one who automatically perched herself on the horizontal wooden beam that made the brim of the hat. She wrapped her arm around one of the metal spokes that suspended the beam from the centre upright.

The others all looked on sceptically as she swung gently towards the centre and back out again. Melody was next to move and sat on the other side of pole Christie clung to.

Paul and Tim were a little more circumspect, standing back and watching the carousel as it wavered freely back and forth from the point of the Witch's Hat.

"You're not expecting me to get on that contraption, are you?" Paul asked.

"That looks like the skeleton of a conical pendulum, and belongs in a Maths or Science lab, not a kid's playground," Tim muttered.

"Have you never been on one of these before?" Christie laughed. "If you go and do what we are doing, but opposite us, it will settle down,"

She and Melody watched, amused, as the two men hesitated. "Oh, stay where you are," Christie said as she dropped one foot onto the sandy snow-flecked ground and gave a push, which sent the beam on a slow spin. When it reached to where Tim and Paul were hesitantly standing, she used her foot as a brake. "Now hop on. It won't bite!" She laughed again. Melody joined in as the two men sheepishly sat on the beam and swung their legs over while the carousel bucked. But soon they were all settled.

"Right then," Paul beamed, and, not too keen on letting go of the metal pole he was holding on to, nodded his head towards Tim. "This here is my friend Tim. He's the one that I've been so worried about. And why I am here."

Tim managed a feeble smile. He knew that the two women would be curious about him, but not having used his limbs for a month or so he was near exhaustion after their trek out of the bush. "Yeah, hullo."

"Hi Tim," Christie and Melody chorused in unison then looked at each other and laughed.

"And that, pretty much in a nutshell, brings us all up to date. Right?" Paul, having related a condensed version of what he knew of his friend's escapade, looked to Tim for confirmation.

"Yep, pretty much," Tim said with a feeble nod. "But what about my plane, and things? You reckon we can go back and get them sometime soon?"

Paul shook his head. "I reckon it's better if we don't go back right now. Your guard will soon see that you are missing and, well, I'm not too sure what will happen when what's-his-face finds you've absconded. As for your plane and belongings ... I'm pretty sure that the plane will be safe, so there's no real hurry. It's too valuable to trash, and you can always replace your personal things.

"But my ELT is in there! And what do you mean, 'trash my plane'?" Tim made to get off the carousel, but Paul restrained him before he fell.

"Just a turn of phrase. Keep your hat on. I'm just saying Horse would be stupid to do anything to your plane. He probably still has a need for it. And you."

"Oh, so that's why he's been keeping me here? Am I supposed to be amenable to further flying for him, after the way I've been treated this past month?"

"Your mate's got a point there," Melody chipped in. "This Horse character you talk about, whoever he is, is not winning any friends at the moment."

"I just hope I'm not being docked for that accommodation."

"Wait, you mean you weren't paid all up at the beginning?" Christie exclaimed, aghast at the idea.

Tim shook his head. "Only a small retainer."

"When were you to get paid?"

Tim shrugged his shoulders, and the others looked appalled.

"Does that mean you don't know?" Melody asked, wondering what sort of man this Tim fellow was. Knowing when she was getting paid for a job would have been the first thing she would have asked about, even before taking on a job.

"Leave it Mel, can't you see that he is totally out of it?" Christie looked up at the clear blue sky. "Of course, it might be sun stroke, or perhaps even snow blindness that has marvellously addled his brain. How long did you say you were tied up back there?"

Tim shrugged again, then looked at Paul.

"Well, it must have been four weeks at least since I had last received any message from you. But I'd also like to know why you don't know when you were to get paid. Not like you at all, Tim. I know that you can live off next to nothing, but you were always looking to the next pay day."

Tim tried to look mollified, but only succeeded at accomplishing a half-hearted sheepishness. He shrugged his shoulders yet again.

"Not too sure. Guess I was all gung-ho at landing such a lucrative offer that payment was a minor detail that slipped my mind. Guess it would have been when I had completed the job."

"And when would that have been, exactly?" Paul asked.

"I guess when I had completed the chartered tour."

"Which would have been when?"

Tim shrugged. "Don't know. No idea even why I flew here."

While he was not privy to everything that was going on he'd had plenty of time whilst being tied up to review his dealings with Richard Ibraham and Harry Harris. And after weeks of reflection, he had come to the conclusion that he was a right dipstick to have been so easily dupped. Almost from the start everything had pointed to the junket involving some clandestine activity, of which he still did not know the depth or ramifications.

He assumed that it was highly probable that the world believed that the plane, *his* plane, carrying Demetrius Popolo, had disappeared and most likely crashed. He also knew where it had disappeared to. And now so too did the three people with him. And if Gee-Gee had trussed him up because of what he knew, how safe were Paul, Melody and Christie now that they knew about him, and the plane?

So many unanswered questions, the paramount one probably being what was publicly known about the staged misadventure in the flight to Sydney? He'd have to ask Paul what the media had reported. Till he knew what was common knowledge, he'd have to play it safe and keep mum about everything, including Popolo, and so hopefully not endanger anyone else.

"Initially I was flying the passengers to Melbourne, but one of them directed me here. Guess you could say I was privately hijacked," he tried to laugh, but the humour was lacking.

If what Paul had seen out by the lake and what Tim had briefly told him about where he'd been kept captive were any indication, he wasn't too sure that he wanted the women to become involved. It might be better to make light of the predicament.

"Well, here's to hoping that your pay hasn't been hijacked as well." Paul laughed.

"I'd say that the charter is well and truly over, don't you?" Melody stated. "But you'd be best to check if you've been paid."

Christie stared unbelievingly at Melody "Why are talking about money? It's either there or it's not. I say we should go to the police. Don't you want to report your assault and captivity?" Christie asked.

Paul looked at Tim, one eyebrow raised in query. If Horse or whoever had gone to the expense of engaging Tim, and altering his plane, and falsifying flight plans, then there was more going on than simple hijacking and kidnapping. This sounded a whole lot more complex than what a country cop could deal with. Besides, police involvement at this stage could hamper his chances of a news scoop.

Tim understood the silent query. He wanted to know what Gee-Gee was up to and having now talked with Paul, felt convinced that the man who had watched over him knew what it was, and that together he and Paul could get it out of him. If they went to the police, they may never know. Better to leave the police out of it, at least until they had the answers they wanted, or things got too hairy.

"So I was roughed up and kept captive? I've been liberated now. I'll go to the police when I get back to Melbourne. I'm with Melody right now – more interested in seeing if I've got some dosh in the bank."

Seriously? Christie thought. Where were their heads? Tim had been subjected to unlawful detention, the perpetrators needed to be apprehended and all they could think about was money? She shook her head. All three of them were hopeless.

"Well, I don't know about any of you, but I'm getting cold sitting here. You can go to the police or the bank, I don't care, but I'm outta here." Christie let go of the pole, swung her legs over the side and jumped off the carousel, causing the others to all yelp as it rocked back and forth. "Watch it, you!" shouted Melody, then she too took a leap, leaving the men to contend with the momentum. Soon they were following Christie as she made her way across the playground and down another street, heading towards the main road. "We could check that out now. There's bound to be a bank in town

"I don't think so Melody."

"What? You telling me that Hemlock doesn't have a bank?"

"Of course Hemlock has a bank. But it will be closed."

Melody pulled the sleeve of her parka up to look at her watch. "How do you know it's closed?"

Christie shook her head, "It's Saturday, you dodo."

"That won't matter if there is an ATM outside," Paul interjected before turning to Tim. "You do have a card? With you?"

Tim stopped walking and looked blankly back at him, then blinked. "Well, I started out with one, wouldn't know if I still have it or if Gee-Gee relieved me of it."

Christie looked at Tim, who was busy pushing his hands into numerous pockets, "Gee-gee? There's another horse?" She was definitely not following this conversation.

Tim paused briefly and looked to Paul for help.

"It's a nickname, along with Horse." Paul shrugged his shoulders, and glared at Tim. "For a mutual friend back in Melbourne. One who was wont to help himself to others' wallets when he was skint." He wasn't sure why he did not want to elaborate on the existence of Horse.

"Eureka!" Tim let out a yelp, and with a weak flourish produced a wallet from the inside pocket of his flying jacket.

"Well done mate." Paul put his hand on Tim's shoulder and gave a squeeze.

"Good. Let's go and take a look at the bank, it might be a branch of yours."

Chapter 41

Nikki chose to wait at the edge of the clearing. The cottage was a poor excuse for somewhere to live, but then what hermit of this man's calibre lived palatially?

She watched as Alex boldly made his way across the clearing, mounted the veranda and rapped on the door with the little-finger side of his fist. She held her breath as Alex waited for a response. But none came.

Alex looked over to Nikki and shrugged his shoulders, arms out in query as to what to do.

Nikki nodded her head and crept forward to join him on the veranda.

Alex put his hand on the door handle, gently turned it and pushed the door open. He waited for Nikki, and they entered together, staying close to the door till their eyes became accustomed to the lack of light.

"He's not here. No one is here."

Alex could feel Nikki relax beside him.

"No. But there are two beds. And that one," Alex pointed and walked towards the one recently occupied by Tim, "looks like it has restraints."

"Well, there's your 'more than one person' to be fed. But what do we do now?" Nikki whispered. "We have no idea who was being kept in this bed, or where they are now, or if they are coming back, or when."

247

"I for one am fed up with this job. It might pay well, but I think it is time to quit with the secrecy. Not that any of us know why there is a need for the subterfuge and secrecy. It is obvious that someone has been kept here against their will, and I don't want to be part of a kidnapping, no matter who they are. I think I'm going to head into Hemlock and talk to the police. A kidnapping needs to be reported, especially now that whoever was tied to that bed is no longer there. Who knows where they are now, or what has happened to them."

"What if you bump into Fletcher? We know that he was headed Hemlock way."

"Fletcher is in this as well. Up to his neck. Has to be. He's the one in charge. And I'm not worried about meeting him in the street. I know Hemlock better than he does I'll warrant. It can't have changed that much since I left. I'll stay well out of his sight. You coming?"

Nikki didn't need a second asking. She absently fingered her neck. No way was she going to hang around on her own, not if this was where The Hermit hung out. For sure she wanted to have the opportunity to quiz him about her sister, ask him if he had anything to do with her death. But to confront him on his own ground? No way.

"Well, I'm not wanting to stay here on my own, in case one or both come back, thank you very much. And I can keep an eye out for Fletcher too."

Chapter 42

Paul and the women hovered discretely behind Tim, and all held their breath as he pushed his bankcard into the ATM and entered his PIN. It did not take long before he turned around and, beaming, gave a fist-pump. "It's there!"

"All of it?" Paul asked while the women chorused their surprise. "Really?" Then followed a collective sigh—they had all been thinking that there was a distinct possibility that, after the treatment Tim had received on arrival in Hemlock, the funds would have been withheld.

"Yes. All of what I was still owed. One huge lump sum all accounted for. I'm flush."

"Must be your shout then," Paul laughed.

It was an excited group that headed away from the bank, talking and laughing as they jostled each other across the footpath and towards the road.

Christie was walking backwards facing the others as they all crossed the road, oblivious to the approaching panel van with a series of skies tied onto the roof-rack. Paul leapt forward and grabbed hold of the sleeve of her parka.

"Whoa, what are you doing?" she asked as she was pulled into what she thought was an embrace.

"Saving you from being collected by that van," Paul indicated the vehicle that had passed behind her.

She spun round as the vehicle continued down the road toward the ski fields, a frown puckering her face. "If they have a van, then why are their skies on the roof and not inside where they'd be safe from falling off?"

Melody rolled her eyes and laughed. "Honestly Christie, where have you been? Don't you know these things? Did you see who was in the cab? A couple of young bucks. They will have set the inside of the van up as a love nest – mattress, pillows, blankets. No doubt plenty of grog in there too. No way would they want skies messing that up."

Christie blushed and Tim and Paul joined Melody in her laughter. Christie harumphed and disentangled herself from Paul's grasp, surprised at how she now felt bereft without the contact. "I'm hungry." It was the first thing that came to her mind as she hurried across the remainder of the road and stepped up onto the footpath outside the Grand View Hotel.

"Wonder if the ..." Tim looked up at the signage above the door, "... Grand View has room service?"

"Room service?" The tone in Christie's question suggested incredulity, as though she was asking an imbecile whatever gave them the idea that the only hotel in town would have the time and staff to provide anything but counter meals.

"Yeah, don't know about you, but I'm not too happy about fronting up to a public dining room looking like this."

"Don't think you need to worry about that," Christie laughed. "I may not have been here for a while, but some things don't change. This is the only hotel, or pub, in town which serves food, so they get all sorts here. Besides there is more than one eatery inside."

Tim shuffled his feet and muttered something inaudible. The women looked to Paul who shrugged. "Or, if you are feeling particularly uncomfortable about the way you are dressed, I don't know about room service, but I'm quite sure it would not take much convincing for me to have one of the staff deliver something up, or, failing that, provide us with something to take up to my room. But Christie and Melody might prefer to eat in one of the dining rooms. Either way, let's go and get you tidied up a bit first."

Chapter 43

Fletcher found himself in quite the quandary, it most certainly was not his day. He stared at the four figures crossing the road, just to make sure. He did not recognize the two women, but he did recognize the men with them. Somewhere in the past he felt sure he had known the better attired one. The other ... the other was the pilot! He looked back at the street the man he'd been following had gone down. He was meant to be back at that dump of his near the boathouse, keeping an eye on the pilot who was here in town, bold as you like.

Fletcher shook his head in disbelief, wondering what was going on. The hermit had assured him that he rarely came into town, he had no need. Part of the arrangement was that whatever the man needed, beyond what he caught in the bush and the lake, would be provided by what was on hand at *Braedon*. And if he did come into town, it was never during the day, when people could see him. Fletcher had never understood the rationale about that. The hermit, who was meant to have assumed the identity of the maldape, was here, large as life, as himself. It did not make sense. Obviously his assurances were worth diddlysquat. Not only was the man himself in town, but so was the pilot. The hermit was meant to be keeping an eye on the pilot, back near the lake, not here in Hemlock. And they weren't even together. Fletcher could feel his ire rapidly rising, clouding his vision as he watched the pilot and his companions nonchalantly walk into the Grand View Hotel.

It was too much to try and sort out those logistics when he was not thinking straight. He stifled the scream he wanted to vent, squeezing his eyes closed while massaging his head in an attempt to clear the confusion festering there.

Would Murphy never leave him alone? There went any chance of him releasing his frustrations by baiting the barman, whatever his name was. For sure he did not know where in the hotel they were headed, but, although he wanted to know what the hell was going on, he did not feel up to an unequal face-to-face confrontation while his mind was all of a jumble. He wanted answers, yes. But that would have to wait. He stuffed his hands into his jacket pockets and turned around. He'd phone his mother. There was nothing or no one who would better be able to ease his shattered state.

He resolutely wove his way through the oncoming tide of people, amazed that so many individuals would be attracted to the snow. He shivered at the thought of willingly spending time strapped to thin planks of wood while negotiating the elements and calling it 'sport' and 'fun'. Once across the road he made his way back to the phone box, expecting to find it as he had left it, with the handset dangling and the few remaining coins still on top of the telephone.

Murphy and the gods of fate were once more against him. A middle-aged woman and her two dogs filled the cubicle and were busy steaming up the panes of glass. He let out a frustrated sigh. It would have to be a reverse charge call now. Any coins he had left in his haste to chase after the hermit would have been a windfall for the present occupant.

He stood in what he hoped would be her line of vision should she look his way. He pulled his hands out of his pockets and made an expansive display of pushing his jacket sleeve up to reveal his watch. But the woman either didn't see, or was not to be intimidated. Either way she did not budge.

Fletcher stood his ground, alternating between stamping his feet and slapping his arms around his chest. He looked at his watch again. 5 minutes, then 10 and still the woman worked on fogging up the windows. Could she not see him there waiting impatiently to use the phone? Did she not care that he was getting frost bite, and that her dogs were getting agitated at his comic antics?

"I wouldn't waste your energy. Mrs Evans will be there for an hour or more yet."

Fletcher turned around and frowned at the audience to his impatience. A lone woman was standing nearby. The voice sounded vaguely familiar, but he could not place who she was or where he knew her from.

She laughed, and to his surprise he saw that it was the woman who had conducted the sale of the property to him. "It's the only time that she gets to talk with her family."

"Can't she use her own phone in the comfort of her home?" Fletcher stuffed his hands back into his pockets and looked down at his feet to avoid her gaze as he tried to recall her name. She would have given it to him, a professional courtesy at the very least. And he ought to recall it, especially as he had entertained the notion of paying her a visit today. He shuffled his feet in the slush of snow. That's how his brain felt – mush. Megan? Mary? Muriel? No, it couldn't be Muriel, she was not old enough to be a Muriel, that would have been his mother's generation. He willed his mind to remember, but the grey cells that monitored that part of his brain were not cooperating.

"I don't think she has one. Besides, for her it's cheaper to come here, use the public phone and reverse the charges. Gets her out of the house and the dogs get a walk."

"Doesn't look like there is much walking going on, other than the dogs circling her legs."

The real estate agent laughed again, and he cursed his numb brain for failing him in remembering her name.

"Come on." She swung her head to the side, indicating that he was to follow her. "If you need to use a phone, you can use mine." She blushed, then laughed again. "I mean the one on my desk, that is. I'm not actually working today, but most of our business is on the weekends so the office will be open."

With that she stepped around Fletcher and headed down the footpath, wondering what had possessed her to be so forward. After all it was not like her to bounce up to someone she had only met once before and initiate a conversation. But he had looked anxious to use the phone and everyone in Hemlock knew that once Gertie Evans started talking there was no stopping her. If that was what happened when a woman lived on her own, then she herself would have to think about how her life was going to end up. She shuddered at the thought that it might be like Gertie's.

"Thanks, but I couldn't possibly use your office phone," he called after her, not sure that he wanted to share his conversation with an audience in an open plan office, but to have use of a phone would be good. He hurried to catch up with her.

"It wouldn't be right. I'm wanting to make a trunk call. My mother. It could be a long one."

"Oh, silly me. I just assumed it would be a local call. Don't know why." She blushed again. It was so, so stupid. Yes, she had found him attractive when she had shown him around *Braedon*. But he was a client for goodness' sake. That's why she had, very reluctantly she recalled, declined his offer to accompany him to the Grand View. That and the fact that she was afraid he might cancel the contract he had just signed. And now she had suggested he use the office phone for his own personal use when that was against office policy for even Mr Spratt, far less the staff. That thought brought her up sharp and she abruptly stopped walking.

Fletcher, realising that she was no longer walking beside him, stopped. He turned round to find that she was several steps behind him and looking most perplexed, lines creasing her forehead. Abashed by his self-centredness, he walked back to her.

"No. Thank you for your offer but it would most probably be a long trunk call, and a private one, so if the office is open it would be inappropriate for me to hog the line, even if I left cash to cover the call."

She smiled, and he felt his face flush as he watched relief wash over her face. He knew he had made the right decision. He wished that he could return the smile, but all he could think about was how the hell would he get to talk with his mother and hear her advice, what with Mrs Whoever She Was hogging the public phone and his conscience not allowing him to use another company's equipment? Oh, why had he not had a phone connected to *Braedon*? But he knew why that was, and until now the decision had proven to be a good one.

She reached her hand out and touched his elbow as she made a decision that was further out of character for her. "In that case, since we can't have you breaking the office policy, I have a better idea." She took a deep breath and clumsily crossed her fingers, not that anyone could tell, her gloves were so cumbersome, and hoped that she would not regret what she was about to suggest. "Come home with me and use my phone, and stay for a coffee. Talk as long as you like and if it will make you feel better you can leave what you think appropriate."

Chapter 44

Fletcher had rung his mother from the phone in the hall, but there was no answer. That hadn't worried him, she was often out of hearing of the phone. But he was disheartened that he had not been able to unburden himself and in return reap the benefit of her wisdom.

Now, as he re-entered the living room he was faced with finding a way to divert the interrogation that he expected would bombard him. Weren't all women gatherers of gossip, anxious to know every little detail of everything that went on? He could not imagine the real estate agent would be any different. To delay the inevitable, he slowly made his way into the room and stood silently beside an armchair, the partner to the one that the woman was already occupying. He tilted his head to one side, effectively indicating the chair. She nodded her head at the same time as putting one hand out, inviting him to sit down.

He picked up a mug of coffee strategically placed nearby. Looking around, he realised that he was sitting, uncomfortably, in the front room of an old timberman's cottage, not entirely dissimilar in style to many of the older houses that he had seen in the past—bull nose veranda, with a solid wooden door standing sentinel between two casement windows and opening onto a hall that bisected the place.

He took a gulp of coffee from the mug and tried to disguise his displeasure – not only had it gone cold, but it was instant – and waited for the dreaded grilling, and wondered if he could get out of it. He was more used to being the examiner, and certainly was not in tune with the wiles of a female inquisitor.

Pamela Ellis, yes, her name had finally surfaced, nothing at all like the ones his brain had been busy suggesting earlier, sat opposite him nursing her own mug of coffee. Heat was radiating from the potbelly stove set in where an open fireplace had once resided. She was leaning forward expectantly. "And?"

He looked up unenthusiastically and he was surprised to see that her smile was a cross between mirth and intrigue. He had been right, she was curious.

"That wasn't long. Is your mother alright?"

"She didn't pick up." Fletcher brought the mug to his mouth, then remembering its lack of appeal, returned it to the coffee table.

"Here, let me get you a fresh coffee. Things can't be all that bad, can they? Maybe she was out."

When she returned, she smiled and handed him back the freshly filled mug. She'd decided that maybe his despondency had to do with the property she had sold him. She hoped that it was not something that he could hold against her. There had been a lot of rumours doing the rounds of the town, but other than a resurfacing of tales of the hermit's activities returning, no one could shed any light on their new neighbours out at *Braedon* maybe this was a chance to find out. "Tell me, have you settled in at *Braedon*?"

"Ah, if I told you, then, as the saying goes, I'd have to kill you."

She sat back in her chair and glared at him. "You can't really be serious. Can you?"

Fletcher looked at her and wondered ... He knew next to nothing about her. How much could, or ought, he share? His head told him not to be so idiotic as to even contemplate telling her anything; but he needed to talk with someone, and his mother was not answering the phone. He could always try phoning his mother again, one unanswered call did not negate the possibility of trying again, after all, that was why he was here. He glanced across at Pamela. She was not the kind of woman he would normally be attracted to, but there was something almost beguiling about her, in a benign way, that he found appealing, and his heart was telling him that Pamela could be trusted. He gave a guttural chuckle as something that C.S. Lewis had said about the heart obeying the head sprang to mind and he frowned as he tried to recall the homily from his schooldays. ... "*The heart never takes the place of the head: but it can, and should, obey it.*" Startled by that notion, his train of thought was brought to an abrupt hiatus. He shook his head. What was he thinking? He was overthinking, that was the problem. Ever since he had left Maxwell's office with the dreaded words of caution that he was on his own, nothing had been straightforward. Perchance it was time for him to stop listening to his brain, and let his gut, if not his heart, take over. Maybe Pamela could provide him with a sounding board. But, as when he was talking with his mother, he would have to be circumspect in what he shared.

"I'm afraid, yes, I am. What is happening out at *Braedon* is, seriously, better for you not to know about."

She leant forward, now gripping her mug tightly. She could feel her heart starting to pick up speed, urging her sweat glands into action. "It's not illegal is it, what you are doing out there?"

Fletcher laughed, he hoped that it would alleviate her concern, but her reaction had also amused him. "Oh, no. Nothing like that. Just that it is highly, er, sensitive, that's all."

"Then why the glum face?" Fletcher watched Pamela as he sipped his coffee. Her relief was almost palatable as she collapsed back in her chair, placing her mug on a table beside her.

Fletcher stretched back in his chair, his head falling back as he closed his eyes and ran his fingers through his hair then cupped his temples in his hands. "Everything's going to custard," he sighed, straightening himself back into an upright position. He looked at the woman opposite.

"Custard?" Pamela laughed. "Since when is making custard a secret operation? Her attempt to add some levity to the conversation seemed to work.

A smile started to invade his face as he now ran his fingers forcefully across his brow and into his hairline. He let out a protracted sigh and broke eye contact with Pamela.

"I'm used to being a man of action would you believe?" he said in an uncharacteristically quite voice, as though he was admitting a failing.

She did. Pamela fidgeted with her fingers and felt herself start to colour as she reached for her mug. Yes, she could well believe that he was a man of action. She remembered admiring his physique and fluid movement when she had shown him around *Braedon*.

"I like to be on the job, going in and getting the job done, then out. All done and dusted as quickly and quietly as possible.

She sat back in her chair. He made his work sound dangerous and clandestine, maybe not the kind of action she had envisaged him being involved in.

"I'm not cut out for this covert organising lark that *Braedon* requires."

"Covert?" Pamela was getting confused and uncomfortable. Who exactly was this man that she had invited into her home?

Fletcher blinked, and looked at Pamela. Had he said too much?

"Covert? Well, maybe more like sensitive. Is there much of a difference between the two? I guess not."

Pamela was shaking her head.

"Anyway, whatever. It is because of the covert, or if you prefer sensitive, nature of the work that I am overseeing that I purchased the property. It is exactly what we needed. Plenty of room and space and away from prying eyes. Mostly."

"Mostly? You mean to say that you have had ... visitors? I can't imagine that they would be locals. None of the locals would dare to go near the place."

Mentally congratulating himself, thinking that his plans—the maldape and latterly the hermit—put in place to deter the locals had proved successful, Fletcher cocked his head to the one side and looked enquiringly at her. "No? What makes you say that?"

Now it was Pamela's turn to be flustered and wonder if she had said too much. She let her mind race through the options she had, wondering which one would be the closest to the truth without leaving herself open to ramifications which she might not want to face. Could she be prosecuted for not disclosing all that lay behind *Braedon* when it was all well in the past? How could she best phrase her explanation?

"Not with them all being brought up with tales of the maldape."

Fletcher chose to feign ignorance in the hope that he might glean more about the history of the property and the strange man with his odd behaviour. Since that first meeting and altercation he had occasionally seen the man about the place, behaving as though he were a dog or some other animal intent on leaving its calling card or laying claim to what was his. By all accounts he never interacted with the team members, and he certainly appeared to be a more reliable deterrent than Nikki McDonnell's robots. While the theory behind their use was admirable, (and thank goodness no one knew that the idea of robots was his idea originally) and it had seemed a good idea in the beginning to use robots, their practicality had been somewhat less impressive. The intention had been for them to not only provide an aural screen—deathly disturbing noises which would deter any local investigation—but a visual presence of unidentifiable footprints and unnatural activity. Still, it had not been an entirely wasted application of money; he had acquired a most efficient team leader out of the exercise, but still ... the hermit had proved to be more reliable.

That was, until now. Fletcher creased his brow and wondered again what the man was doing in town. He would have to pay him a visit. He smiled. "Maldape?"

Pamela sighed. She knew that she ought to have been more upfront when she had shown him the property. Keeping quiet about The Hermit was one thing, he was a tangible entity, but the maldape? One did not go about telling out-of-towners about the legend of the local bogeyman, not unless you were looking to be called a nutcase. That would surely have cost her the sale. How was she to have known that stories about hauntings and mythical beasts, which may or may not be real, would have sealed the deal with ease?

"A maldape is a mythical monster that the local parents have used for decades to deter their children from venturing anywhere near your property." She stared into her mug and slowly moved her hands, wrapped tightly around the outside, in a circular movement until the liquid inside started a slow swirl, hoping, unsuccessfully, that that would assuage his curiosity.

"Why would the parents want to do that?"

"Safety. You saw how dilapidated the place is. And then there is the lake."

"But the place must not have always been a dump. You said 'decades', and there were once children there—they left their drawings on the walls. They must have had friends in town, at school ...? Who had the place before I bought it?"

Pamela stopped swirling her mug and raised it to her lips before pulling a face at the tepid coffee. She reached down and put the mug on the floor beside her chair and sighed.

"The history of the property is, well, rather unusual. As you can see from the style, it is quite old, but it has only ever had two owners, well, I guess really three – the first two were still the same family, before you. The original owner was a well-to-do man, and a pioneer of the area. I'm told, because it was long before my time, that he was quite the philanthropist and *Braedon* the site for many community activities. When he died his only child inherited the property, but not the philanthropy. He thought himself a cut above everyone else. Had his children educated in Melbourne and barred the locals from accessing the lake. It wasn't until he lost all his family, tragically, that he tried to mend his ways, in his will. He left the property to the town. That brought about a lot of enmity within the community one way or another and the place was left vacant. A commune of squatters moved in, and then ... Well, you."

"But why the need for a bogeyman?"

"Oh well, over the years the place developed a certain mystique about it. First there were the drownings. There was speculation about them seeing as how all the children apparently were good swimmers. Then there were the hippies, and all sorts of strange reports, more likely rumours, of unconventional behaviours that generally appeared around the counter-cultural communes that were emerging.

When the hippies left, the place was regarded as contaminated. All of which intrigued the older children, the teenagers, you know, but which frightened the adults. So, stories of the aboriginal monster, which had always been prevalent in the area, became an obvious vehicle by which to deter exploration."

"But did it work?"

Pamela laughed. "It certainly did for me and my friends. Oh, for sure there was always the intrigue, but over the years there have been sufficient reports of strange 'goings on' to deter all but the very brave to go anywhere near the place, or the surrounding bush. Of course, those older boys who were adventurous enough to defy their parents always came back with, what would have been bogus, reports of what they had found, seen or heard in the area and that only increased our fear of the place. Silly really, but there you are."

Fletcher nodded. Her version of the maldape pretty much tied in with what the hermit had shared with him.

Pamela bent down to retrieve her mug then stood up, putting her hand out to receive Fletcher's that he was still holding. "Another cup?"

"Er, yes please, thanks." He handed over his mug.

"I'll grab us something to eat at the same time. I've a quiche in the freezer. Or are you one of those people who believe that 'real men don't eat quiche'?" Pamela stood in the doorway with a suggestive smile on her face.

He looked across at her and wondered how he should best answer. Was she flirting with him? Or did she seriously think that he was a 'real' man but would still want to eat quiche? He had several in his own freezer, ones that his mother had made and would periodically give him 'one to take home for when you don't feel like cooking'.

She saw him hesitate. "It's homemade. Or I could heat up some soup for us. That's homemade as well."

Another adage from his mother rose to the surface of his thoughts – 'the way to a man's heart is through his stomach' and he now wondered if Ms Ellis had been stalking him in the street and had an ulterior motive for offering him the use of her phone. He knew only too well that the charms and ploys of women were strange, and that was one of the reasons why, over the years, he had tried, not always successfully to his chagrin, to stay away from any female entanglements. With his mother he knew where he stood, but with this woman standing in the doorway, he wasn't sure what was happening. Neither with her, nor with himself. She was not what he would normally be attracted to, yet there was something there that he felt drawn to. Oh, what the heck, it was only something to eat – quiche or soup. There could be no entanglement. He'd be out of here soon enough. Out of both her house, and Hemlock. He was reading too much into her hospitality and his own state of mind. Yes, that was it, his jumbled state of mind. Besides, he was hungry so why not enjoy something to eat here in pleasant company? Far better than returning to *Braedon* with unanswered questions, or risk going to the Grand View Hotel and having a face-to-face with the pilot – his mind was not in the right space for that confrontation. He needed to know what the pilot knew. Better to have it out with Ibraham or Harris, if he could now track them down. As planned, once they had completed their task and handed over 'the patient' to his safe keeping, they had headed off into Hemlock and he hadn't seen them since. He screwed up his face. They too were supposed to have disappeared in the plane crash, and, knowing their expertise and connections, they were probably well and truly out of the country by now, using one of their aliases. The pilot. He sighed. What was he going to do about him? What if the pilot had gone to the police? It is what he would have done in his circumstances. And the people with him. who were they? God life was a mess. Yes, a much more palatable alternative was to stay, eat, and try to nut out what to do next.

"Quiche is fine, thank you. So's soup. Whichever is the easier."

Chapter 45

One look at the dimensions and furnishings in Paul's room was enough to convince them all that one of the eateries downstairs was the better option, providing that Tim could scrub-up a bit.

Christie and Melody, laughing, left the two men to fight over which of Paul's clothes Tim would fit into without it being too obvious that they were way too big, and they couldn't wait to see what apparition would greet them once Tim had been cleaned up.

Downstairs they looked into all three bars and the two eateries before deciding that the Snuggery, which offered a snack menu, would meet their needs. They could sit at four chairs around a table, and being less busy than the Eatery or Bistro, they would have more privacy.

Everyone's plates were empty before constructive conversation returned.

"So, what do we do now?"

The other three looked at Christie, bemused.

"What do you mean 'we'?" asked Paul.

"Well," Christie looked at each of the others in turn. "It seems to me that while we all came to Hemlock with our own agenda, fate, or rather ..." she shivered, choosing not to look at Tim, nor wanting to say what came to mind next for fear of bringing back memories

269

he'd no doubt rather leave well and truly buried, continued. "The maldape has contrived to lump us all into a shared quandary. Wouldn't you say?"

"Speak for yourself Christie. You didn't even want to come here. I came to investigate this haunted house that Paul wrote about, remember?" She looked at Paul and beamed proudly, after all it was she who had discovered Paul and his article on Shangri-La.

Christie sighed. "How many times do I have to tell you Mel, there is no haunted house, no matter what Paul wrote. He can't even remember writing the article!" She glared at him, resolved to extinguish the crush-like admiration she had for his work.

"Now wait a minute," Paul straightened up in the chair. "I never forget the things that I write about."

"Is that right?" Christie snapped.

"Yes, that's right. I never forget. Do you want me to start with my first article? It was about dingoes ..."

"There is no need to go on. I can tell you. It was about dingoes that were returning to someplace where they were thought to have been eradicated 100 years ago," Christie smirked across the table at Paul.

"It was Tasmania, and they weren't eradicated, they were just never found there, so now who can't remember things that I wrote?"

"Tasmania? Is that because the devil or the tigers killed them all?" Melody looked from Christie to Paul, eyes wide and innocent.

The other three at the table all rolled their eyes and chose not to respond.

"Well, if you can remember what you wrote, how is it that you *claim* not to have known about the lake? Huh?" Christie snapped.

Tim gave a discrete cough and turned to her. "So, um, Christie? What brought you to Hemlock this weekend?"

Christie quickly swallowed what was in her mouth and laughed. "She brought me." Christie jabbed her thumb in the direction of Melody beside her. "Or rather, I brought her in my car. Melody here believes in ghosts, *and* believed his story about there being a haunted house in town," she spat with another thumb jab across the table to Paul.

"You did not!" Melody looked around the table. "Well, alright, you drove us here. But," She paused and took a mouthful of beer from the glass in front of her before continuing. "But Christie's mother lives here, so she came to visit her mother and I just tagged along for the ride." She beamed at the men, then turned to face Christie and muttered, "And to take a look at the haunted house."

Tim, fearful that his turn to be interrogated by the women would be next, and not wanting to endanger them by having them privy to the real reason for he and Paul being here, took the opportunity of Melody's opening. "Speaking of haunted, what's all this maldape stuff?"

He'd heard the man who had held him captive prattling on about a maldape, but he had never really had the energy, nor the inclination to engage him in conversation so had let it slide. The man hadn't seemed a monster, but Tim had often wondered if he was the full picnic, that maybe he was a kangaroo or two short in the top paddock. He certainly didn't always seem to be completely with it, but he had never felt afraid of him, even with his wild and erratic quasi-masturbating sessions. The first time the man had flashed him, he had not reacted and after that the man had seemed to take pleasure in relieving himself by putting out the dying embers of the fire at the end of the day, before resetting and then relighting it each morning. Tim had come to the conclusion that there really was something amiss in the man's cognitive pathways.

Christie sighed. "The maldape ..." Melody leaned into the table and settled her elbows either side of her now empty dinner plate. "Is a figment of everyone's imagination."

"Christie! I was going to tell Tim about the maldape, and now you've spoiled it."

"Okay then. You tell him. And then I will explain what it *really* is."

"Thank you." She nodded her head at Christie and turned back to Tim while Paul listened in. He had yet to fathom the complete story behind the word that the women had repeatedly interjected their conversations with.

"So, you're telling us that while this maldape thing is not really real there is something out there trying to convince us that it is? Have I got that right?" Paul asked.

The women nodded.

"And Tim, you believe that this is somehow tied up with your ..." Paul stopped and searched for the right word. The word that would not give too much information away to the two women. "Your er, charter?"

Tim nodded his head thoughtfully. "That would make sense, somehow. I don't know what Gee-Gee is up to, and I don't think I want to know. But what I do know, is that I had better go back to that wretched place."

"What?"

"Why?"

The women asked. Paul just nodded. He and Tim had talked about it earlier in Paul's room. Tim was anxious about his plane's welfare, especially as he now knew that the key had been removed. And while it was not exactly a manifestation of Stockholm

Syndrome, he was concerned for his captor's welfare should Horse learn of Tim's escape. Knowing Horse as they did, they dreaded to think what he would do to the man who was so obviously not firing on all pistons.

"But I think I'll wait till the morning. First, I'm going to have a decent night's sleep in a well sprung bed with clean linen and blankets."

"And a proper breakfast," added Paul.

Chapter 46

For the briefest of moments Bradley gaped at how busy the place was, with people filling the footpaths both sides of the main thoroughfare. It wasn't until he saw the cars with skis on roof racks that he realised that it must be a weekend. They would all be strangers, so there was no need to be concerned about people seeing him and reporting his presence in town to That Man who was now of the understanding that he never came here during the day.

Buoyed with that thought, he stepped out onto the road and negotiated his way between the cars heading towards Ruby Street. It was only a short street which led nowhere. Unless, like him, they had a particular need and the knowledge of what was to be found there. There were only a handful of old timber workers' cottages, occupied by old timber workers who were well past their prime, except for the one that he was heading for, and the those either side. The one that he was heading for was, like all the others, showing evidence of time and the elements, and was almost entirely secreted away behind a wall of engulfing vegetation. That had been one of the things that had appealed to him when he had reacquainted himself with the property a decade ago—no one could see in.

He pushed his way past the tangle of jasmine and happy wanderer smothering the struggling fruit trees that edged the crazy paving path to the front door. Having no need to knock, he pushed the door open and walked in. As always, he tried to resist the temptation to feel that he had 'come home'. This cottage was not home. Even though he had been brought up here, it was not his home. His home was currently being occupied by That Man, but it would soon be his. That Man had given his word that it would be his. Soon. Would he then sell this place, he wondered, then shook his head. Plenty of time to work through that. He smiled and looked through the doorway to the front room. It was empty. Still smiling he quietly walked to the back of the house, wanting his arrival to be a surprise. But there was no one there either, nor in the mess of the tiny back yard.

Less joyfully he slowly made his way back to the front of the cottage. To the bedroom, but why she would be there at this time of the day he did not know. The door was closed, and he wondered why he had not noticed that on his arrival. He turned the knob and slowly pushed the door open.

Instead of the pristine lavender candlewick bedspread that he expected to see, what greeted his gaze was bare buttocks smiling at him as their owner rhythmically ground into *his* woman.

Growling, he leapt forward and grasped the man's shoulders, pulling him none too gently away from his business and flinging him across the room. The man landed against the wall below the window with a satisfying thud.

Rage filled Bradley's face as he confronted the startled woman who was now clutching blankets to her neck. He stabbed the air with his finger. "You!" he bellowed, spittle flecking his beard. Then his mouth opened and closed as though fighting grizzle as he tried to form the words that were cascading through his mind. Unable to express what he felt, he turned back to the man now scrambling around as he tried to retrieve his clothes and a modicum of decency.

"What the hell do you think you are doing here?" Bradley walked towards the man on the bare boards of the floor.

"What does it look like he was doing?" the woman spat. But Bradley wasn't sure if it was venom or hysteria that tinged her tone.

"I'll come to you in a minute," he growled over his shoulder. "So shut your mouth for now. I'm talking to this scumbag here."

The man looked over to the woman in the bed. She shook her head. He quickly gathered his clothes to his chest and, hunched over, fled from the room without saying a word, narrowly escaping the kick that Bradley had aimed for his chest. Instead, Bradley kicked the shoes that the man had not had time to pick up. Two kicks and they were out the door and across the hall into the front room where the man, his eyes wide and haunted, reminding Bradley of a spooked horse, was now busy struggling into his clothes.

Bradley then turned to the cowering woman. He leaned forward and stripped the blankets away from her. She wrapped her arms across her bare chest.

Bradley laughed as he bent closer, trapping her against the headboard, one hand either side of her shoulders.

"No need to cover them up. I know them well. They are mine. You are mine. Mine!" He leered at her and stood up and started pacing up and down the room, taking glaring looks across the hall.

"How long has this been going on then? Huh? And you," he shouted across the hall. "You can get out. And don't even think about coming back." He turned back to the woman in the bed. "Aren't I good enough for you?"

"Please Bradley. Please."

"Who is he? Are there others?"

"No, there are no others. It has only been this once." She reached for the blankets now at her knees and pulled them up and tucked them under her armpits. "You have to believe me." As the front door crashed closed, she jumped and swiftly looked out the window.

Bradley turned from watching the man scamper down the crazy paving. "And you expect me to believe that? Where'd you meet him? He's not local. Don't tell me that you fell for some cock and bullshit tripe from one of them ski-fellas. Thought there would be enough eager snow-bunnies to go around without that slimebag calling on you. Did you go out of your way and encourage him? Aren't I good enough for you?"

She rose up onto her knees still clutching the blankets to her chest. "Bradley, please."

Something in her cajoling stirred memories in Bradley. Memories from many years ago, when he had been younger, now played in his mind and he realised that, sadly, his more recent exploits were not as enjoyable or effective. He shook his head. He had lost his touch. He came back to stand beside the bed. He looked down at the woman on the bed, his hand unconsciously making its way to his crotch. Maybe he could rekindle the thrill today.

"I didn't go looking for him. Honest. He knocked on the door, not knowing this is a private house. He'd come looking for one of the other places. She waved her hand in the general direction of the cottages of ill repute that sandwiched the one they were in. "It has been so long since you have come to visit me. I couldn't help myself. I was missing you." She sat down on her ankles and reached up to Bradley.

It was true, she had been missing him. But she had not been expecting him to turn up on a weekend, and during the day. His usual routine was of an evening, and until recently he had been as regular as, well, her periods. She let out a soft laugh and stroked his arm, mirroring the movement of his hand, silently pleading.

It was true, he realised. He had not been here for a while. Not for four weeks and a day or so. His face darkened and his eyes clouded. His absence had not been his fault. Mentally, and not for the first time, he cursed That Man. It was his fault. His and that pilot man. And now, because of That Man he'd been cuckolded. Damn him. Bradley dropped his hands and clenched them into fists as his libido faded to be replaced by anger. He'd been cheated of the two things that he held most dear – his house and now his woman.

Her hand moved from his arm to rub his chest in circles before dropping lower. A warm glow followed the movement of her hand, and he could feel primordial desire overcoming the flare of resentment and a smile started to bloom across his face at the prospect of promised delights.

"Come," she rose once more to her knees and sashayed away from him, across the bed, her hands holding the rope belt threaded through the stays of his baggy trousers. As she pulled him closer, he saw her wrinkle her nose.

"I think you might prefer if I had a shower first. It's been a while, and you have hot water." He pulled away before he toppled across the bed and the smile which proximity and memory had brought to his face froze as he righted himself.

There on the cabinet beside the bed were several $20 notes. He glared at them, and then at the woman. Her gaze followed his. She let go of his belt and slowly moved further across the bed, away from him.

Bradley picked the notes up and slowly counted them before anchoring them under a dogeared paperback copy of *Lady Chatterley's Lover*. He smirked. He had given it to her, thinking that she might enjoy it. But the irony had been lost on her.

She shuddered and tried to pull away as he yanked her to him, then pushed her hard up against the headboard. There was no way she could fight him; all she could do was use her feminine wiles to try and placate him as she had often done before. She reached up to stroke his face, but he grabbed hold of her wrist with one hand before she could make contact.

He shook his head sadly and turned her hand palm up and lightly kissed it before letting her hand drop. He then cupped her face with his hand, rubbing his thumb against her jaw. "You were the only one, you know?" Bradley's voice had softened, and she smiled coyly into his steely eyes. "You were the only one who didn't scream or run away. You were the only one who was not afraid. Instead, you were curious. And that made you different, and I wanted to know why. I brought you to this cottage, let you live here. It cost you nothing. I nurtured you. I taught you to be a woman." His voice grew hard again as he let go of her face and stood back from the bed. "And this is how you repay me?"

He picked up the notes again and waved them in front of her face. "Was it he, or was it you who suggested that he pay for the pleasure of *my* woman?" Bradley reached across the bed and grabbed her by the shoulders. "I AM NOT YOUR PIMP."

He stood up straight and stomped around the room. His mind was in a turmoil. He had been betrayed. Betrayed! In the bed that he had bought for *his* woman. And she had violated it. She was no better than the prostitutes with whom she shared the street. He could never have her again. And neither could anyone else.

His pacing was interrupted when his boot became entangled in something. He looked down at his feet and saw a ski jacket on the floor, peeking out from under the bed, taunting him.

Rage surged through him again as he saw in his mind the woman slowly and tantalizingly slipping it off the man's shoulders the same way she would strip him of his clothes. Once discarded, she would then lay them on the end of the bed, never on the chair by the door. And it would always end up on the floor, as this jacket had. He kicked his foot free and spat on the jacket with contempt.

He turned back to the cowering woman on the bed. With one stride he was back beside her. He peeled her fingers from the blanket she still held up against her chest and grabbed her wrists. She winced with the pain as Bradley then smashed her hands up against the headboard.

She gasped, looked up at his face towering and glowering above her, and tried to smile engagingly at him. But he was too busy looking at his own hands plastered over hers.

He smiled. He still had his gloves on. That made things all the better as an idea sprang to his mind. He moved her left hand so that he could hold both her hands in his one hand above her head and fumbled with his trouser leg to reveal the ankle knife holster he was never without. Slowly he slid the knife out. The pocketknife of his earlier escapades had long since been replaced by a hunting knife.

"I have only ever used this to scare and warn them. The girls. That was usually enough to terrorise them, make them compliant with my desires. If it was not enough, then I would give their necks a taste of this." He waved the knife in front of the woman's face and touched the point to her neck. "And, of course tell them that it was to be our secret, that no one would believe them that the maldape would do such a thing. Of course, that alone went a long way to perpetuate the myth of the maldape." His laugh rippled around the room. "Till now I have only ever used it once to actually harm anyone and that was because she talked too much. I made sure that she shut up. So now, why don't you shut your mouth? And your legs. You are of as much use to me as she was. I don't need anyone squealing on me and my pleasures. You are of no more use to me."

He looked down at his woman. Pity. Things could have been different. He shrugged and turned to leave. The ski jacket lay accusingly on the floor, he kicked it towards the head of the bed and saw the notes under the book. He wiped his knife over the cover of the book and pocketed half the notes.

Bradley closed the front door behind him. He wished the owner of the ski jacket good luck once the police became involved/ the woman was found. Life on Ruby Street had been good, and it should have lasted. But now he had to get back to the hovel and concentrate on doing his duty to That Man and so reclaim *Braedon*.

Chapter 47

Fletcher felt much refreshed after the congenial lunch with Pamela, and he had found her a receptive sounding board for his current dilemma, which he had been successful in couching in anonymity.

The day had not been wasted, and held the promise of enjoyable things to come, but not today. He had been away from *Braedon* too long as it was. He might be excused for missing lunch, but the boss going AWOL would be harder to explain. Besides, it would be bad for morale if it ever came out that he had not adhered to his own dictum.

"I'd offer to stay and help you with the dishes," he smiled across the table at Pamela, who was collecting the spent dishes together. "But I really must be going. I'm not even meant to be here, in town. No one is."

"Oh? Then how do you explain the other new faces in town this weekend?"

Fletcher's face puckered. New faces? They couldn't be from *Braedon*, could they?

"Other new faces? They are all over the place, these skiers."

"Oh, I didn't mean them, we are used to seeing them around. Besides, they may be strangers in town, but they are not considered 'new' faces. They are the faces that bring business to Hemlock."

"Then what do you mean? I would have thought that strange faces and new faces would be pretty much the same thing?"

"New faces are those that have not been seen here before, or those who are only here for a short while. The skiers are strangers passing through, never staying, and besides, their faces always stick out as belonging to the skiing fraternity." She paused, perplexed at Fletcher's sudden agitation, and tried not to look at his discomfort before she continued. "The couple of non-skiing new faces I saw earlier today were heading to the Police Station. A man and a woman."

"The Police Station?" There were two 'new' people going to the police? Could they be two of the four he'd seen earlier, or could they be from *Braedon*? If they were from *Braedon*, then the woman could only be Nikki, but then who did she have with her? And why would they be going to the police? Had something happened back at *Braedon*? Had he been found AWOL and Nikki was coming in to report him missing? Surely he hadn't been gone that long. He looked at his watch, and rummaged in his pocket for a handkerchief and wiped away the beads of sweat which were now glistening on his forehead. Murphy had a lot to answer for.

He really needed to get moving. Back to *Braedon*. No, the police station to call off the search. But what if that wasn't the reason for Nikki and whoever to go to the police? Had someone squealed? Had the subterfuge been blown? He took a deep breath. He could not let his emotions betray the quandary that he now faced. He had succeeded in whitewashing the cause of his dilemma when he had sought the unscheduled counsel from Ms Ellis. Yes, he must think of her with a title. He could not afford for them to be on first name terms, even if it was only in his head. He had to think. To remain calm, in control. And think. First things first.

He had to get out of this house.

"Then there were the other four new faces, though, mind you, one of them did look a bit familiar, then again I didn't see them up close, so I was probably mistaken."

Four more strangers. Thinking no further than his own operation, the only other new faces he could think of being in Hemlock were the pilot and his companions that he had seen earlier going into the Grand View Hotel. While they were a problem, they were no longer the priority.

First the police station, then Nikki. No *Braedon*, then Nikki. And he also had the hermit to confront. He groaned inwardly. He could not afford to show emotion in front of Ms Ellis. She would start to ask him more questions and would want to console and advise him. And while a part of his mind acknowledged that he could do with a lot of that consoling and advice at the moment, he needed to get back to *Braedon* and get his house back into order.

"They are probably locals," continued Pamela, "returning for the long weekend. They do that. Leave town for study or work and come back to see family. That is probably who they were. Besides, I did only see them fleetingly, before seeing you at the phone box.".

Phone box? Yes! That gave him the out that he was wanting. He could say that he needed to make another phone call. One that required the privacy of the phone box. Collecting his composure, something that he had learned to do to perfection when he had been a student at high school, Fletcher pushed his chair back, stood up, then pushed the chair in under the table.

Taking a deep breath, he rested his hands on the top rung of the chair back and hoped that he looked remorseful. "I'm grateful that you saw me champing at the phone box, and stopped to advise me of the potential wait I would have had. So thanks. And thanks for letting me use your phone. And for lunch. I wouldn't have come in to town if it had not been for the fact that I needed to make a couple of phone calls. But I am glad I did."

"A couple? You only made one from here."

"Yes, I managed to make half a phone call before I was called away from the phone box. I need to go back to the phonebox and complete that call ... er, to my boss." Fletcher blanched. Maxwell! He imagined Maxwell back at his home – staring at the hand piece in his hand and wondering what the devil Fletcher was up to. He supposed he ought to actually phone Teddy-Max back. But what would that achieve? There was no way that he was ready to admit to him that things had gone pear-shaped. He tried to remember how much he'd said before he'd rushed out of the phone box after the hermit. Update. On schedule. Should be ready. That had, really been the essence of the phone call to Maxwell. Would he have expected more? Then again ... Better not to phone him. Besides, his coins would well and truly be all gone by now. He looked at his watch, then back at Pamela.

"Sorry, I really do have to get back."

Chapter 48

Fletcher waited to catch his breath as he stood looking at *Braedon*. He felt weary. Weary and tired. Was this to be the albatross that ended his career? He took a deep breath and sighed. Whichever way it went, all this would soon be over and *Braedon* would be signed over to its rightful owner, and he would be glad to see the end of it. Of it all. A smile caught the corners of his mouth. All of it, except maybe for Ms Ellis. He wondered if maybe this could be the start of a new career in real estate.

He shook his head as he remembered that there were still things to be done before he started to contemplate a future far removed from what he knew. For starters he needed to have a word or two, and fists if it came to that. He brought his hands together in a loud clap and ground them together. That man needed a talking to, and a good bollocking. Yes. He really did need to pay the man a visit sometime soon. But standing here, getting cold, was not the best idea. He needed to get back inside, and hope that his absence had not been discovered.

He walked slowly across the vestiges of what had once, many decades since, been a manicured circular drive, and wearily climbed the front steps, pushed open the front door and stepped inside.

Funny that it should feel like coming home, but it was somewhat of a relief to feel the now familiar walls enclose him and give him a respite from the ravages the day had thrown his way.

"There you are! Where have you been? I've been looking everywhere for you."

Fletcher gave an involuntarily shudder as despair clothed him and he consciously halted his shoulders slumping as the aggrieved voice thundered down. He looked up the staircase to see David Lapaine bearing down on him. Fletcher sighed and pulled himself together. Now was not the time to radiate the desolation he felt enveloping him.

Fletcher's initial impression of the head nurse, gained from the original file photograph, had been neither cancelled nor improved upon on their physical meeting. He still exuded a macho force unrivalled by any of the security team, and Fletcher had been pleased that contact had been minimal.

Fletcher grimaced. What the hell could Lapaine want? And did it have to be him that had been left when the rest of the medical team, their expertise no longer required, had, under the cloak of darkness, left *Braedon* and Hemlock? Hadn't Murphy's Law exacted enough flesh from him today without more angst being pitched his way?

"What is it Lapaine? It better be good. I'm in no mood for tales of splinters or blisters from the men. Or, don't tell me, the cook has gone and lost a finger in tonight's dinner."

He watched the nurse bristle, and Fletcher afforded himself a silent chuckle. He knew that Lapaine liked to be addressed by his title, but today he was simply too tired to be bothered with kowtowing to the giant of a man who, having reached the bottom of the stairs, now loomed over him.

"It's the patient. Upstairs. Says he needs to speak with you. If you'll come with me. Sir."

Fletcher didn't know why he had to be accompanied. It wasn't as though he did not know where to go. He may not know the current precise location of where the patient was to be found. But for goodness' sake, his own suite of rooms was on the same floor, just the opposite wing to that which he had been instrumental in setting up the other wing as a dedicated hospital unit. Admittedly, since Popolo had arrived he had not been into the hospital wing. There had been no need. But it could not be that hard to find the sole patient.

With an audible exasperated sigh he slowly followed Lapaine across the foyer and up the stairs to the hospital wing, wondering the whole time what Popolo could possibly want him for. Maybe it was to complain about the food. Being put on a stringent diet for over a month was probably driving him nuts. His girth on arrival had certainly reflected an appetite for meals of a higher gastronomical star and calorific intake than anything the kitchen team had been serving up.

Lapaine stopped outside the doorway to the hospital wing. "You will find him through there, out on the veranda," he said, pointing to the left before striding away to the right.

Fletcher watched him go before taking his time to walk through what he knew to be Popolo's suite. It was both pristine and spartan, giving nothing away as to the personality of the occupant. He stood at the door to the veranda with its wooden shutters, currently open, and observed the man who was sitting in a wheelchair and looking out toward where snatches of the distant lake could be seen through the flickering leaves of the mountain ash.

Although he could not claim to be intimately conversant with Demetrius Popolo's original back view, Fletcher would not have guessed that this was the same man. Where Popolo, on arrival, had been dark haired and well-padded to say the least, the man in the wheelchair was a redhead and slender.

The bare boards of the veranda creaked as Fletcher stepped out onto them and Popolo turned his head. Fletcher stopped his advance and gaped. This most definitely was not the Demetrious Popolo he had welcomed to *Braedon* four weeks ago.

"You will excuse me if I do not stand. This contraption is devilishly hard to get out of, especially now that pain of a nurse has trussed me up in all these blankets." He plucked at the tartan rug pulled tight over his legs.

The man in the wheelchair stretched out his hand in Fletcher's direction. "I see you don't recognise me. That is a good thing. Let me introduce myself. My name is Phillipe Du Pont. And despite the beauty of this place, I think that I am ready to get out of here." He laughed as Fletcher stepped forward, still opened-mouthed and took the offered hand. He then stood back and closed his mouth.

"I am glad to see your reaction. It confirms what I see in the mirror. Your medics, they did a good job do you not agree?"

Fletcher appraised the man in front of him and marvelled at what his medical team had managed to achieve in the short time allocated to them. Here certainly was no Demetrius Popolo. Phillipe Du Pont' green-blue eyes met his gaze through large wire-framed glasses perched on a pert, upturned nose. His sideburns and moustache reminded Fletcher of a red-headed Burt Reynolds from *Smokey Bandit*. The whole change gave him such a comical look that Fletcher was hard pressed not to laugh out loud.

"I most certainly do. You look nothing like the man who arrived here. No one would guess."

"But those that share these premises? What about them?"

"No need to worry about them, your secret is safe. And even if they were tempted to divulge, the repercussions would not be worth any amount of money or coercion that they might encounter. It would not be worth it, if they wanted to live, that is. You have no occasion to be concerned on that front.

"Thank you. I really want to leave that life behind. I'm getting tired, and too old to be running away all the time."

"You always could have curbed your writing you know?"

"Yes, yes, but no, that was never possible. I was never able to do that, the words, they simply came out by themselves. I could not control them. Now, when can I leave?"

"What are your plans for when you do leave? Have you organised something?"

"Oh yes, that's all sorted. First thing will be a holiday with a friend of mine. Might take a tour and see some of the country. I know that I was taken on that flying jaunt, but I was too preoccupied, worried about what was coming up to take in much of the sights. While I'm here in Australia, I really ought to experience some of it. You know, cuddle a koala or two."

Fletcher nodded, his mind a blank as how best to answer or placate the man sitting in front of him with a mixture of anxiety and euphoria shining from his face.

Fletcher scratched his chin and walked over the to the veranda rail. He gave it a tentative shake, before leaning against it. He stared out, unseeing of the view. He knew had known that this moment would come, but he had not yet untangled the best way to approach this man's re-entry into the world, so to speak. Maxwell had never given any indication as to what was to happen after the event.

Damn him. Was this simply another orchestrated part of the trial? A test to see what he would do, all the while hoping that it would prove to be nothing less than another nail to his coffin? Fletcher could just see Maxwell, sitting back comfortably in his insular tower, malevolently twiddling his thumbs, watching and waiting for the fatal decision. If that was the case, then he would not be party to it. He would make another trip to the public phone box and dump the decision into Teddy-Max's lap. After all, it was Teddy-Max who had stuck him with this abnormal operation. And if it was going to cost him his job anyway, then he had nothing to lose.

And if that was the case, then Maxwell, and Du Pont could wait. He needed to get to the cottage and sort out the hermit, and only then would he go into town and phone Maxwell. Then, and only then, he might have an acceptable answer for Du Pont. Damn, he was fed up with this assignment. The sooner it came to an end, even if he lost his job, he would be glad when it was over.

Fetcher turned back to face Phillipe Du Pont and smiled.

Du Pont released the blanket from his fingers and returned Fletcher's smile and said, "Sounds good to me. The sooner the better."

"We'll get you out of here as soon as we can. There are a couple of things that need to be ironed out, but things must be looking good if they have left you with only Nurse Lapaine to care for you."

"Ha! That imbecilic excuse for a carer. Lapaine by name could not be more appropriate. He is a sadist."

Fletcher nodded again. "Yes, he would make anyone anxious to be discharged. I will see what I can do to expediate things." Fletcher patted Phillipe on the shoulder and walked back through the suite and down the stairs to his office. He opened the door and stopped. Strother and his sous chef were in there waiting for him. What the hell could they be wanting? He walked to his desk, hoping that his smile was in place.

Once Fletcher was seated Strother stepped forward and presented him with a handwritten note.

He took the note and looked quizzically at the chef who grinned and flicked his head in the direction of the sous chef. Fletcher read the note and sighed. As if he didn't have enough to work through.

"He wants to apply for *citizenship*?"

The sous chef beamed, and the two men nodded their heads.

"You've told him that residency comes first?"

Dave shrugged his shoulders.

"I'd have thought clemency would have been the next step. After fronting up to immigration and sorting out his current status. An illegal, isn't he?

Dave shuffled his feet and shrugged while the man beside him looked at his shoes and tried to make himself look smaller.

Fletcher closed his eyes in a grimace, he could feel a real doozy of a headache coming.

"Okay. Leave this with me, though I'm not sure what I can do. But I will see."

Dave beamed and nodded his head in thanks while the sous chef backed out of the room in a flurry of bows. Dave gave him a shove which had the two of them stumbling out the door.

Fletcher ran his hand up through his hair and back down to massage the back of his neck. There were definite knots there. He might go for a short lie down before heading out and confronting the man in the cottage, and phoning Maxwell. The idea that Mrs Whoever She Was would once more be phoning her family briefly surfaced, but he quashed the notion – he had no time at the moment to entertain thoughts of another visit with Ms Ellis.

He retraced his steps back up to the first floor and was making his way to his room when Nurse Lapaine called out. Fletcher turned and watched as Lapaine walked towards him.

"My patient is telling me that he will be leaving soon. Do you think that is wise?"

Fletcher shrugged. "I would have thought you would know the answer to that. I have no expertise in such things. That is why you are here; you are the one with the medical knowledge."

David Lapaine stopped a few paces from Fletcher, momentarily flummoxed. Yes, he did have the knowledge, and that all bore out the fact that the patient was recovering very well, but if the patient was discharged then he himself would be out of a job. Not that he was being paid by the day or the hour. His remuneration was a large lump sum at the conclusion of the job, and one that he had agreed on, and was not to be further negotiated. But he did not like the prospect of being unemployed.

"So? He wants to leave. Can I stop him? No. He is not a prisoner here. He is a guest."

"That may be true, but he is one who has undergone surgery."

Nurse Lapaine was definitely an irritant and on one of those 1 to 10 scales that the medics used he was undeniably a 9.9. Fletcher squeezed his eyes closed and rubbed his forehead. He was totally exasperated by ... well ... by everything. And the nurse in front of him was no exception.

"Surgery of which I can see no evidence, other than the excellent results," he said, wondering what else he could say that would get Lapaine out of his personal space.

David Lapaine frowned. While he had had little to do with Fletcher since arriving, he had not seen him as perturbed as now. He wondered if it was his place to offer some relief.

"Er, yes. The patient has responded to our ministrations far better and quicker than any of us had imagined. Will you excuse me for a minute? I need to get something to show you."

Lapaine abruptly turned around and retraced his steps to the hospital wing, leaving Fletcher perplexed, head bowed and vigorously massaging his forehead. What in the blazes did Lapaine mean? And ought he to stay here and wait for the nurse to return? Showing him anything medical would be a waste of time and he didn't have the energy to feign understanding or interest.

It was only a couple of minutes before David Lapaine was once more standing in front of Fletcher, both hands stretched out.

"Here," he said, depositing a couple of tablets into Fletcher's hand, then offering the tumbler of water that he held in the other hand. "Take these." He held his breath, waiting for the reprimand that he recognised as his due. But it never came.

Fletcher looked at the tablets now in the palm of his hand, then quizzically at Lapaine. The man had compassion spread all over his face. Maybe he was human after all.

"What are they?"

"Quite safe. You look a tad bit frazzled; I thought a couple of analgesics might help."

Fletcher put the tablets in his mouth, reached for the tumbler and a mouthful of water, then threw his head back and swallowed.

"They work best if you rest up for a bit. Maybe lie down for half an hour."

Fletcher handed back the tumbler, nodded. "Thanks," he muttered. "I might just do that."

Fletcher rubbed his eyes and peered at his watch, wondering why he struggled to read the hands. "Damn!" He sat up and swung his legs off the side of the bed before quickly steading himself with his hands either side of him. He had slept. Slept! He looked out the window. No wonder he'd had trouble seeing the time – it was dark outside. He slumped back across the bed and let out a long sigh. Too late now. Having it out with the mad man at the cottage would have to wait till the morning, as too would the phone call to Maxwell.

Chapter 49

Bradley stopped as he came to the edge of the clearing, "What the blazes?" he scratched his head and looked around. Everything appeared to be in order, and undisturbed. Except for the door. The door to the cottage was open. He was sure that he had closed it when he left. Positive. Closing doors was a habit from childhood. So, he would have automatically closed it when he had left. So why was it now open?

He bent down and took his knife out of the ankle holster. He walked cautiously towards the cottage and as quietly as he could, climbed onto the veranda. He grimaced as a board creaked under his foot, and he stood still, waiting. He closed his eyes, knowing that inside would be dark, and he wanted to see what awaited him once he entered. Nothing other than his own breath disturbed the quiet.

Carefully, one foot at a time and keeping his back to the door, he edged into the room, opened his eyes and looked around. The place was undisturbed and as he had left it. Except for the bed at the end.

"What the ...?"

Bradley raced to the bed. It was indeed empty. And by feeling the bedding it had been empty for some time. Where the hell was his prisoner, the man that he was in charge of keeping captive? How had he got free? Bradley grasped the rope that was dangling from the bedframe. The unravelling ends taunted him. Who had freed the man that he had been entrusted to watch?

Then he remembered the man and woman back at *Braedon*, when he had first been nabbed. While he had no idea who they were, he was sure they had recognised him. Were they locals? He had not

297

seen either of them delivering his regular food supply. But that did not mean that they didn't know where he lived. But why would they bother coming here? Certainly not to visit him. If it was them, and for whatever reason they had come here, they would have seen his guest, and it was logical that they would have set him free.

Not that it really mattered who had it been, the main thing was that his guest was missing. He had not been able to resist the urges that had plagued him his whole life, and now he had let down That Man by disregarding his duties. Duties that would have brought *Braedon* back into his hands. Bradley started to shake uncontrollably. Unless he could find the pilot-prisoner and get him back here, tied up, That Man would know that he had reneged on his word and disobeyed him. But how would he even know where to go looking for the escapee? He could not have escaped without help so it would be unlikely that he would be on his own. And even less likely that he would return willingly. Whichever way he looked at it, it was not looking good.

He sat down on the now empty bed, knees akimbo, elbows resting on his thighs and dropped his chin into his hands. He looked around the cavernous room. It had never been home, only ever a convenient temporary substitute for what was rightfully his. And now what were the chances of that ever coming to fruition? He did not expect That Man to honour their gentleman's agreement, as that balanced on the captive presence of the pilot.

He sighed with resignation. "Well, that's Ruby Street gone and me now truly buggered."

Chapter 50

"I wonder if it is always this busy on a Sunday morning?" mused Tim, hands stuffed into his armpits to keep warm as he looked out onto the empty main street. "I'd have thought there would have been a stream of cars heading to the snow by now."

Paul stamped his feet and blew into his cupped hands before answering. "It's the middle of a long weekend, and it's 10am. If anyone was going to the snow, then they are already there." He stepped down from The Grand View Hotel's front door and looked up and down, waiting for sight of Christie and Melody, who were to join them.

"Is that them?"

Paul followed Tim's outstretched hand.

"Yeah, that's them." The two men headed down the pavement. "You sure you want to do this?"

"What? Go back to the place of my captivity you mean?"

"Yeah. What good will going back do? By now that guy will know that you have scarpered, so why go back? I can understand your concern over the plane, but you can get there without having to actually go into where you were kept."

Tim shrugged his shoulders. "I guess I feel bad for him. He didn't hurt me. Not physically at least. Sure, he tried to torment me with his innuendos. Drove me nuts the way he carried on. But I think he is a decent enough person. He needs an explanation."

"Who needs an explanation? For what?" Melody asked as she came to a halt in front of the men.

299

"Morning guys," Christie muttered. She was not happy with anything this morning. And certainly not about the morning's intended excursion.

"I was just asking Tim if he was sure he wanted to go back and apologise for escaping."

Tim glared at his friend, but did not have time to respond before Melody, almost skipping with excitement, interrupted. "I don't care if he apologises or not, Tim has to go back."

"Melody! How can you say that? You saw how he'd been treated. Besides, it is up to Tim what he does." Christie wondered for the millionth time why she had allowed Melody to persuade her. Even though she had come to terms with the need to slay her personal dragons, the idea of confronting The Hermit would not have been her choice of how to spend her time.

"Yes, but if Tim doesn't go back, then how am I ever going to get to see the inside of that hovel."

"Why'd you want to see that?" Tim asked and shook his head in disbelief. Yes, he wanted to go back, but only because he felt strangely guilty for escaping; even though anyone should understand the reasons for wanting to get away from any captivity, especially an unexplained one. He also hoped, now that he was free, that the man would finally explain why he had been so detained. Asking from his tied and prone position on the bed had been like talking to himself and had not loosened the man's tongue.

"It might be the closest that I get to see anything like a haunted house."

"The only thing that is haunted about that place is in Tim's mind. I can't understand why either of you would want to go investigating the place. And what sort of reception do you think you would get from the man living there? You saw him. Who knows what he'd do to you if you waltzed up there full of curiosity. 'Excuse me, I want to appease my curiosity, can I have a look around your place? Is it haunted?' Get real Melody. Isn't being here, and meeting the maldape enough for you?"

"Never. Come on. Let's go."

Christie and Paul exchanged looks of resignation and fell in behind Melody who had tucked her arm through Tim's.

They stood by the edge of the clearing and looked at the cottage. The whole place was eerily silent.

"Something's wrong." Tim sounded perplexed, and the others all looked at him, then at the place in front of them.

"What do you mean?" Paul asked. The place looked exactly the same as it had the day that they had first visited.

"The door's open," Tim pointed. "And there's no smoke from the chimney."

"There wouldn't be if the fire had been lit a lot earlier," Christie murmured, fed up with everything and everyone.

"Maybe the man has gone out," offered Melody hopefully, relishing the idea of being able to explore inside without having to ask permission.

Tim shook his head. "He never left the door open when he went outside. Not even when he went to relieve himself."

Cautiously the four approached the cottage. Then equally cautiously they each stepped up onto the veranda.

Tim moved towards the door, "Hello?" his voice echoed back to him as he turned to look at Paul and shrugged his shoulders.

Paul pushed past his friend and stepped into the room, then, as he waited for his eyes to adjust he felt the others enter and stand beside him.

"Oh Tim! Really? This is where you have been holed up for the past, how many weeks?" Melody tentatively walked towards the iron bed at the end of the room. When she reached the bed, she sat down on it and gave a couple of jumps. "Ugh. That's horrid. Poor you." She looked towards where the others were still gathered by the door and screamed.

Christie started to run towards her but was brought up sharply as Melody pointed wildly toward the other end of the room. The others all followed her gesticulating arm.

"No!" yelled Christie, running back to the men and grabbing hold of Paul's arm. "Quick! Do something."

"Like what?" muttered Tim, walking almost reverently towards the man suspended above the floor.

"Get him down," Melody whispered as she unsteadily came and stood beside Christie.

"Too late for that," Paul stated.

"What do you mean?" Melody demanded, suddenly recovered and feeling benevolent.

"Well look at him. Does he look like a person who can be revived? He's as stiff as a board, and I don't imagine that skin with that bluish or mottled appearance is particularly healthy," Paul said as he stepped beside Tim and reached his hand out to give the body a gentle push, setting it off in a pendulum swing.

"Well so would you be if you were just hanging around in the middle of winter with the door open and no fire going."

The others all looked aghast at Christie who had yet to realise her gaff.

"I suppose we ought to let the authorities know, or someone." Paul looked around the room then walked over to a table and pulled out a chair for Tim to sit down.

"Then let's go," Melody said, moving toward the still open door, suddenly anxious to get away.

Paul shook his head. "Tim needs to ch... needs time to purge himself of his ... and I want to be here to support him. And I thought I might take a look around, see if I can find a rifle, or gun, one that might have shot at us the other night."

"Oh. Sorry. I meant to ask yesterday if you had taken a look at the damage to the car, and if you had reported it."

"It's all right Christie, no need to apologise. The damage was minimal, just needs a bit of touch-up paint. It was not worth bothering the police, not when I had other, more important things on my mind."

"Firearm?" Tim asked anxiously, looking at Paul and making to get up. "You never told me that you'd become a target."

"Don't panic. I'll fill you in later." Paul went over and put a hand on Tim's shoulder. "Did you ever see any evidence of a weapon while you were ... in residence?"

Tim, panicking, looked around the room. "No, no weapons were ever used in my presence. Unless of course you would consider manipulation by coercion on the part of those two who engaged me in this enterprise, or that madman's," he looked at the women now both edging towards the door, "er ... his appendage."

"Um, I think that at times it could have been considered a weapon," Melody said quietly as she looked at Christie.

Christie stood rooted to the spot unsure what to say or do as the rumours of her childhood, and her recountings to Melody, started to swarm around her.

Melody might have liked the idea of exploring a haunted house but being in close proximity to an actual dead person, and one which she had seen alive and well only the day before, was stretching it. Plus, she could see that she needed to get Christie out and away from the place. She grabbed hold of Christie's arm. "We'll go," she announced.

Christie let herself be pulled away. She was having a hard time coming to terms with the fact that the tormentor of so many children, girls and women was now dead. Their silence could now be broken, and the trauma openly shared. She wondered how many would feel assuaged.

The two jumped off the veranda and stumbled across the clearing and onto the bush track towards Hemlock.

Paul joined his friend at the table.

"Well, that solves that then."

Paul dragged his gaze from the man at the end of the rope and looked at Tim questioningly. "How so?"

"I've now no need to confront him and come up with a plausible explanation of why, or how I escaped." He paused and looked up at the man again. "You don't think that he killed himself because I escaped, do you?"

"Don't give yourself airs and graces over your importance. I doubt it. Do you think he left a note?"

Tim stood up and looked around the surfaces nearby, careful not to disturb anything.

"Doesn't look like it. What do we do now?"

"I'm still interested in finding that firearm, but after that we could follow the women, or we could go take a look at your plane. That is what you wanted to do, wasn't it?"

Tim returned to the table and sat back down. He rested his hands on his knees under the table and dropped his head. In all honesty he didn't know if his legs could hold him upright for much longer and didn't want to admit his weakness. He looked up and out the door that still stood open. "It looked like there was snow in the air earlier. I think staying here is the better option. Melody and Christie ought not be too long getting the authorities out here, and then we will be here for them."

Chapter 51

Fletcher came to a halt. There were two women hurrying away from the cottage and heading into town. What the blazes? First the man contravened the conditions he had placed upon him by going into town yesterday. Something which he had assured Fletcher he never did in daylight, yet he had seen him. And now here he was entertaining not one, but two women.

Seething, Fletcher strode across the clearing in front of the cottage. In his rage he was looking forward to tearing strips off the man. He would have his guts for garters.

He came up short, he had not used that phrase since he was a senior back in high school. He smirked at the memory. The junior students would always tremble when so threatened. That had given him a feeling of power and authority. That's what he needed now. He needed to get things back under control. Banish Murphy and his Law and get things back to where he himself wanted them; with him in charge.

Taking a deep breath and drawing himself upright, Fletcher looked across to where the two women had disappeared then continued towards the cottage. Feeling buoyed with the confidence of his younger self and filled with a desire for revenge he mounted the veranda.

Tim and Paul spun round from their musings over Tim's tormentor dangling in the corner, then stood up and focused on the silhouette in the doorway.

Fletcher heard their movement and turned in their direction, willing his eyes to quickly acclimatise to the dark interior. He could see their form, but not distinguish who they were, other than that there were two of them and neither were the man that he had come to chew-out.

"What the devil do you think you are playing at?" He bellowed as he stormed through the open door.

Tim and Paul had the advantage, and as Fletcher further entered the room recognized him first.

"Will you look who's here? Gidday Gee-Gee." There was a tinge of laughter in Tim's voice.

Paul reached out and stopped Tim but could not help himself from adding to the insult. "What are you doing here, Horse?"

Tim took one look at Fletcher's face as it infused with anger and could no longer hold back his laugh.

"You!" Fletcher, pointing his finger at Tim, took a step forward, but Paul stepped in front of him and placed a warning hand on his chest. Fletcher brushed Paul's hand aside and moved closer to Tim, expecting him to step back and cower like he had as a young teenager. But Tim was no longer that small scared new kid at school and stood his ground. Fletcher halted. "Why are you not restrained? I told him to keep you restrained. Where is he, by the way?"

"You mean the bastard that you had imprison my friend?"

Paul once more instinctively moved to stand between Tim and Fletcher. It was just like old times, decades ago, when he would defend the smaller Tim from the bullying meted out by the senior Fletcher and his cronies.

Fletcher glared at Paul then turned to Tim. "I see you still rely on your friend in shining armour then?" he laughed bitterly, and a ~~brief~~ frown creased his brow. How could this second man be here? Fletcher's contact in Search and Rescue was supposed to have dealt with any unwanted interest in the disappearance of the plane. He'd need to have a serious talk with them, later. "But my questions still remain. Why are you not restrained? And where is he?"

Tim might have earlier held a certain empathy towards the man who had held him captive, but Gee-Gee had been the instigator. He had always appreciated Paul's interference when they had been at school, but he was now big enough and old enough to fight his own battles. And now he was in fighting mode. He pushed his way in front of Paul and stared Fletcher in the eyes.

"If you mean the fellow you had strip me and tie me to a rotten bed with nothing but some rat-eaten mouldy old blankets, then there he is." Tim flicked his head in the direction of where Bradley was.

Fletcher looked to where Tim had indicated. An unexpected sense of dread and vulnerability enveloped him as he saw the hermit hanging.

"What have you done to him?" he spat.

"Not us mate. Though Tim had cause enough," Paul sneered and braced himself for the attack that he could see coming.

"If Christie is to be believed, then so too did half of Hemlock." Tim added assuming a fighting stance.

"Why?" Fletcher asked as he pushed his way between them to stand looking up at Bradley. He turned back to face Tim and Paul who had now moved around so that the table was between them and Fletcher.

They both shrugged, neither wanting to add the usual response of 'search me' for fear that Fletcher might take that as an invitation.

"No idea. We found him like that," Paul answered, instinctively taking the lead.

"When?"

They gave another shrug. "When as in when did he do it? I'm guessing yesterday? Last night? Or when did we find him?" Paul looked to Tim. "We got here just shortly before you turned up."

Fletcher looked back at Bradley then pulled a chair by the table closer and collapsed onto it. His mind was in turmoil. He slowly shook his head. He was now faced with two, no three, new problems. The hermit had provided him with extra security and the solution of what to do with *Braedon* once this operation was complete; and had solved the problem with Tim. Now he had to deal with Tim, as well as his friend.

He ran his fingers through his hair and sighed. When Tim and Paul had been juniors at school, they had provided him with game to be taunted, and he had relished in the power it gave him. Now they were thorns that he had to deal with but on more equal terms. He looked up at the two men who had not moved. They were standing side by side, feet apart, and arms crossed over their chests, glowering at him.

"Why did you have him keep me tied up? I don't really blame him Gee-Gee. The order came from you. You. It was you who told him to 'look after' me. He didn't want to. But you gave him no choice." Tim slammed his hands down on the table and leaned across to face Fletcher. "What was your hold over him? Are you the reason why he is now dead? Did you kill him?"

Paul placed a hand on Tim's shoulder, "Easy there. You know that all bullies are cowards. I don't think Horse has the guts to kill anyone. Maim them maybe, but not kill."

Fletcher laughed and stared into Tim's eyes before looking up at Paul. "You don't know the half of it. But no, I did not kill him." He thumbed over his shoulder. "Not him."

Tim and Paul exchanged looks which pretty much reflected what each was thinking—that there was no knowing some people. Could the man opposite them really be a killer?

Paul stepped closer to the table. "You haven't told us what brought you here this morning. Tim never mentioned you as being a regular visitor. In fact, other than seeing you from a distance when he landed his plane, he hasn't seen you. So why come here now?"

Fletcher shrugged his shoulders and inclined his head in the direction of the body. "He had reneged on our deal, and I wanted an explanation."

"Your deal? To keep me a prisoner? How had he reneged on that? Until yesterday he had been most meticulous in keeping up his end of the arrangement. I've been tied up the whole bloody time!"

"Ah yes. Meticulous. Then it was his charity that allowed him to take you into town yesterday was it? I saw you."

Tim and Paul exchanged glances and Tim shrugged. So he'd seen them in Hemlock. What of it? And what did Gee-Gee mean about them coming in with the man from the cottage? None of anything made sense. The charter, the faked crash, his being held captive, Gee-Gee being here, a deal? Tim was at a complete loss.

"And you were with your mate here," Fletcher wagged his finger at Paul. "And a couple of women. He set you up with them, did he? And brought them back here last night, did he? How do I know that the whole lot of you weren't at it all night? A right orgy, and then, when you didn't like sharing, you topped him. Is that how it went?"

Paul sighed. "We told you. We only got here a few minutes before you did."

"I saw the girls slinking away. Looked right scared they did. What, you threaten to harm them as well?"

Paul silently seethed. Horse deserved a good walloping. He clenched his fists and took a step forward, then stopped when Tim put out a restraining arm.

"I'll have you know, those women you saw with us, they are not what your filthy mind might think. They are our friends, and I'll not have you besmirch them," Tim said.

Paul looked at Tim and felt like whooping. It was good to see that Timid Tim from school days no longer needed him to stick up for him.

"How do I know that you're telling the truth?" Fletcher snarled. He knew that he was getting carried away, but he couldn't help himself. Everything was turning to custard and his brain couldn't keep up. He had to vent, and the two men opposite him were a convenient target.

"Listen Gee-Gee," Tim yelled. "The four of us had only arrived just before you. The women have gone back to town to alert the authorities. The police and the doctor."

Fletcher stared at them. He stood up abruptly, knocking the chair over as he did so. If only he could think straight. His thoughts were a piece of flotsam being buffeted through rapids. He started to pace the room. He had to prioritise his actions. He had to think.

For the umpteenth time Fletcher mentally cursed Murphy, and cursed himself for ever accepting the assignment. But if he hadn't, he would have still been stuck at the desk that had become his burden. At least he *was* out in the field, just not the way he wanted it to be. He continued pacing, muttering to himself and trying to fathom when it was that his career had taken the nosedive. Where, and when had he gone wrong? But nothing came to mind. He kicked out at a pile of rubbish that sent empty cans clattering across the floor and was roundly miffed when Paul just moved aside and let them roll past. Even that simple action was working against him. He felt like screaming. When would Murphy be satisfied?

That brought him back to the present predicament that Murphy had landed him in. What was he going to do about the two men? And the women? And now the police and a doctor were soon to be involved. He had to distance himself from all of them. He didn't know how much the four knew about what he was involved in. Between them, would they have enough to rip to shreds the whole project? He stopped and spun round to face Tim. "How much do you know? What have you told them?"

Tim stared at Fletcher. "About what? What's there to tell, other than that you had me trussed up like a Christmas chook, and left me tenderising for a month? Who'd I tell, and who would believe me, other than Paul here? Oh, and him." Tim pointed to the corpse.

Fletcher, who had once more started his pacing, took a shuddering look at the hermit suspended from the roof joist. At least he was no longer in a position of potential threat. Though there was no knowing if or what he had divulged to anyone when he had gone into Hemlock.

Damn, this place was turning into a veritable sieve. Not counting the damage that the hermit might have created, there was Nikki, if it was her, and whoever, who may have gone to the police. Then there was the pilot and his lot. And now he might also have to contend with the police. He was overwhelmed by the thought. The bottom line was that he could not risk anything leaking out, Not now. Not with the operation so close to closure. He was not ready to lose his career. If Ibraham had done his job properly then he would have known that Tim was a potential threat and not employed him.

He continued to pace, periodically stopping to glare at Tim and Paul. He could feel them watching him. even if they had not yet blabbed, they were still a threat. Did he take them with him? If he left them here, would they stay? What would they say to the police? The police. They would be here soon. He had to think of something, and fast. Fletcher turned and strode back to the table.

Clarity came out from the jumble. He couldn't be here when the police arrived. He needed his own space to think this through.

"I've got to go. You deal with the police. After all, you were first on the scene. Or so you tell me." His sneer, the other two men noticed, had not changed since their school days and they smirked at each other as Fletcher walked to door.

"Some things, apparently, never change." Paul muttered under his breath, and Tim snickered.

Fletcher turned around when he got to the door. His stare silenced the two men. He pointed menacingly at first Tim, then Paul. "Mind you, I was never here. You don't know me. If I learn that you have spoken to anyone, *anyone*, about me being here, or anything that you may or may not have heard or seen, then, then ..." He wagged his finger at them, then made his hand into the shape of a gun and fired it. "Then I'll have your guts for garters." There, he had said it. And he was sure saying it to Tim and Paul had more effect than if he had had the opportunity to say it to the man he had come to chew out.

With a final glance at Bradley hanging silently from the roof joist Fletcher turned back and was out the door before either of the men left in the cottage could blink. They stared at the still open door, heard Fletcher jump off the veranda, then watched as he almost ran away.

Chapter 52

"Well, what do you make of that?" Paul asked.

Tim sat down and shook his head. "Pity it never worked like that back at school. Would have made life a whole lot more pleasant." He grinned up at Paul. "While you're on your feet why don't you take a better look about the place for a farewell note or something.

Paul wandered about the room. "I would have thought that most people, when they write a suicide note, leave their final message somewhere obvious, but we've both taken a look and all the surfaces are clear."

"Have you thought about his pockets?"

Paul turned back to look at Tim. "I might have some adventurous bones in my body, but my fingers are not going anywhere near that man's clothes. I'll leave that to the police, or doctor, or whoever it is that the women bring back with them."

"Yeah, you are probably right. If Gee-gee is prepared to suspect us, then we'd best not leave any incriminating fingerprints about the body. We might be accused of fabricating the note and all. If there is a note somewhere about his body."

Paul looked at his watch. "They can't be too far away."

Christie and Melody had made it back to Hemlock in record time considering the tangles they had had with the blackberries, which grasped out at them with prickly fingers at every opportunity. They arrived at the police station only to find that it was closed.

313

"Now what?" gasped Melody as she slumped down on the top step of the station.

"We go around the back and bang on the door."

"Police stations have back doors?"

"No you dodo, the cop's house is round the back of the station. Come on, let's see if," Christie reached down and pulled Melody to her feet before peering more closely at the notice, "Constable Walter Mosley's at home." It didn't surprise her that she did not recognise the name, the cop she'd known growing up had been an old fossil back then, so of course he would have retired and been replaced.

She was surprised to see that the policeman who opened the door was in uniform, and she frowned. "Sorry, I thought that you were off duty." She pointed back down the path that they had come, "The notice on the station door said that you were closed."

"Yeah, well, it is Sunday. And yes, I'm supposed to be off duty, but there's been a rash of incidents so ..." Walter raised one arm and scratched the back of his head.

"Well, we have another one for you," Melody piped up. "We've got a body for you. We would have gone to the doctor first, but there is little that the doctor can do for him now, being dead, and besides Christie here said that the station was closer."

Not another body. Walter sighed. Who is it this time? As if he didn't have enough going on. Yesterday an indignant skier had stormed into the station to report an assault. He'd stated that he had mistaken a private residence on Ruby Street for one of the other houses when an irate man fitting Mr Gentian's description had assaulted him. Walter had found that interesting as Mr Gentian had not been seen around town for a while, so he had dismissed him as a suspect. That was, until he had later gone to corroborate the skier's story and he had found the woman's body. She'd been murdered. She was, by all accounts, Bradley Gentian's mistress. Though who was to know for sure?

Walter scratched his head again and felt his body sag with exhaustion. Now, when he needed to locate Mr Gentian, here were two women telling him that they had found a body.

'Then I guess you had better make your way back to the front door and I'll take particulars. Don't suppose you recognise, the, er, body ...?'

Melody looked to Christie as Constable Mosley pushed past the two women and led the way down the path.

Christie shrugged her shoulders. Oh, she knew who it was, just didn't know what his real name was. She had only ever known him as The Hermit or maldape, and she doubted that would mean anything to Constable Mosley, he didn't look old enough to have been around for long.

"Er, Constable Mosley, how long have you been here in Hemlock?"

Walter stopped and turned to face the two women. What the hell was going on? How long had he been here? What did that have to do with the body? "Why?" he growled.

Christie took a step back. "Well, I kinda know who the body is, but I don't know his real name, so, if you have not been here long then you might not know what I'm talking about."

Walter rolled his eyes. He really had no patience with time wasters. And that is what these women were turning out to be. For sure, a body was a body and he needed to attend to that, but that body was apparently dead and therefore wasn't going anywhere. He needed to find Bradley Gentian.

"You could always tell me what you know, and I'll determine if my time here has any bearing on this body of yours."

Melody sensed the irritation bubbling in Christie, and she took a step towards Constable Mosley, stuck her arms on her hips and took the initiative. "According to my friend here he's known by you locals as 'The Hermit' and has been terrorising the females of the area for decades, so it's a good thing that he is dead."

Walter involuntarily gulped. He may not have been stationed in Hemlock for decades, but he thought he knew all about The Hermit. He had heard the hushed rumours about The Hermit's antics, but had never been able to find anyone prepared to make a statement. Now it appeared that whatever this Hermit fellow had been up to was at an end.

"Right," Walter said as he turned to face the front door of the police station and bounded up the steps. "We'd better get in here and you can tell me about your hermit body. Then after I contact the doctor, I guess you should show us where this body is."

Christie gaped at the man who opened the door to the doctor's residence. The doctor was far more wizened than she remembered him to be. She had thought him old and due for retirement when she still lived in Hemlock.

He chuckled at her surprise. "Yes, indeed young Miss Rowlands. You are not hallucinating. It is I, and it is good to see you finally make it back up this way again. It's been too long. Your mother is not getting any younger. Then again, neither am I." He chuckled and turned to the policeman. "Hello Walt, I take it this isn't a social call then?"

"Sorry to disturb you Doc, and you're right. No social call this, but no rush. It's a stretcher and certificate case this time."

"Dear me, do we know who it is?" He looked to all three for a confirmation. Then zeroed in on Christie when the policeman inclined his head in her direction.

"I'm pretty sure I know who he is, just not his name, other than The Hermit."

"The Hermit, indeed? Now there's one for the books."

"What do you mean?" Melody piped up.

"Well now, Miss ..." he looked to Christie. "A friend of yours, is she?" Christie nodded. "It's good to see you have a friend." He turned back to Melody. "One for the books? Yes indeed. Never thought that he'd make an appearance in this manner." The doctor tutted, then remembered why there were three people at his door. He turned around and looked down the hallway behind him, tutted again and stepped back against the door.

"Go on ahead Walt." He let out a deep sigh. "You know where the stretchers are. Go grab one while I put my dirty plates in the sink, then get my bag and coat."

The doctor had instructed Tim and Paul to release the body from where it was suspended and now it lay on the table.

"Well?" Walter Mosley asked. "What do you reckon?"

The doctor looked at the policeman, who was standing at the end of the table where Bradley's legs dangled from the knees down. "I'd pretty much hazard a guess that he is now deceased. Yes. Pretty much I'd say he is dead."

Christie clasped her hands over her mouth to stifle her laugh, Melody was not so circumspect, and her guffaw echoed in the room. Tim and Paul were also trying to contain their amusement. Walter glared at them.

"But what about who he is?"

"Oh, yes. It's definitely him. The Hermit. Only I always knew him as Bruce Gentle."

"But is he Bradley Gentian? That's what I want to know. What are you going to put on the death certificate?" asked Mosley, anxious to know if this was the same person that had assaulted the skier. Of course, he would get the skier in to identify him. But did that mean that Mr Gentian was the person who had killed the woman in Ruby St? This man on the table was not of the usual calibre of those who frequented the establishments on that street. Maybe the murderer was the skier, and he was only filing the assault complaint to provide himself with an alibi. It would certainly explain his injuries, sustained in a fight with the woman. So much to think about. But first, best to bring the body back to town.

"What's your hurry? He's dead. Does it really matter, here and now? Think you'd be better occupied in helping get this body onto that stretcher, then maybe these two strapping young men," he waved his hand in the direction of Paul and Tim, "could help the two girls man-handle Mr Hermit out of here and back to the surgery."

And with that he headed for the door.

"And when you get there," Mosley hurried to get his piece in before everyone disappeared, "You'd all better come round to the Station and make your statements."

Chapter 53

Fletcher was almost in sight of *Braedon* and had walked off most of his anger by the time he saw an agitated Nikki approaching. Although he would have liked to blast the dickens out of her for leaving the property yesterday, he could not be sure that it had actually been her that Ms Ellis had seen entering the Police Station. Far better to pussyfoot and trick the truth out her and save the bollockings till later.

"You look a bit flustered there Nikki. That's not like you. Is everything all right? He tried to inject a sense of bonhomie into his greeting, masking the subsiding rage that was competing with the jumble of alternative measures that were tumbling through his brain with this latest blemish to what he had hoped would be a peaceful conclusion to the fiasco of an operation.

Nikki could not be bothered with his attempt at flippancy. Now was not the time for such familiarity. She had her own quandaries to cope with, the malfunctioning automatons for one thing, then there was The Hermit, and what he was doing here, and now the strange man in the flash car. But right now, it was Fetcher. She was too worked up over his duplicity to give thought to the others at the moment.

'I wouldn't be flustered if you'd been here earlier', she thought uncharitably. She fell into step with Fletcher, not wanting to face him when she delivered her message.

319

"Thought you might like to know, before you get back to the house." She stopped walking and hesitated briefly before continuing, unsure what his reaction would be. "There's a man come to the house."

Fletcher stopped walking and turned to look back at Nikki. His brow puckered. Why was she coming to him with this? He had enough to worry about. It felt to him that the acid in his stomach was curdling, though even he knew that acid didn't curdle. He looked ahead, towards the house, and slowly counted to ten. He had appointed her head of the security team to deal with such matters so why was Nikki bothering him now? While he'd like to scream and yell, he also knew that, with his position already in jeopardy, it would be best to temper his feelings and show the leadership he was meant to be displaying.

"And? You are telling me this, why? He hasn't been dealt with? Who is he?"

"He didn't, or rather wouldn't say. He asked for you. By name."

"He knows who I am?" Fletcher almost screeched. There was only one person who knew he was here, and that was not a 'he'. If he ever had occasion to be in close proximity to Ms Ellis again, and he would make sure that he would be, he would tear such strips off her that ... he didn't care if she was a woman. What he had shared with her was in confidence. Off the record if you wanted to call it that. He wondered what information she had shared with someone else. And who? Was it the police? Why would she have done that? Thoughts and theories jumbled in his brain as he started to hurry towards the house, with Nikki easily keeping pace behind him, despite her stride being shorter. "Where is he? What did you do with him? What did you say to him?" Fletcher hissed back at her.

"We divulged nothing, and he wished to remain in his car."

He noticed that Nikki didn't identify the car as anything but 'car' so if it was the police, then they were detectives or undercover. He did not imagine that Hemlock's police had any vehicle other than the standard yellow commodores with all the standard antennae, sirens and lights perched on top.

Fletcher stopped when he saw the large black sedan that was pulled up at the base of the steps leading up to the front door, and his stomach churned.

Nikki caught up to him.

She saw that Alex was standing on the veranda where she'd left him after telling him to maintain surveillance over the strange man in the car. She gave him a backwards nod and he came down the front steps and walked towards them car.

"Er, I'll leave you now, better get back to work," Nikki muttered and grabbed Alex's arm. "Come on, now's our opportunity to go visit the cottage again. The Hermit might have returned." She glanced towards Fletcher and the car. "I'd imagine that these two will be occupied for a while." Whatever was happening, she had done her duty in suggesting that the visitor remain in the car before taking off to find Fletcher. She had no idea why Fletcher had suddenly taken it into his head to thwart his own rules. First yesterday and now today. Had there been other occasions? Was it some sort of test of her abilities as a security team leader? If so, then she hoped that this morning's effort was worthy of a pass. Finding Fletcher had been a challenging effort. Not wanting to arouse suspicion among the others she had made a secretive and futile search for Fletcher in and around the house, the outbuildings and the immediate area. It had only been on a hunch that she had headed toward the cottage by the lake and had found him on his way back from there.

Fletcher didn't hear Nikki; he was scrutinising the car. He approached the car slowly, his mind in turmoil. Maxwell had never showed up on any of his other assignments. Mind you, none of them had been like this one. This one, where he was categorically on his own. And, theoretically no one in the organisation knew where he was. And those outside of the organisation who did know, namely Ms Ellis and Tim and his pals, had no links to Teddy-Max. Or did they? His heart started a fast tattoo that had Fletcher catching his breath. What had he done that warranted Maxwell to come up here, now, today? More to the point, how did Teddy-Max know where to find him? He took another deep breath and prepared himself to be dismissed for failing in his job.

Maxwell had been looking out for Fletcher to arrive and was exiting the driver's seat before Fletcher could open the door for him.

"Where is he?" Maxwell boomed.

Fletcher, trying to mask his heavy breathing and almost standing to attention blinked. That was not what he had expected the opening gambit to be. "He? Sir?"

"Yes. Your guest."

Fletcher continued to blink while he tried to pull his thoughts into line. Maxwell was here to view the raison d'être of this whole fiasco of an escapade; not to haul his butt over the proverbial coals. Or maybe that was still to come. Guest. Yes. Fletcher had always had to remind himself that even though Demetrius Popolo resided in the hospital wing he was not a patient, but a guest, and since yesterday had thought of him under the new name that he had assumed – Phillipe. Phillipe Du Pont.

"Oh. Yes, of course. Phillipe. Come this way. He's inside." Fletcher stood to the side and postured a royal welcome before following Maxwell up the steps to the front door.

"Phillipe, is he?" Maxwell turned and looked beyond Fletcher, taking in the view from the house. He took a deep breath. "Don't you just love the smell of the bush?" Then looking to Fletcher, he continued. "How is he? Phillipe?"

"Yes. Phillipe Du Pont. He is well. But sir, if I may ask, what are you doing here?" Fletcher gestured for Maxwell to enter the house.

"Well, after your aborted phone call yesterday I decided that it was time I came to see how you were. What was it that caused you to end the phone call so abruptly?"

"Er, something came up that I needed to attend to immediately. Sorry that I did not get back to you. Seeing as how I had need to be in town, I thought that I would phone and give you an update, that was all."

Maxwell harrumphed and came to a stop just inside the door, making it difficult for Fletcher to enter and close the door behind them. He looked around the foyer, it was evident that efforts had been made to rectify the decades of neglect, and he imagined the grandeur that would have once graced the place. All it needed would be a bit of TLC, and an infusion of funds. He smiled as his mind started tweaking ideas.

Fletcher succeeded in fighting the door and stepped up beside his boss. "How'd you know where to find us?"

"Really Fletcher, you must realise by now that there are ways and means, for just about everything, and we use them. As have you. Take this for example," he made a sedate twirl and waved his arms encompassing the foyer. "Mr Joe Average would not have succeeded in pulling off this job. But you have. As for getting here. Finding you was almost as easy as looking in the Yellow Pages. After all, you didn't actually hang up on me, did you?" Maxwell smiled sardonically.

Fletcher felt his stomach drop. Of course, Mrs Whoever She Was with her two dogs must have arrived at the phone box directly after he had left it to chase after the man. She would have picked the hand piece up and, on being asked by an irate Teddy-Max, informed him of where she was. All his subterfuge and calling in of favours, and in one callous sentence Maxwell brought all that he had achieved crashing down. He wondered how long he would have to wait before the axe was brought down on his neck.

"Now, where is this Phillipe Du Pont?"

Fletcher straightened up and pushed thoughts of defeat aside. "Up this way." He made his way over to the stairs and started up them. "Mind the fourth step, it's a bit loose."

Fletcher waited for Maxwell on the landing at the top of the stairs. Maxwell was taking his time mounting the staircase, busy looking around him, and running his hand casually along the banister.

Subconsciously Maxwell was once more imagining what the place could look like if cared for. Meanwhile Fletcher was only too consciously willing his hands to stay in his trouser pockets—it would not make a good impression to be caught gnawing on his fingernails. He could only hope that Maxwell would be pleased when he met Phillipe.

He quietly cleared his throat as Maxwell reached the top step.

"This way," he held out his arm and indicated the passage that led away to the right. The two men walked side by side past a couple of doors before Fletcher stopped outside the door at the end of the corridor. He cleared his throat again and gave the door a couple of knocks before opening it. He stepped back and indicated for Maxwell to enter.

Maxwell walked into the room, surprised at how clinical it appeared. He had had no idea what to expect. But this was not it. This room could have been the clone of any private suite in a major hospital. He looked to Fletcher and surprised him by smiling and giving him a 'thumbs up'. Then he walked purposefully to the commodious armchair set facing a window that looked out towards the lake. toward where snatches of the distant lake could be seen through the flickering leaves of the mountain ash.

At his foot fall the occupant of the chair turned to watch Maxwell approach. A smile lit up the man's face.

"Teddy-Max! You will forgive me if I don't stand up to greet you. How wonderful it is to see you. You are indeed a sight for sore eyes, and my eyes are sore, let me tell you.

Maxwell's advance was halted. The beaming man was not who he was expecting to see. He looked back at Fletcher, a worried frown on his face.

Fletcher, still standing in the doorway, was puzzled by Phillipe's greeting. Teddy-Max? He'd thought that was only a derogatory term used by the minions in the office. Was there something more to it? That speculation was interrupted when he saw the uncertainty that played across Maxwell's face was all the assurance that Fletcher needed to know that the surgery had been successful. He stepped forward and with his hand on Maxwell's arm and ushered him forward.

"Mr Maxwell, allow me to introduce you to our VIP guest, Phillipe Du Pont." He stood back and watched as Maxwell struggled to both contain and hide his emotions as he stepped forward with an outstretched right hand.

Phillipe reached out and grasped Maxwell's hand with both his.

Fletcher gave a discrete cough and excused himself then retreated downstairs, his mind and emotions a fairground carousel on steroids. What the hell had he just witnessed?

Maxwell joined Fletcher in the front room. "Right. Let's go."

"Go?"

"Yes. Er, Phillipe will be joining us as soon as that nurse – Nurse Lapaine? – helps him down the stairs and into the car, and then we need to get going."

Fletcher stood up. "Where are we going?"

"Lunch. I've booked a table at the Grand View Hotel. We have some things that need attention, then I must get back to Melbourne."

"You've booked a table already?" Fletcher sat back down. His world was collapsing around him, and he was having difficulty finding his balance. All he could see was his career, and his life going down the gurgler like an unforgiving tsunami.

"Certainly. Country pubs are known for their Sunday roasts, and I had no idea what provisions you would have on hand."

In less time than Fletcher could come up with an acceptable excuse, he found himself uncomfortably sat at a table in the Bistro facing Phillipe and Maxwell and beyond them the doorway to the foyer. He certainly felt like the third wheel on a date as the other two men engaged in an embarrassingly exclusive conversation. They didn't need a chaperone, so why was he here? He fidgeted in his seat and dragged his knife through the residual gravy on his plate, making patterns of infinity. That's what it felt like. Infinity. His future would be dragged out into infinity if Maxwell and Phillipe would not stop talking. He wanted to know where he was to go from here now that the project was finished.

Maxwell looked up at Fletcher and smiled. How Fletcher hated that smile. It usually preceded a pronouncement that never boded well.

"Well Fletcher," Maxwell meticulously placed his knife and fork together on his plate. "It's come to that time." He lent back in his seat and looked to Phillipe who, with all but a beatific smile inclined his head.

Fletcher, as he steeled himself for the inevitable, was surprised to find himself thinking of *The Mikado* where Nanki-Poo, confronted by Katisha, proclaims 'Now comes the blow!' He would have laughed out loud if he had known how appropriate the next line was – *Prepare yourselves for news surprising* – as what Maxwell was about to reveal came as a total surprise.

"I have been watching you for some years now and after coming here, and talking with Phillipe, I have decided that the time is right."

Fletcher watched, mesmerized, as Maxwell reached across and put his hand over Phillipe's where it rested on the table. He felt his stomach heave but was not sure if that was a result of what he felt sure was his impending dismissal—though what that had to do with Phillipe he had no idea—or the unexpected realization that he had missed something. His colleagues calling their boss Teddy-Max behind his back suddenly made more sense. He recalled with embarrassment his goading several months back of the barman in The Den and squirmed in his seat. He'd have to be more circumspect in future and not wear his bigotry on his sleeve. Each to their own, but why would Maxwell want him to be the witness to his coming out of the closet?

"Yes, I'm going to retire. And I'm appointing you as my successor."

Fletcher blinked. Had he heard right? Teddy-Max was retiring? And had chosen him to be his successor? He shook his head and looked at Maxwell.

"You what?"

"Yes, I'm taking early retirement. We, ..." he looked at Phillipe and they shared a smile, "want to enjoy life. And you are going to be replacing me. Effective as of this weekend. You have shown yourself to be most admirably suited to take over my responsibilities and I feel that I can unreservedly leave the business in your capable hands. Of course, I say effective this weekend, but there will still be a certain amount of bureaucratic paperwork to wade through once this project is finalized and wound up. Which leads me on to the next thing."

Fletcher stared, tight lipped and straight-faced across the table at Maxwell. Next thing? He was still trying to take on board the news that Maxwell had just promoted him. No by your leave, or would you like, simply a statement. And now there was more to come? What more surprises could the man have up his sleeve? He wondered, his head already reeling from the shock of this unexpected revelation.

"What were your plans for the property once this, do we call it an operation?" Maxwell looked at Phillipe and they exchanged a mirthful smile. "Yes, I think that is the most appropriate word. What were your plans for the property once this operation was completed?"

"Er ..." Yes, what were his plans now that the hermit had gone and topped himself? Not that he felt like sharing that debacle with Maxwell. If Maxell knew about the recent trysts he had had with Murphy's Law, then he might well rescind the offer of promotion. It had only been a few minutes in the making, but after the initial shock Fletcher could feel himself growing into the role.

The reminder of the hermit brought the remaining problem of the pilot and his accomplices to mind. They might not know what had transpired at the house, but they would, after the pilot's treatment, know enough to still be a threat if they squealed. Then there was the hermit's body and the police. That was another minefield if the pilot and his cronies squealed. The silence from the other two men at the table finally filtered into Fletcher's mind. Those were potential problems, the more pressing one was how to answer Maxwell's question about *Braedon*. He looked at Maxwell, and Phillipe who had now covered Maxwell's hand with his. A pact was in the making. If Maxwell had asked about the property, then it was obvious that he had something in mind.

"... um, probably sell it. What would you suggest?"

Maxwell glanced at the man beside him and smiled "Phillipe likes it here, and I thought it might be a nice place to retire to. You know, quiet, secluded, fishing on the lake. Might even take up skiing again." He gave a soft chuckle. "Do you think the funds could stretch to this becoming a company retreat, maybe?"

Fletcher's mind was a whirl of fractured thoughts. Things were happening so fast that he did not have the time to catch onto an idea and run with it to its fruition. But Murphy appeared to have slunk into oblivion.

Chapter 54 – Five years later

The gentlest of breezes tickled the swathes of banners and garlands that bedecked the front of what had once been *Braedon*. George Ellis, the mayor of Hemlock, stepped out from the front door and walked across the veranda to stand at the top of the steps. Maxwell and Phillipe quietly followed him and stood either side of the front door. The mayor looked out at the gathering of people blanketing most of the immaculate lawn and spilling over onto the gravelled circular drive. He felt sure that the whole population of Hemlock, and more, were in attendance and was grateful that the day had blessed them with beautiful weather. He leisurely scanned the crowd till he saw his daughter Pamela towards the front of the guests, her husband standing beside her. He smiled at them, then raised his arms and waited till the general babble had dwindled into silence.

"Welcome! Welcome, one and all. How lovely it is to see so many familiar faces here today on this special occasion.

"A special occasion which has been a long time coming. As most of the older codgers here will know, *Braedon* was once an architectural delight and the hub of Hemlock's pioneering community. A community founded by the original owner and early pioneer. Frederick Gentian. Not that I would expect any here to remember him personally as that was a good century or more ago." He waited till the titter of laughs drifted away.

"What most of you are more likely to recall are be the tragedies that befell the later generations of the Gentians, but what you may not know is that it had been the wish of the last incumbent, Jim Gentian, for this property to become a park and memorial to the tragedies that had befallen.

"Members of a previous council were not impressed with the bequest. And we who are locals, rather than the weekend wanna-bes here" Once more he waited for the laughter to stop before continuing. "All know this property was left to the wiles of the maldape and the hands of unrelenting Mother Nature."

People were nodding in agreement, and many were touching their necks. The weekenders and those who were not locals looked around and wondered what secrets were being silently rekindled and shared. While neither Tim nor Paul fitted comfortably into either category, they knew only too well what was being referred to. Paul reached over and gently kissed the top Christie's head, while Tim pulled Melody closer to him and smiled at her upturned face. He was happy that his wife had not had to suffer the trauma and indignity of growing up in this community.

"Today it is my utmost pleasure, on behalf of Hemlock's Council, to categorically state that the maldape has been put to rest and, through the generosity of some nameless gentlemen here in our midst, I welcome you all to *Maldape Manor*." He raised his arms once more to quell the ripple of appreciation.

Melody shivered as she remembered her obsession with haunted houses and maldapes. She had finally managed to visit the property before its transformation and could now say that she had seen the place in both its incarnations. She was pleased that it had been given a new name, and smiled up at her husband remembering what part the maldape had played in their meeting.

"While this property may not be called *Braedon* anymore, *Maldape Manor* has become more than old Jim Gentian could ever have imagined. The outbuildings have been redesigned as self-contained holiday chalets. A children's adventure playground has been developed, revolving around a massive interactive rendition of a maldape. The lakefront has been groomed to be the envy of any resort beach and the old jetty has been extended."

Once more the mayor paused for the public's reaction to settle.

"And that's not all! I don't know how many of you even knew there was a jetty, so probably even fewer of you knew of the existence of a boathouse and cottage. These too have been extended and renovated to accommodate conference facilities. While the upper floor of this magnificently restored building is a private residence, the lower floor has been converted for public use as community meeting rooms with dining facilities if required and a café."

This time the response was unanimously explosive, and it took a lot of arm flapping to bring the crowd's attention back to him.

"But wait, there's more!"

The laughing from those standing on the lawn was thunderous.

"The boathouse is no longer a 'boat' house, but is an 'aeroplane' house. And that aeroplane has a purpose. During the summer weekends, and for a donation—philanthropy only goes so far—you will be able to take a joyride over our marvellous location." He spread his arms wide and turned from side to side in a lavish demonstration of the area, then turned around and reached out to Phillipe Du Pont who handed him a large pair of scissors from off a table by the door.

"And now, without further ado, I declare ..." Maxwell had stepped up behind him and whispered in his ear. "Er, yes. Before I continue with what I was about to say," there was quiet twitter from the audience. "I've just been reminded that refreshments will be served inside, or you may prefer to try out the grounds' camping area barbeques. And now, back to where I was ... I declare *Maldape Manor* open!" And with that he walked down the steps and cut the ribbon that was strung between the bottom balusters.

As the ensuing applause died down Maxwell and Phillipe quietly withdrew back into the house and made their way up to their private quarters upstairs. It was done. It had taken five years, but they had transformed the dilapidated property into a retreat and a resort. A place where they could enjoy each other's company, pursue their own interests and collaboratively write thriller novels under the pen name Ted Du Pont.

Fletcher looked up at the property's new name emblazoned across the top of the veranda, and smirked. *Maldape Manor* seemed ironic, but somehow appropriate. He then walked Pamela across the grass and into her father's keeping before turning to look out across the townsfolk mingling on the lawn and smiled. Changed times. The maldape was gone and Hemlock's residents' curiosity about *Braedon* had been put to rest. He glanced across to his wife and gave her a grateful smile before he entered the house, 'just to check' that everything was in order with the logistics pertinent to such a grand opening as this.

All was well with his world.

Epilogue

Fletcher had felt pleased with how things had turned out and was justifiably rather proud of how he had circumvented any breaches of security and secrecy.

It was wonderful how money and influence could set the wheels of loyalty into motion. While he could never be confident of how much the members of his original teams knew about the clandestine operation they had been involved in, he had been more than pleased when most of the catering and security teams had readily agreed to stay on as bona fide employees of the trust that Maxwell and Du Pont had set up to run *Maldape Manor.*

The medical team had not been a problem – they had been only too happy to receive a generous remuneration and slink back into their nefarious lives. And for once Murphy had not stuck a finger into that pie—none of the medics knew who Demetrius Popolo was. They only knew that they were involved in creating a new identity for someone.

No, the real fly in the ointment had been the four people who had never been part of the plan. And his promotion had been the coup to clinch that problem. Lady Luck had booted Murphy and his Law out of his life the moment Maxwell dropped his bombshell.

It had taken Fletcher a few moments to take in what had been said, but it was in those moments that he had seen Tim and his cronies walk past the Bistro door and the mental light globe had exploded—he would employ them in return for their silence. He still wasn't sure how much they knew, but better to have them

335

on-side than him cultivating ulcers wondering if they would squeal about anything. Yes, better to suck it up and offer the proverbial olive branch.

He had known it was a risk to bring these two men into the organisation, but it had paid off.

Tim McNaulty, who had never been confident enough to dream of being a fulltime pilot, was happy to forget about the years of torment that Gee-Gee had meted out on him. He was now happily engaged as the company's pilot, not only of the Cessna residing in the boathouse, but also of the Metroliner in a hidden hanger beside a private airstrip.

Paul Edgar had been tricky, until he learned that he was a journalist or something. What a life-changing opportunity for him to be offered a lucrative, not-to-be-ignored exclusive. Then it had been easy to set up an interview for him with Phillipe Du Pont aka Demetrius Popolo for a posthumous exposé, and add the carrot of him heading up the organisation's media relations. Public Relations was too passé for *his* organisation, Media Relations Department sounded so much better.

He was quite puffed up with the knowledge that he could dictate and control what was made public.

Initially the two women had been a concern, especially with him not knowing anything about them, how they fitted in with the two men, or what they knew. But that too had been resolved when it became apparent that a romantic element was entering the equation. That, along with their administrative skills, made it easy to offer them lucrative positions, which they were very happy to accept.

When it came to what to do with Nikki and Alex – well, he had to laugh. Murphy may have thought that he had upset things there, but Lady Luck had won out in the end. Neither of them knew anything beyond their own involvement in the project, they had only been concerned about the hermit and his part in a murder that had happened when they were both kids living in Hemlock. The policeman (he still shuddered at his lucky escape there) had gone back to the cottage and conducted a thorough search. He had come up with no firearms on the property, but he had found the man's stash of diaries in a metal box behind the chimney. They went back decades, documenting his tortured childhood and later retribution on the females of Hemlock. They had also provided enough evidence to posthumously confirm that The Hermit, aka Bradley Gentian, aka Bruce Gentle had been responsible for two murders. After that Nikki and Alex had been more than content to wash their hands of Hemlock.

Pamela had replaced his mother as his sounding board which made his relationship with his mother as a son-mother ought to be. And his mother loved Pamela as much as he did, for which he was forever grateful.

Yes, Lady Luck was his companion now, and life was good.

Don't miss out!

Visit the website below and you can sign up to receive emails whenever Nolan MacKenzie publishes a new book. There's no charge and no obligation.

https://books2read.com/r/B-A-DQKM-GYRZB

BOOKS 2 READ

Connecting independent readers to independent writers.

Did you love *If They Squeal*? Then you should read *Eenie, Meanie, Minie, No!*[1] by Nolan MacKenzie!

The diaries of a dead man call. Can Sandie resist? Where will reading them take her?

Sandie's husband and his university nemesis compete for the affections of a man long since gone. She turns to the old man's diaries for assistance. It began in academia but it won't end there. Because university can be murder.

Sandie uses the diaries to decode a mystery stretching across decades and continents. She might pay with her marriage and her life.

Kidnapping and murder form the backdrop for this fast paced thriller set in 1990s New Zealand.

---

1. https://books2read.com/u/bzeYA9

2. https://books2read.com/u/bzeYA9

Also by Nolan MacKenzie

The Tag Series
Eenie, Meanie, Minie, No!
If They Squeal

About the Author

Leigh lives in the South Island of New Zealand but still calls Australia home, even though she left when she was a pre-teen. Educated in Australia, Africa, Europe and New Zealand she has seen a lot of the world.

No matter where in the world Leigh was living, she has always been surrounded by books. As a child, when she was not being read to, she would be an avid listener to the tales that either her maternal grandmother or her father would weave.

Leigh never considered writing until she was encouraged to attend a U3A Creative Writing course in the 1980s. She has been writing ever since. Now, after many years of traveling, teaching and working in a school library, among other careers, she is ready to share her writing with the public.

Leigh writes under her own name, as well as the pen names Nolan Mackenzie and Jacklyn Harris.

Leigh has two adult children, who are also voracious readers and write when they can find the time.